ZEN
AND THE ART
OF MURDER

063

OLIVER BOTTINI

ZEN
AND THE ART
OF MURDER

A Black Forest Investigation

Translated from the German by
Jamie Bulloch

MACLEHOSE PRESS
QUERCUS · LONDON

First published in the German language as *Mord im Zeichen des Zen*
by Scherz Verlag in 2004, and reissued by DuMont Buchverlag, Cologne, in 2015

First published in Great Britain in 2018 by

MacLehose Press
An imprint of Quercus Publishing Ltd
Carmelite House
50 Victoria Embankment
London EC4Y 0DZ

An Hachette UK company

The translation of this work was supported by a grant from the Goethe-Institut

A CIP catalogue record for this book is available
from the British Library.

ISBN (HB) 978 0 85705 766 2
ISBN (TPB) 978 0 85705 735 8
ISBN (Ebook) 978 0 85705 737 2

10 9 8 7 6 5 4 3 2 1

Designed and typeset in Minion by Libanus Press, Marlborough
Printed and bound in Great Britain by Clays Ltd, St Ives plc

For Chiara

A wise man knows his fellow human;
an enlightened man knows himself.

GUIFENG ZONGMI (780–841)

PROLOGUE

It was a snowy Saturday morning in Liebau. When Johann Georg Hollerer took his first glimpse out of the kitchen window at the high street, he was confronted by a vision. Dressed only in a dark robe and sandals, an oriental monk had emerged from the driving snow. His virtually bald, wet head glistened in the gloomy morning light as he walked slowly past Hollerer's window towards the church. In his left hand he gripped a head-high staff for support, in his right he held a small bowl. Amelie has sent him to me, Hollerer thought, as the vision dissipated back into the snow.

Hollerer returned to his breakfast table where he sat for several minutes, pondering the message Amelie had been trying to send. It confused him that she, a life-long God-fearing Catholic, should have chosen an oriental Buddhist to deliver it.

Eventually he stood up, irritated. Even in death Amelie spoke to him in riddles and put him in a bad mood.

It was another half hour before Hollerer realised he hadn't been duped by a vision.

As he buttoned his uniform jacket over his protruding belly, he remembered noticing a large dark mark above the monk's right ear. In the initial shock he hadn't paid it much attention, but on second thoughts it was strange – a rectangular, dark-blue discoloration of the skin. Hollerer knew marks like that only too well, in all their stages of bruising, in every size, on all parts of the body.

The monk had an injury to his head. As if he'd knocked it against something – or had been hit.

Unsettled, he went to his bedside table. In the drawer beneath a

7

dusty copy of the Old Testament lay his service pistol. He had not carried it once in thirty years, let alone used it. But now he picked up the gun with his thumb and forefinger.

Hollerer found the monk in the church square. Even though snow was still falling heavily, the man was sitting cross-legged on the steps of the Catholic church. His eyes were closed. His mouth moved as if he were saying something. But no sound issued from it.

The small bowl stood in front of the monk. It appeared to be made of wood, and was empty. Snowflakes formed a white circle on the rim.

Twenty-five or so villagers had assembled in a semi-circle around the man. Hollerer nodded to the others. The mayor was there, both priests, other notables, a few farmers, a handful of children. No-one was talking; Hollerer couldn't even hear a whisper of astonishment. He sensed that everyone was waiting for something to happen, for the monk to open his eyes and explain what he was doing there and where he'd come from. Or for someone to grasp the initiative.

Hollerer moved in from the side until he was a couple of metres from the monk. The injury was ten centimetres wide, five centimetres high. A blueish mark, yellow-green at the edges and purplish in the centre. Caused either by a hard, accidental knock, or a deliberate blow. He would not have been able to say why, but Hollerer was certain it was a blow. A shiver ran down his spine.

He rejoined the semi-circle. Now he saw that the monk also had a wound on his left cheek, a laceration that had only just stopped bleeding. A scab had formed, but the snow stopped it from drying out.

"We've got to do something – he'll freeze to death otherwise," Hollerer said to nobody in particular. The crowd stirred, there was a muted muttering.

The monk moved too. He raised his head and opened his eyes. They were very narrow; they seemed sad and lifeless. They roamed slowly across the villagers, now and again alighting on a particular face before moving on.

The narrow eyes rested briefly on Hollerer too. A strange expression. Not unfriendly, but strange. Knowing. Hollerer couldn't put his finger on it. The monk gazed at Hollerer as if he knew him. As if he knew something about him that Hollerer didn't know himself.

Then the monk looked away.

"But what *can* we do?" asked Ponzelt, the mayor. "Are we going to tell him it's illegal to beg in Liebau?" A handful of villagers snorted in amusement.

Hollerer approached the monk again, stopping a metre away from the bowl. Water had begun to collect in it. Bending his knees slightly, he stooped and propped his hands on his thighs. The holster grazed his elbow. All of a sudden he felt ridiculous. "You've got to get into the warmth," he said. "You're soaked; you'll catch your death of cold."

The monk gave the hint of a smile. He was still a young man. Or he looked young, at least. Hollerer's colleague Niksch was in his early twenties and he didn't look much younger.

The monk pointed at the bowl, then at his mouth, lowering his head several times as if bowing, expressing thanks or simply nodding. "He wants money," someone said from behind.

Hollerer grunted, picked up the bowl and turned around. He tipped out the water and dried it as best he could with the sleeve of his jacket. Then he dropped in a two-euro coin and set it down again in front of the monk, who had watched him without stirring.

Hollerer pointed to his own left cheek, then to his right temple. "What happened?"

The monk simply put his hands together in front of his chest, gave a slight bow and closed his eyes. Hollerer was about to ask him to open them and look at him again, but because the monk would not have understood he just said, "Leave him be. I'll be back in a minute."

When Hollerer returned from the bakery with two cheese rolls, at first glance everything seemed to be the same as before. The monk was sitting there with his eyes closed; the villagers, now numbering around forty, in a semi-circle around him. But Hollerer sensed that the mood had changed.

As if to confirm this, Ponzelt took the police officer by the arm, pulled him beneath his umbrella and moved a couple of paces aside. "People are getting nervous," he said, his gaze fixed on the monk. "You've got to get rid of him."

Hollerer stared at a drop of water hanging from Ponzelt's nose.

"They're wondering," Ponzelt said, "if there are more of his sort where he came from, or wherever he's going to. If people like that are going to be coming to beg in Liebau every Saturday morning. You know, the Hare Krishna and Bhagwan types. Our lot reckon they've got enough problems without some sect making itself at home here."

The drop of water finally detached itself from Ponzelt's nose. Hollerer now turned to the monk as well.

"Do you see?" Ponzelt said. "In times like these people get nervous. How can we be sure that he and his comrades aren't planning something?"

Hollerer nodded but said nothing. He wondered whether, like Ponzelt, he too was an opportunist who instigated all manner of things, but was never to blame. Someone so slippery that blame did not stick.

Since Amelie's death he had often been visited by peculiar thoughts. Am I a pessimist? An optimist? Am I an egotist? An opportunist? Without such thoughts life had been simpler, he mused. He had eaten, worked, slept and argued with Amelie. But he'd never had odd thoughts.

"It may also be . . ." Ponzelt said, pausing when the monk opened his eyes again.

In silence they waited for something to happen. Hollerer had a vague sense that the monk knew what was going on around him. Knew that the mood had turned.

"The best thing," Ponzelt said, "would be if you showed him your

I.D. and took down his details . . . that sort of thing. Then the village will see that you're not leaving them at his mercy. And his Hare Krishna mates will realise that there's no chance of them setting foot in Liebau."

"The best thing," muttered Hollerer as he went over to the monk, "would be if you kissed my arse." Disgruntled, he wondered if merely having voted for Ponzelt made him an opportunist. He decided to postpone this question until the next election. If he voted for Ponzelt again, that would be the time to subject himself to greater scrutiny.

The monk followed him with his gaze. Once more Hollerer felt that this man knew him to the core. That in fact he knew everybody and everything. Despite this – or maybe because of it – his eyes looked sad and exhausted.

And Hollerer fancied he detected something else in those unfamiliar eyes: fear.

He offered the monk the sodden paper bag with the rolls. "Here's something to eat," he said. His voice sounded unintentionally reassuring.

The monk nodded and peered inside the bag.

"Local cheese," Hollerer said. "I assume you're a vegetarian."

The monk took one of the rolls and held out the bag with the other one. Hollerer was about to protest, but the monk nodded again and shook the bag impatiently.

Hollerer took it. Baffled, he folded the paper around the roll. "O.K., then. Goodbye."

With the roll in his right hand he went back to Ponzelt, but didn't step under the umbrella.

"Well?" Ponzelt said.

"He's just having a snack," Hollerer growled, and plodded off into the sheet of snow.

I

THE MONK

1

Louise Bonì hated snow. Her brother had died in the snow, her husband had left her in the snow and she had killed a man in the snow. It was the memory of this man that particularly discomforted her. Last summer she'd managed to suppress it at times, but during winter it haunted her mercilessly. At home, down at the station, out and about. A bloodhound that refused to be shaken off.

Even now, as from her bed she pushed the curtain aside and stared into the snow flurry for minutes on end, this man dominated her thoughts. She pictured him lying on a snow-covered road in the middle of an expanding pool of beautiful, bright-red crystals. René Calambert, a teacher from Paris, handsome, married, one daughter, one bullet in his leg, one bullet in his stomach, both from her service pistol.

She let go of the curtain and sank back into her pillow. It had been snowing non-stop since yesterday lunchtime and there was no prospect of an improvement in the weather today or on Sunday. Freiburg was suffocating in the snow. Her colleagues were looking forward to skiing, her colleagues' wives to a winter break with the family, and her colleagues' children to snowball fights. Bonì was looking forward to a moment without René Calambert bleeding to death.

She glanced at the digital clock. 11.30. She closed her eyes.

An hour later the telephone rang. Louise went into the sitting room and saw Bermann's number on the display.

"Yes?"

"Luis?" Some of her colleagues called her "Luis", effacing both her French background and her gender. Bermann chanelled all of his bodybuilder's strength into the "u", perhaps because he was head of Section 11, the Serious Crime Squad. "Luis, you've got to go to Liebau."

"But it's Saturday."

"Still."

"I won't," she said, hanging up. Louise was surprised by her own nerve. For a few weeks now she'd been resisting Bermann's habit of exploiting her, ordering her around. Something seemed to be coming to an end, but she had no idea what. She didn't get the impression that her courage would lead her into a new life. More likely into the abyss.

She looked out at the snowstorm. Three faces flashed through her mind. Two belonged to dead people, one to a painful memory.

My three men, she thought. My snowmen.

As she stood under the shower with her eyes closed she found it difficult to keep her balance. Louise opened her eyes slightly but it didn't get any better. Through the gushing water and the closed door she heard the telephone ring again.

A few minutes later she was sitting with wet hair on the sofa in her dressing gown. Bermann had left two messages on her answerphone. The first consisted of a single command: "Call me back Luis, *immediately. I need you.*"

The second message was a threat: "Luis, if you don't call back in five minutes I'll start disciplinary proceedings and strike you off the task force list." Bermann's voice sounded icy with rage.

She suppressed the urge to reach for her mobile and instead returned to the bathroom, trying not to think about the task force list. For a detective it was painful enough to be absent from it for special investigations. But to be struck off the list entirely was the worst punishment imaginable. You would remember the two or three task forces per year for the rest of your life; everything else was just routine.

By the time she rang Bermann the clock read 13.00. He answered at once. "That's *twenty* minutes, Luis," he said. "I've started disciplinary proceedings." She could hear chatter in the background, an announcement over the tannoy highlighting special offers. Bermann was in the supermarket.

She closed her eyes. "Rolf, I have a day off."

"And I've had it with *you*," Bermann said.

Bonì was beginning to understand his irritation. For a moment she wondered why that didn't surprise her, or even depress her. "What are Ops saying?"

"Nothing. They haven't been there."

"Operations haven't been?"

"Nothing has actually *happened*," Bermann panted angrily. "And because nothing has actually happened, and because the operations department is undermanned, it hasn't paid a visit. And because we're undermanned, *you're* going to take a look."

"Can't Anne do that?"

"No." While Bermann gave a lecture on the staff situation in the operations department as well as in Section 11, detailing illness, parental leave and regular holiday, she wondered how he could have started disciplinary proceedings in a supermarket. Was there a special counter beside the meat one? Forms in metal containers behind a rounded glass screen? Bargains to be had on disciplinary proceedings today, said a woman wearing blood-stained disposable gloves.

She grinned.

"So?" Bermann said gruffly.

"Alright," she said. At least she'd have some company. Better than spending all weekend alone at home. It might stop her thinking about René Calambert.

Then she concentrated on Bermann, who was talking about Liebau and the extraordinary things going on there.

She was still feeling dizzy fifteen minutes later in her red Mégane, squinting into the dim light of the underground car park. The ramp was wobbling, the concrete pillars were moving. She shut her eyes, opened them and waited for a moment. She had heartburn and a headache.

In a wall to her right the lift doors opened, flooding the garage with a harsh neon light. Ronescu the caretaker stepped out of the glare and his blurry figure shuffled past her. She screwed up her eyes but he was still fuzzy. The contours of his substantial body were duplicated, as if he possessed a spiritual aura. She gazed at him in fascination. The mysterious Ronescu was revealing his secret: he was a medium.

She giggled and got out. She'd take a taxi.

To avoid startling him she closed the door softly. "Herr Ronescu," she said.

Ronescu turned. "Ah, Frau Bonì." He nodded, and his long, grey, canine face came alive. His fleshy jowls quivered, the deep furrows on his brow smoothed out momentarily. The aura remained.

"I've got a bottle of ţuică."

Ronescu raised his grey-brown eyebrows. "Let's sink it together, then." His eyes remained watery and lifeless. He rolled his "r"s, while in his small mouth vowels became broad, dark and wistful. To Louise it seemed as if they were trying to slip out of German and back into his native Romanian.

Nobody knew for sure where exactly Ronescu came from, or what he had done there. A few vague rumours were doing the rounds of the neighbourhood, suggesting that he was a former secret agent who had once spied for Israel in Romania.

Now he was old, widowed and poor.

Ronescu raised a hand to say goodbye and turned away. For a moment the contours of his body merged into each other, then became body and aura again.

She walked up the ramp. Wet tyre marks looked black on the concrete floor. She went through the narrow opening set into the garage door. Outside everything was white and snow still fell thickly. She cursed and tramped off to the taxi rank.

*

As the taxi slid through the city, she tried to make sense of what Bermann had told her. A Japanese man walking through the Black Forest in his sandals. A "Jap", he'd said. Bermann wasn't racist, just lazy. He said whatever came into his head. He had neither the time nor the inclination to think before he spoke. And he'd been furious with her.

"A bald Jap in a black robe," he'd said, before whispering, "Do you take credit cards?"

Hollerer, the officer from Liebau, had called police headquarters. He was at a total loss. The monk hadn't actually done anything wrong, but if he kept wandering through the snow with "barely anything on" it was almost certain he would freeze to death.

Besides, Hollerer had said, the village was in a lather. They were worried that a sect might be about to settle in nearby. Something had to be done – and quickly, Liebau demanded. The mayor was putting pressure on him. He'd assembled the local dignitaries, telephoned around and refused to leave Hollerer in peace. He wanted the case that didn't exist to be investigated.

"Look serious, jot down as much as you can and bugger off again," Bermann had said, his words accompanied by the beeping of the checkout scanner.

Bonì realised that she'd been staring at the headrest in front of her ever since getting into the taxi. Cautiously she looked up. The giddiness seemed to have subsided. She noticed with regret that things seemed to have lost their aura.

She wondered whether she knew Hollerer. The name sounded familiar. Had she met him before? She couldn't remember.

The journey dragged on. Because of the heavy snow, the Saturday traffic had slowed to a snail's pace. With bowed heads and white umbrellas, pedestrians struggled across the bridges spanning the Dreisam. Aristotle and Homer had disappeared beneath a shapeless covering of snow. They passed the scene of an accident and got caught up in chaotic jams. Gritters were out in force, yellow breakdown vehicles helping people to start their cars. The young taxi driver was unperturbed, casually whistling monotonous tunes through his teeth.

When there were no longer houses on either side of the road, the whiteness became almost unbearably dazzling. The taxi driver put on a pair of sunglasses, while Bonì screwed up her eyes. They were driving into the void.

René Calambert had died in the void, on a narrow road outside Munzingen. Bermann and the others had run in the wrong direction. Only she had run the right way.

No. *She* had run in the wrong direction.

"What?" the taxi driver asked.

"I didn't say anything."

"You said: wrong direction."

"Didn't mean to."

"O.K." The driver nodded. She sensed that from beneath his dark glasses he was eyeing her in the rear-view mirror. He was young – he looked like a student – with wild curly hair. She noticed that his earlobes were unbelievably large, about the same size as the cap on a vodka bottle. They'd turned faintly red in the car's warmth. All of a sudden she felt an urge to touch his right lobe, take it between her thumb and forefinger and play with it for a while.

She'd already raised her hand when the earlobe moved. The driver bent forwards and took another pair of sunglasses from the glove compartment. "Here," he said.

"Thanks."

The glasses were freezing, the lenses two dark, narrow rectangles. For some reason they reminded her of Bob Marley, Rastafarians and vast quantities of hash. Fifteen years ago she would have worn a pair like these to go clubbing.

"You can give them back to me when we next see each other," the driver said.

She put the disco glasses on. "What's your name?"

"Anatol Ebing."

"We won't be seeing each other again, Anatol."

"Seeing as this must be the fourth or fifth time you've been in my taxi this year, I'd say it's a fairly safe bet that we will." Anatol gave her a brief smile.

She stared at him in horror. He didn't look even vaguely familiar.

In her mind a different man's face began to materialise: round, friendly and tolerant. The face was joined by a body which was equally round, friendly and tolerant. Fat white fingers, which every couple of minutes hoiked up trousers that were slipping down. In her memory the face suddenly lost its friendliness and turned a dark red. The man it belonged to was standing in a small kitchen–diner, panting, next to a father who had taken his ex-wife and daughter hostage. Could you really kill someone you love? the man with the red face said angrily to the father. The father looked at him, confused, then quickly lowered the hand that gripped the kitchen knife. I'm glad you couldn't, the man growled.

Hollerer.

Hollerer wasn't in Liebau. In his patrol car he was following the monk who had by now moved on. He'd been relaying his positions via radio to the small police station in the village.

A keen young officer with the unusual name of Niksch took Bonì deeper into the void along invisible roads. It seemed as if she were gliding across an endless field of snow. Here there were no houses, no trees or fences. Just pylons and crows.

Not even René Calambert would stray here.

Niksch had dandruff and delicate hands and drove too fast. At virtually every bend the rear of the police car swung off the edge of the road. Beaming, he brought the vehicle back under control.

"Great reflexes," she said, wondering whether he was trying to impress her because she was a woman, or because she was almost old enough to be his mother.

"I go rally driving," Niksch said.

"Not now, please," Louise said.

Ten minutes later a police car appeared to their left in the white waste-land, parked at the foot of a bare hill. Halfway up, directly above the car, Bonì could make out a black dot. It took her a moment to realise that the dot was slowly moving upwards.

Niksch pressed a button on the radio and said, "Boss? We can see him – he's right above you!"

"*You don't say.*" Hollerer's voice sounded muffled, as if he was talk-ing with his mouth full. "*Have you got the camera there, Niksch?*"

"Of course," Niksch said, beaming, and wrenched the steering wheel to the left.

Hollerer was standing by his car. As she walked up to him he nodded as if he recognised her straightaway. They shook hands. "Let's sit in the warmth for a bit," he said a little dourly, holding the door open forher. When they were inside he said, "I see you came on your own."

Through the windscreen they watched the monk in silence. It had stopped snowing, the sky had brightened. Thank goodness for the sunglasses; Hollerer was having difficulty even when squinting through his eyelids. The monk was now about three-fifths up the hill and no longer climbing vertically but diagonally. He was several hundred metres away.

"Where on earth is he going?" Hollerer said, sounding as if he'd been pondering this question for hours.

"What's beyond the hill?"

"Nothing," Hollerer said. He switched off the engine, but the fan kept whirring.

Niksch had climbed about ten metres in pursuit of the monk. He put the camera to his eye, then turned and raised his shoulders. Hollerer gestured to him to continue. He pointed left, right and shrugged. Niksch shrugged too.

"Niksch has many talents," Hollerer said. "He's a good driver for one. Unfortunately he's a crap policeman. He works like he drives a car: with concentration but far too fast. And he's addicted to twists and turns, with no desire to proceed in a straight line. He prefers to work cross-country, if you see what I mean."

"Not entirely."

"Well, let's just say his results are creative, but ineffectual."

Bonì smiled.

They'd met in the summer before René Calambert. Hollerer was already pretty portly back then, but if her mind wasn't playing tricks he'd put on even more weight since. And he looked dishevelled, almost as if he'd gone to seed. He'd shaved badly and the jacket of his uniform was stained. Breadcrumbs stuck to his belly.

"Why am I here?" she asked.

"There are some people who have a sixth sense for danger," Hollerer said. "They see something or someone and the alarm bells start ringing: 'Danger Ahead'. They see someone like that guy over there," he said, nodding towards the monk, "and sense that something's not quite right."

"And you're one of those?"

"No, but Ponzelt is. Our mayor."

Louise laughed and Hollerer joined in grimly. But he soon turned serious again.

In Ponzelt's head, he explained, the monk had become the Antichrist smoothing the path to Liebau for a pack of devils. "*That's* why you're here," he said. "To reassure Ponzelt and put the wind up the Antichrist. Mind you, Ponzelt isn't entirely wrong . . . something funny *is* going on up here." Again he nodded in the direction of the monk. "He's frightened. And injured."

Hollerer described the injuries. He admitted that they could have resulted from an accident. Who knew how long the monk had been wandering around in the open? He might have run into a tree in frenzied enlightenment. Perhaps some youths had beaten him up. "And yet," Hollerer said.

"You *are* one of them," Louise protested.

Hollerer laughed. "And what about you?"

She shrugged. I used to be, Bonì thought. But ever since René Calambert she didn't trust her inner voice so much.

Hollerer looked down at the crumbs on his belly, but didn't brush them off. "Right, then," he said, opening the door.

She had no desire to follow the monk through the cold. What she most wanted was to drive back to Liebau with Hollerer, find a bar and have a nice chat. Louise felt she had a right to defy obstinate buggers like Ponzelt and Bermann, at least at the weekend. With a sigh, she got out.

At the bottom of the hill they trudged side by side, sinking to their ankles in the snow. After twenty metres Hollerer was panting loudly. Niksch had moved on and was now photographing the monk from a different angle. Hollerer waved to him. "That's fine," he shouted. "You can come back down now."

Bonì sensed that Hollerer wanted to be alone with her. Something was weighing on his mind and she had an idea what it might be.

They watched as Niksch returned to his car. Then Hollerer said, "I've heard about that thing with the French guy."

"And?"

"That's always been my biggest fear. That I'll arrive too late."

"That you . . ." She hadn't thought about the girl in a long time. She'd only thought about Calambert, not the dead girl.

Calambert had folded up the girl like a piece of paper so she would fit in the boot of his car. Annetta. Raped, beaten, strangled. And still she had survived for four days.

There had been a sticker on his rear window – IT'S A MAN'S WORLD.

She couldn't remember how she'd found Annetta. Couldn't recall opening the boot, untying her and calling the doctor. It was all in her report so that's how it must have happened. She'd forgotten everything except Calambert's face as he was dying.

"It seems to have taken its toll on you too," Hollerer said, glancing over her face and body.

She blushed. You couldn't hide four and a half kilos. Or insomnia, or all the rest.

But she was grateful to Hollerer for having reminded her of the girl.

When Niksch got into his car they went on. Louise's trainers were soaked and the cold crept up her legs. Her anorak offered little protection against the icy wind. Hollerer, wearing only the jacket of his uniform, was visibly freezing too.

She put her hand in her right pocket. "Well, well, what have we here?" she said, pulling out a miniature of Jägermeister.

"Bloody hell!" Hollerer said.

"Just to warm me up." She opened the little bottle. Hollerer took a swig too.

As they continued on their way, Hollerer called out several times, telling the monk to stop and wait where he was. But the monk did not react.

They began their ascent of the slope. Bonì soon broke into a sweat, but she was freezing at the same time. The wind seemed to be growing ever colder. She glanced at Niksch's patrol car as it swerved and hurtled into the distance, then at Hollerer, whose face was now the same shade of red as when they'd met two and a half years ago. She couldn't help smiling as she recalled how furious he'd been at the time. Could you really kill someone you love?

After another few metres Hollerer could go no further. Gasping for breath, he rested his hands on his thighs for support and motioned with his head for her to continue alone. "But . . . be careful. Have you got a . . ." He coughed.

". . . a weapon?" She shook her head.

"There's . . . something . . . funny," Hollerer wheezed.

She looked up the slope. They'd gained quite a lot of ground; the monk was now only thirty or so metres away. With his staff he laboured up through the snow. He looked small and thin. He didn't glance even once in her direction. Did Hollerer really think this guy was dangerous? The father in the kitchen had been dangerous. Calambert had been dangerous. But the monk?

Far off in the distance Niksch turned onto the main road. From up here she could just about distinguish it in the landscape, the carriageway slightly raised above the snow-covered fields it cut through. A narrow dark strip running parallel to the horizon marked the lower edge of the road.

"Here." Hollerer passed her his gun. It was Sig Sauer, not a Walther P5. Having checked the safety catch, she stuck the pistol into her waistband. Bermann had loved the Sig, a great piece of kit, he'd called it. The first weapon she had held in her hand since Calambert's death was Bermann's favourite pistol.

She thanked Hollerer and trudged onwards.

2

Louise caught up with the monk a few minutes later. He nodded, but did not stop. She cast Hollerer, now forty metres below her, a look of exasperation. The monk gave off an odour of sweat, body, something unfamiliar. She put a hand on his arm and eventually he stopped. Beneath her hand his robe was damp. Smiling at him reassuringly, she examined his injuries, and the monk simply stared at her. She felt silly in the Rastafarian sunglasses.

Hollerer was right. It was impossible to say for certain that the bruising had been caused by an accident. If so, why did the monk seem so afraid? Not of her, nor of Hollerer, but of something they couldn't see. She sensed that he wanted to get away from the ridge.

Instinctively she looked around. About a hundred metres to her left began a forest. On the other side, where Hollerer was, lay fields. Besides him there was nobody to be seen.

"I'd like to talk to you," she said.

The monk looked at her in silence. In spite of his exhaustion and fear he exuded serenity, a sort of composure that was unfamiliar to her. That was a composure you could never lose, she thought, no matter what happened.

While the monk's eyes floated across her face from an apparently vast distance, it felt to Bonì as if he was *reading* her features. He was reading what had happened with René Calambert, and reading what had happened since. How she had changed. Without thinking she lowered her gaze and the monk turned to go. She hesitated briefly, then followed him.

*

27

Ten minutes passed. The monk seemed to have forgotten Louise. He didn't turn to look at her or try to dissuade her from tailing him. Slowly but purposefully he headed for the forest.

Hollerer hadn't forgotten his new colleague, she could hear him shouting. After they'd left the ridge and were heading down the other side the snow swallowed his calls.

She had no idea why she felt such a keen desire to accompany the monk for part of his mysterious journey, despite the cold and her sodden feet. She hadn't felt anything as strongly since Calambert. Perhaps she wanted to protect the monk, or take away his fear. Perhaps she wanted to discover what he'd read in her face.

My fourth snowman, she thought, grinning.

Hollerer's voice grew louder again. "Hey!" he called crossly, and she stopped. He'd struggled painfully up to the ridge and was now standing diagonally above them, bending over to recover his breath. "What do you think you're doing?"

"Accompanying him for a bit."

"You're doing *what*? Where to?"

She pointed to the forest.

"But that's utter madness!' Hollerer exclaimed. "It'll be dark in a couple of hours."

"I'll keep in touch," she said, turning to go.

Hollerer bellowed two or three more times before giving up. When she glanced over her shoulder a few minutes later he had vanished.

The monk stopped at the edge of the forest and raised his eyebrows at her. Only now did Louise begin to consider how they might continue. The forest floor was covered in snow. The trees were bare and not very close together, and the wind whistled through them almost un- impeded. Her shoes and socks were wet, her trousers damp to the knees, her T-shirt and bra soaked with sweat. She was beginning to feel hungry. And she needed to pee. She smiled to herself.

The monk said something in a language she didn't know, his voice high-pitched and slightly shrill. His expression was stern.

"English? Français? Italiano?" Bonì asked.

The monk answered in his own tongue.

"To-ky-o?"

A fleeting smile, then his lips reassumed their grim pose. "*Tokyo*," he said.

She nodded in satisfaction. The question of his nationality was settled.

He led her along the edge of the forest, evidently in search of a path or a way in. She didn't get the impression that he was heading in a particular direction, he just wanted to be inside the forest, away from Liebau. Where he went didn't seem to matter.

She followed him, frozen by now. Her feet were blocks of ice, her trouser legs stiff. Well, well, what have we here? she thought, taking the bottle of Jägermeister from her pocket. Warmth briefly returned to her belly.

From time to time she scanned the countryside around her. Once she spotted a distant walker in the infinite expanse of white. Leaping around the figure was a large dog. The monk had caught sight of them too and paused for a moment. He spoke to her in his high-pitched monotone. Although she couldn't understand him, she knew what he was saying. "Don't waste your breath," she grunted. "I'm coming with you." He shrugged. That's that sorted out then, she thought.

Between scraps of cloud stood a sickly, pallid moon. The sun was nowhere to be seen.

About forty minutes after Hollerer had vanished down the other side of the hill Louise heard the revving of an engine. A patrol car was approaching, careening across the field. At the wheel she recognised

Niksch, and beside him Hollerer. Niksch was radiating concentration, Hollerer gripping the dashboard with both hands. The monk glanced at the car but didn't stop.

While she waited for the two men, she felt anger brewing inside her. What business was it of Hollerer's what she did? Had he rung Bermann? Bring that madwoman back! he would have said. She also imagined Bermann saying, Hey, it's a man's world. With a big grin across his face. It dawned on her for the first time that Bermann *had* used this phrase on occasion, before and after Calambert.

Hey, it's a man's world, he'd said, throwing up his hands in resignation.

The police car stopped beside her. Hollerer got out, while Niksch kept the engine running.

"Bugger off!" she said.

"Hang on a minute," Hollerer said. He opened the boot and took out a rucksack. "Blanket, jumper, undergarments, walking boots, socks, hot tea, hunting knife, radio, salami roll for you, cheese roll for him. Have I forgotten anything, Niksch?"

"My very expensive Maglite torch," Niksch said.

"Look after it, won't you?" Hollerer leaned the rucksack against her legs. "With Amelie's compliments." He smiled grimly.

"Thanks."

"Do me a favour and use the radio once in a while." Hollerer got back into the car. "Oh, you might come across some reporters. Ponzelt was just on the radio talking about the monk."

"Tell him to back off."

"No need. He's going skiing tomorrow with his sons. And when he's got something planned with his sons nothing will stop him, not even oriental terrorists. The crusade will kick off on Monday."

"We'll see about that. Say hi to Amelie."

Surprised, Hollerer raised his eyebrows and nodded.

*

Fifteen minutes later they came across a path that led into the forest. After a few metres the monk stopped and looked blankly at Louise, then at the rucksack on her back.

She narrowed her eyes. "What now?"

He didn't reply, but went on.

Darkness descended in the forest. Although flashes of bright grey still appeared between the trees behind them, night already seemed to be oozing from the narrow trunks. Bonì removed her sunglasses and it struck her that soon it would be too late to turn around. Not that she wanted to. For some inexplicable reason she was enjoying tailing the monk. She didn't mind where they were heading either, at least for the moment. He was taking her away from something, after all.

He's taking me away from Calambert, she thought. From Bermann. From *myself.*

It struck Bonì that he was leading her away from her life in more than just a symbolic way. He was escorting her through the snow from one life to another. The narrow path through the forest was like a bridge, at the other side of which lay something different. They were passing through an intermediate realm.

She shook her head. Jägermeister meditations. Not as nutty as vodka meditations or even țuică meditations. That was the worst. When she drank țuică with Ronescu and listened to his dark vowels, everything in her head went haywire. Faces, memories, fantasies and visions hurtled through her skull like a meteorite storm. Connections and relations changed, faces switched names, heads swapped bodies. Germain, her brother, dashed from life to death and back again. Mick, her ex-husband, was elected pope. Nobody was what they'd been a few seconds before.

Only the end was the same each time. When the țuică bottle was empty and Ronescu lay snoring on the sofa, her father would barge his way into her consciousness. You've got to look after me! he'd scream, You've got to look after me, do you hear? You've got to look after me right now!

In real life he was more subtle, especially since Germain's death in 1983: he said nothing at all.

The monk had stopped. To their left, a little further ahead in the forest, rose a five-metre-high vertical mass of earth. There was no snow on the narrow strip that ran beside this elevation. Laying his stick and bowl on the damp ground, the monk disappeared between the trees into the dusk.

Louise went in the opposite direction and relieved herself behind some rocks before changing her clothes. She briefly felt as if she were getting herself ready for a ceremony.

But Amelie's clothes weren't quite right for a ceremony. She was clearly the same dimensions as Hollerer. You could have fitted a basketball inside the extravagant briefs, and she couldn't feel the long johns against her skin until she put the slacks on top. The length was right at least. She passed on the flesh-coloured bra. Hollerer must have been mightily amused when packing the rucksack, if it hadn't been too annoying a task. Amelie's fleece jumper hung in folds from her body. But the walking boots were a perfect fit.

Hollerer had thought of the monk too. At the bottom of the rucksack, as if he'd hoped Louise wouldn't find them, was a rolled-up pair of men's long johns.

When she returned to their camp the monk was sitting on the ground with his back against the earthen wall. His eyes were open but he wasn't looking at her. In the gathering darkness his two injuries looked like dark plague marks.

She tossed Hollerer's long johns into his lap and turned away. Rustling noises told her that the monk was putting them on.

They shared the rolls, and it turned out the monk was not a vegetarian. As they ate she offered him a cup filled from the thermos, but he shook his head. He said something then rapped his chest and coughed gently. She nodded, poured tea into his bowl, then drank from the cup.

"Origami," she said. "Sushi. Harakiri. Banzai. Samurai. Er . . . Mikado." She grinned. "Kawasaki."

"Yes," the monk said gruffly in English.

"Sorry," she said.

The next hours passed agonisingly slowly. For some reason she'd expected the monk's presence to keep her ghosts at bay. But as she sat beside him on the narrow, snow-free strip of forest floor, wrapped in the blanket, they all paid a visit: Calambert, Germain, Mick . . . even her father.

Not moving, but with her eyes open, she surrendered to the images. Calambert amidst the crystals of blood. The weight of the smoking Walther in her hand. The acrid smell from the pistol. Germain, who overturned his car on an icy French highway. Mick, who as they went up the mountain in thick snow in Scuol confessed to so many affairs that the chairlift ride wasn't long enough to enumerate them all. Who looked at her with such naivety and resignation that she whacked him on the side of his head with a ski stick when they got to the mid-station.

At some point she was overcome by tiredness.

When she woke again, barely an hour had passed.

Louise lay on her side facing away from the monk, freezing miserably. Well, well, what have we here? she thought and searched through the pockets of her anorak. But they were empty. Half-heartedly she drank some tea, which was also running low.

The monk was still sitting upright. His eyes were closed, but she didn't think he was sleeping. He looked tense and alert, coughing gently now and then.

She was about to lie down again when she heard a muffled crackling from the rucksack and Hollerer's voice. "*Frau . . . er . . . Boni? Can you hear me?*"

She took out the radio. As she looked for the push-to-talk button

in the torchlight she heard Niksch whisper, "*You've got to say 'Over',*
boss."

"*My, my Niksch, what would I do without you?*"

"*'Over', boss.*"

"*Leave me alone.*"

"Everything's O.K.," she said. Her watch read ten o'clock.

"*She's got to say 'over' too,*"

"*For Christ's sake, Niksch!*" Hollerer lowered his voice. "*How are you?*"

"Freezing, but still alive!"

"*What about the monk?*"

"He's wearing your thermals and sends his thanks." She heard
Niksch giggle. Hollerer growled something incomprehensible.

Suddenly she felt the monk's hand on her arm and she turned. He
moved his head closer and put a finger to his lips. There was urgency
in his eyes. Softly she said, "Hollerer, I have to go now."

"*Wait . . . Your boss rang, Bermann. Want to know what he said?*"

The monk was tugging roughly at her sleeve.

"No."

"*I'll tell you anyway. He . . .*"

"Hollerer, I'm absolutely fine. That's all." She took her finger off
the button and switched off the radio. And then her mobile in the
chest pocket of her anorak.

She looked thoughtfully at the monk. His finger was still pressed
to his lips. What was he afraid of? She felt goosebumps forming. Now
the monk dropped his hand and leaned back.

Louise stared at the trees in front of them. She became aware for
the first time of the sounds of this winter night. Icy branches cracked
while the rising and falling of the wind produced a soft rustling.
Nothing could be seen.

Unsettled, she drank the last of the tea and it was a long time before
she fell asleep again.

*

Bonì woke as the first traces of the morning light appeared in the sky. It took her a moment to understand what had woken her. She could hear a man's voice talking softly nearby.

The monk was awake too and wide-eyed with fear. He put a finger to his lips again and gestured for her to follow him. Her unease intensified. Quickly, and as quietly as possible, she gathered up her things and packed them into the rucksack. The monk waited impatiently.

When she stood it was silent again; she could no longer hear the voice, but she became aware of other sounds.

The muffled crunching of snow.

Footsteps.

The monk waved frantically to indicate that they should leave and pointed to the ground. She must stick to the snow-free path.

They walked along the wall of earth, which became lower after a few metres as the slope fell steeply. At the point where it levelled with forest floor the monk stopped. He signalled that they would walk on the snow to the left, but backwards. She smiled: what an idea. He raised his eyebrows – O.K.? She nodded.

Before Louise turned, she scanned the rows of trees in front of her. The crunching of footsteps was getting closer but still she saw no-one. Who was it? Hollerer and Niksch? Knowing she was armed they would have called out to her. The reporters Hollerer had spoken about? Possibly, but unlikely. Ponzelt and a mob from Liebau? Hardly.

A hissing sounded behind her. The monk motioned to her to get moving. Carefully Louise took one step back, then another. She clenched the right pocket of her anorak with both hands to stop the empty Jägermeister bottle from clanking against her keys.

After a couple of dozen paces she stepped onto soft, snow-free forest floor and turned. Before her towered rocks covered in moss and earth.

The monk had disappeared.

Anger and panic rose inside her, anger most of all. Cursing to herself she walked a few metres alongside the rocks. It was as if a temperamental god had shaken the boulders like dice in his huge hand and let them fall at random.

The hissing again. She spun around. Two metres above her the almost-bald head of the monk bobbed amongst the rocks. A hand waved her up.

Noiselessly Louise hurried back and climbed in amongst the heap of dice. When she'd almost reached the monk she glanced in the direction from which they'd come. On impulse she crouched down against the rocks. A hundred or so metres away several dark shapes were moving in front of the white tree trunks that faced the wind. She held her breath and closed her eyes.

When she opened them again the shapes had vanished.

Jägermeister visions, she thought with relief.

But the figures reappeared. She counted three. She blinked. Four, or only three? She was unwilling to believe that these were people. People who might be after the monk. Three or four Calamberts, maybe armed, maybe intending to kill him. A man as defenceless as Annetta, who would end up folded like a piece of paper in someone's car boot if she didn't prevent it.

Hearing a voice in her ear she lookeded at the monk in astonishment. "What?" she asked softly.

"No," he whispered. "*No.*" He shook his head vigorously.

Only now did she notice that he was clinging to her arms. She was holding Hollerer's pistol in her right hand and had moved as if about to run off. She closed her eyes and let the monk pull her back down.

It was dark behind the boulders, and not as cold. Three or four people could have fitted into this cavity. Huddled together they waited, arms clasped around their knees. Bonì noticed a pleasant warmth emanating from the monk. She heard and saw nothing save for his deep breathing and the second hand of her watch. Had the figures moved on? Were they climbing over the rocks?

She closed her eyes and concentrated, but her ears picked up no sound. As the seconds ticked past, she found the silence all the more unnatural, like the artificial silence of a soundproofed room.

Mick's drum kit had stood in a soundproofed room. Annetta had lain in a soundproofed room for four days. A room with a large, square window. That's the porthole, Annetta's mother had said. She's on a long voyage and she can look out whenever she wants. And we can look in.

Louise tried but failed to visualise Annetta in the soundproofed room. Had she visited her in hospital? Had Annetta ever been in such a room. And if so, why? She couldn't remember. Whenever she thought of Annetta she pictured Calambert. The victim faded, the murderer remained.

She could clearly picture Annetta's mother, however. And her father. A short, muscular man in an elegant, grey three-piece suit. Thanks, the father told her after Annetta had disembarked in her ocean liner. He placed both hands on her right hand and said, "Thanks for doing away with that bastard." No agitation in his voice, just contentment. He could just as easily have said, "Thanks for bringing the pizza round."

Jägermeister memories.

It seemed to be getting warmer in the hollow, as if the monk had an internal heat source. She shifted closer and felt a thin arm, a leg. The now-familiar smell of sweat, dirt and foreignness grew stronger. She resisted turning away. What might his name be?

Calm, deep breaths, the ticking of her watch. Darkness in the soundproofed space as day broke on the other side of the rocks. Nothing else existed. No Calambert, no Bermann, no Mick, no loneliness. Nothing. She was overcome by a feeling of inner peace.

Then she fell asleep with Hollerer's cold pistol in her hand.

She woke at around nine. A ghostly grey light seeped into the hollow. The monk was awake too, gazing at her with a serious expression. He looked helpless, without hope. But maybe it was just the light.

She thought they had waited long enough. Whoever had been out there, they must be long gone by now. She needed something to eat and drink, to organise some protection, have the evidence secured. Pee. She stretched and began to get up.

"*No,*" the monk whispered. He tapped his wrist with his finger. Not yet. Let's wait a while longer.

She shook her head and placed a hand on her stomach.

"*No,*" the monk repeated.

"Yes," she said, pulling herself up. He yanked her firmly back down. Anger surged inside her. "Fine," she hissed. "You'll have to watch me pee then." On her knees she shifted a little away from him, then opened her belt and zip.

For a moment the monk stopped breathing, then quickly looked away.

"Look at me," she said. But he didn't react.

At 9.30 a.m. they left the crevice. For minutes they crouched against the rocky wall and surveyed their surroundings. Nobody to be seen or heard.

They didn't return along the path, but hurried alongside the rocks in the opposite direction. It felt warmer than the day before. Somewhere in the grey above them Bonì sensed rays of sun, and the snow gleamed gently.

She found herself wondering whether they were still in the intermediate realm. Or had they reached the other side of the bridge?

If so, this new life looked just the same as the previous one.

3

Hollerer and Niksch arrived at around eleven o'clock. Louise was waiting at the edge of the forest. She had tried in vain to stop the monk, but he had put his hands together, bowed and continued on his way. Her eyes flicked uneasily between the approaching patrol car and the monk heading into the distance. The dark robe was easy to make out against the white of the snow. A simple target for a marksman, even from far away.

"Your boss is right about you," Hollerer said when he opened the passenger window.

Louise slipped off the rucksack and sat in the back. "No doubt." She gave Hollerer back his Sig. It was warm inside the car, almost as warm as sitting beside the monk in the hollow. All of a sudden the tiredness returned, the exhaustion. She sank back. She needed sleep and something to eat. She thought, soberly, that her excursion into the other world was over.

They watched the monk.

"If someone really is after him, we've got to get the guy to safety," Hollerer said eventually. He sounded vexed. It seemed he had given up wanting to wait and see what happened.

"He won't want that," she said.

Niksch glanced at her in the rear-view mirror. He whistled a tuneless melody through his teeth and looked away again. "So what *are* we going to do with him?" Hollerer said to the windscreen. Then he asked Louise to give a more detailed account of what had happened.

As she talked, Niksch drove back along the snow-covered road, which ran close to the forest a couple of hundred metres further on.

Louise didn't let the monk out of her sight. "*Slowly*, Niksch!" Hollerer roared.

They waited where the road almost touched the forest. Turning to Louise, Niksch said, "If he continues at that pace he'll be outside the Breisgau–High Black Forest district soon. Whose responsibility is he then?"

"No idea."

"Depends where he's going," Hollerer said. "Is he heading towards Emmingden or Black Forest–Baar?"

"Black Forest–Baar, looks like."

"Then it's the Villingen-Schwenningen team."

"Let's guide him to Emmendingen, boss. Karlbert Maurer's there. He'd love to grapple with our monk, don't you think?"

"Good God, Karlbert Maurer." Hollerer laughed.

Louise felt her anger returning. Anger at Hollerer and Niksch, who didn't seem to understand how serious the situation was. Who didn't understand how special the man in the dark robe was. Anger at Bermann and at herself. At the monk who just went on his way, refusing help. At Mick and René Calambert and Annette's father.

She got out.

Hollerer wound down the window. Now serious, he asked, "Did you say three or four people? And you're sure? I mean, that there *was* someone there?"

Louise stared nervously at the white horizon. "What's Bermann been saying about me?" She realised she had her hand around the empty bottle in her right-hand pocket. There was a tired, almost bashful clinking.

"That you're loopy."

She laughed. Niksch giggled inside the car, then sneezed. "Either believe me or don't," she said.

"But I do," Hollerer said, getting out too.

Louise was still gazing at the horizon. Something looked odd, but she couldn't figure out what it was. On the left was the forest they'd walked through. Adjoining that was a wide field blanketed in snow, and to the right stood a wooded hill. A typically bleak, frozen winter landscape.

Behind her Niksch got out of the car and blew his nose loudly.

Then she saw it. About fifty metres ahead a thin dark line cut diagonally through the snowy field. She tramped off towards it. The line became a busy criss-cross. The criss-cross became footprints.

At least three people. The tracks went left to right from the forest to the hill. The snow at the edge of the prints was crumbly. "Hollerer!" she shouted. Louise stared at the hill, but couldn't see anything.

Hollerer spent several minutes examining the footprints. He leaned over them, frowning. There's a difference between believing and knowing, Bonì thought as she looked him up and down. Suddenly she thought of Amelie. Amelie placing dishes of pasta parcels onto the table in a silent dining room, after the father had put down the knife and released his wife and daughter. Amelie didn't stop talking; Hollerer didn't say a word. When she went into the kitchen he looked down, exhausted, and smiled at his hands.

"Could have been walkers or hunters," Hollerer said. But there was doubt in his voice. He looked over at the hill. Today he was wearing a crumpled ski jacket over his police coat, with blue gloves and a bobble hat that was too small. He stood bent at the waist, as if unable to straighten up immediately. He didn't seem to notice that twenty metres behind him the monk was walking past at the edge of the forest.

The monk would spot the footprints too, but he didn't react. She waited, but he didn't look at her.

"Someone's coming," Niksch called out behind them. Holding a tissue he pointed in the direction from which he and Hollerer had come. In the distance a dark dot was visible against the white, and it was slowly coming closer. Hollerer and Bonì hurried back to the patrol car. Mesmerised, they watched as another car approached. Hollerer felt for his Sig.

"Dark-red Daimler, C-Class, T-Model," Niksch said.

"Lederle," Bonì said, relieved.

Reiner Lederle had been a happy man until eighteen months ago when the doctors diagnosed his wife with bowel cancer. Ever since that moment he'd changed along with her. He'd been getting ever greyer, thinner and slower. Sometimes he would disappear for a week. When he came back it looked as if he'd been through the chemotherapy himself rather than his wife. Louise could have sworn he'd even lost some hair. And she thought that he'd begun to smell ill too.

Lederle was there two years ago in Munzingen. Like the others, he'd gone off in the right direction.

"Don't talk to him about illnesses, women or God," she told Hollerer. "Talk about Freiburg football club, skittles and politics. He's Green to his core and the best thing that ever happened to him was when Salomon was elected mayor."

"Christ," Hollerer groaned.

"And keep a close eye on the monk."

"What do you want me to do?" Niksch asked.

"You're going to get me back to town as quickly as possible."

Niksch laughed. "As quickly as possible, or as quickly as I can?"

Lederle shook their hands, including Bonì's.

"Sorry," she said. "I've ruined your weekend."

He shrugged without letting go of her hand. "Doesn't matter."

Lederle used to call her "Luis" too. But ever since he'd known his wife was ill he'd reverted to "Bonì". She stared at her hand, confused, because he hadn't let go. For an instant the world seemed to stand still. Nobody spoke, nobody moved. Lederle gazed at her with dark eyes, as if about to leap into her arms. In two weeks he'd accompany his wife again to her chemotherapy.

"O.K., Bonì," he said finally, releasing her hand. "What can I do for you?"

Louise didn't feel comfortable leaving Hollerer and Lederle alone together. An elderly, overweight village policeman and a depressed detective did not add up to a promising team.

"Hurry," she pleaded.

Niksch grinned. "I've been thinking," he said, as the back end of the car swerved and the road danced in front of them. Bonì closed her eyes. When she opened them again, Hollerer and Lederle were still watching them go. They stood two metres apart and looked helpless, small. Lost in this bright whiteness that brought forth secrets and concealed answers. Now they moved over to Lederle's Daimler and got inside. Two strays on a winter Sunday outing.

She could only pray that the strangers from the forest wouldn't return until more officers came to protect the monk, Hollerer and Lederle.

She looked at Niksch. "What have you been thinking?"

"Well, there are three possibilities. The monk's going to be killed, kidnapped or beaten up. Two years ago in Baden-Württemberg we had a clearance rate for murder and manslaughter of 94 per cent, for kidnapping and false imprisonment almost 92 per cent and for grievous bodily harm it was . . . I think only 87 per cent. That means . . ." Niksch broke off.

"That means," she said to complete his sentence, "it would be best if he were killed, because statistically we'd be more likely to find out who did it." She forced a smile. "Niksch, is that an attempt to *comfort* me?"

Niksch blushed. "Well, you did spend the whole night with him and . . ."

She pulled up her leg and turned half towards him. "And?"

"And . . . and you formed some social ties with him."

"Keep your fantasy in check, Niksch."

"O.K., I'm sorry. I just wanted to say that you're very brave. I mean, what you did was very . . . erm . . ."

". . . brave."

"Yes."

"Thank you." She clapped him on the shoulder.

Niksch turned onto a wider road. His cheeks were bright red.

It looked as though the snow was starting to thaw. In some places on either side of the road patches of black were visible. But as the car raced past, they rose into the air and became crows. Yesterday things moved that shouldn't have. Today things were changing identity. And she existed somewhere between these two poles, she thought with a touch of amusement.

It had all begun with Calambert. Calambert, who kept rising from the depths of her memory in an icy sea of blood. Sometimes he settled on her retina and then she saw the world through a veil of Calambert.

At the time Bermann hadn't questioned her actions. He'd never asked whether she had operated in accordance with the regulations. He could have said, "Did you warn him you were going to shoot? What did you say, exactly? Did you order him to stand still? How many times did you shout out?" He had also made sure that nobody else asked her such questions. Strange, she thought, even when he was being nice she found Bermann unpleasant.

Calambert and Bermann. Sometimes she visualised them in a twin pack.

"Niksch, would you stop at the next petrol station, please?"

Louise spent the minutes that followed in a half sleep. Chaotic images and thoughts bustled through her head. Calambert and Bermann were gone, Hollerer and Lederle soon disappeared. Only the faces of Mick and the monk popped up, as well as Anatol, the taxi driver from yesterday, who was now wearing the rectangular sunglasses himself. Inside her head, nobody said anything; only she spoke. She was naked and said to them: Look at me.

Although the traffic was beginning to get heavier, Niksch barely slowed down. He seemed to enjoy talking because every time she was jolted awake he was speaking. Once or twice she managed to listen for a few seconds. He was telling her about his fiancée, Theres, the daughter of the Liebau butcher.

Theres went rally driving too.

"Theres," Bonì said in disbelief. "Theres and Niksch."

Niksch smiled and said, "Can you get a doner kebab in Freiburg?"

When she woke later they had stopped at a petrol station, but the engine was still running. The first thing she noticed was that Niksch was talking differently. He seemed gentle and relaxed. Looking at her with glowing cheeks, he raised his eyebrows and nodded, as if to say: Well, that's how it is with the world in general, and with Theres and me in particular.

The second thing she noticed was that she'd stopped at this same petrol station a few weeks ago. At the counter behind the glass partition stood a chubby young man with cropped hair. She didn't recognise him, but she knew this meant nothing.

"Keep driving, Niksch," she said. "And tell me more – it's fascinating."

In Freiburg the snow was indeed thawing.

They stopped at the first petrol station that was open within the city limits. Bonì was almost certain she'd never been here before. On the counter she put three cartons of orange juice, three bottles of coke and two each of vodka and bourbon. "A little Sunday evening party," she said with a wolfish smile.

The bearded Turkish shop assistant grunted without looking up. She paid in cash, asked for three bags and packed away the bottles with an exaggerated yawn.

Then she asked where the loo was.

During their drive through the city she learned that Niksch had become a policeman because it had been his mother's dream. A policeman in the family brought security. Nobody would try it on with a family who had a policeman for a son. Not even God or fate, his mother said. When Bonì asked if his mother lived in Beirut, Niksch chuckled. Then he said that last year in the Breisgau–High Black Forest district, 11,397 crimes had been recorded, a 9.8 per cent rise on the previous year. Sexual offences had seen an 18 per cent increase. Niksch had three younger sisters, and a policeman in the family brought security.

"Does your mother live in Beirut?" Louise said, realising as she spoke that she'd already asked this question. Niksch frowned. "Left turn there," she said briskly. "We'll go to my place first."

Once inside her apartment she put the alcohol in the cupboard beneath the sink, and the coke and orange juice beside the dustbin. Then she changed and strapped on the holster with the Walther.

On the answerphone was a message from her father, demanding that she call back. "It's Sunday morning, Louise," he said with feigned levity, "where the *hell* are you?" After forty years of living in Germany his French accent had almost faded entirely. The hard "ch" sounds were no longer accompanied by an "s", while the short "i" no longer sounded like an "ee". His voice came across as simultaneously smug and obsequious. She hadn't heard him speak French in years.

"In the forest," she said to the answerphone.

"When are you going to come to Kehl?" her father said.

She shrugged.

On the way back down she bumped into Ronescu. Leaning on a snow shovel, he was standing in the middle of a group of tenants from the fourth floor. Today the bags under his eyes were drooping almost to the corners of his mouth.

She jostled her way through the group and passed close by him. "Eight o'clock tomorrow evening?" she whispered into his ear.

"Perfect, Frau Bonì," he whispered back.

When she was in the hallway the stairwell lights went out. The grey gloom reminded her of the dimness in the rocky cavity in the forest. She stopped. Where the *hell* are you? her father said in her head, and all of a sudden her eyes were flooded with tears. Louise let it gush out, a wave of mysterious grief that subsided as rapidly as it had risen. She blew her nose and left the building.

When she got into the car, Niksch said, "I could murder a doner."

"O.K."

"Or is it a döner?"

"No idea." She switched on her mobile. Bermann had left five messages since yesterday evening. She kept it on voicemail and put it in her anorak pocket.

"Might be a bit of traffic around here," Niksch said, concentrating hard.

Louise looked out at the street. Sunday afternoon in the snow, only a few cars out. "I thought you were a rally driver."

"They all go in the same direction."

She laughed.

On the way to police H.Q. she thought on more than one occasion that she could hear Bermann yelling in her anorak pocket, but perhaps she was only imagining it.

As they were parking outside headquarters she called Bermann. It was a moment before he picked up. "I'm here, Rolf," she said.

"Good," he said.

When they entered the office she shared with Lederle, Bermann was already waiting in the middle of the room with his hands in his jeans pockets. He looked overtired and gave the peculiar impression of being lost. He didn't appear cross. "Who's he?" he asked, looking at Niksch.

"A colleague from Liebau," Bonì said.

Bermann nodded in the direction of the door. There was no contempt in his gesture, just exhausted fatalism. Friendliness à la Bermann. Niksch opened his eyes wide. Stroking his arm, Bonì said, "Please wait outside."

Through the frosted glass she could see Niksch standing with his back to the door, as if trying to stop anyone from coming in or leaving. Maybe he just wanted to protect them.

Bermann watched her switch on the coffee machine. Even now he didn't turn into the fire-spitting demon she'd anticipated. In an almost soft voice he said, "A new phase has begun, Luis. From today everything is going down the official route . . ."

She turned around. "You waited until today?"

"I did."

She nodded. Bermann seemed unsure as how to interpret her nod. He sat on the edge of the desk and adjusted his tight jeans. "There'll be a few discussions," he said. "You'll be on sick leave for a while, go through some therapy, followed by desk work. And then in two or three years we'll fetch you back."

"Therapy?" she said, surprised.

"Rehab, Luis."

"Coffee, Rolf?"

Bermann hesitated before shaking his head.

She apologised and picked up the mobile from her desk. As Bermann didn't know she'd asked Lederle for help, she called Hollerer. He answered on the second ring. She heard the whistling of the wind and Lederle coughing in the background. They seemed to be standing in the open. Louise pictured the two of them, then the monk and herself sitting on the strip of forest floor where there was no snow. They walked on and were sitting in the cavity in the intermediate realm. It took a while for her to realise that she and the monk were talking to each other.

No change, Hollerer reported, the monk was traipsing through the snow and there was nobody else to be seen.

"Get back into the car, for God's sake," she said.

"We just wanted to stretch our legs. Is Niksch behaving himself?"

"Of course."

"Niksch isn't a city boy, he's a country bumpkin," Hollerer said. "In town he goes astray – make sure he doesn't get lost."

They hung up.

"Have you understood what this is about, Luis?" Bermann asked patiently. "Have you understood that it's serious now?"

"Later, Rolf, O.K.? We don't have time." She poured coffee into her mug while she explained to him what had and hadn't happened. She was glad to see that her hand wasn't trembling.

The mug had been a present from Bermann. On it was written: EVEN THE BEST SECRETARY SOMETIMES NEEDS A BREAK. She turned it in her hands and stared at the inscription so as not to have to look at Ber- mann. Why had she kept the mug? Why did she use it almost every day? To avoid giving Bermann the satisfaction of having managed to goad her into his petty war? Nice yellow, she'd said as she weighed up whether to smash the mug against his or her skull. The yellow of dawn.

Behind the door Niksch suppressed a sneeze.

"We need between four and six patrol cars," she said, "a Japanese interpreter, a helicopter." She sounded frantic and Bermann appeared to notice this, for he lowered his eyes and frowned. She took a sip of coffee and waited.

"Luis?" Bermann looked up. "Do you understand that it's serious?"

"You're repeating yourself."

"Come and sit next to me."

"Are you afraid I'm going to lose it?"

"Let's *talk*, Luis."

"Talk?" she said. "Coming from you that sounds perverted."

"I just want to find a solution, Luis."

She went over to her desk and sat down. Bermann seemed tense, and for a moment at a loss.

Niksch stood immobile outside the room. Even though she knew it was him she was unnerved by the tall shadow at the door, as if something dark and threatening was waiting to come in.

Bermann watched her. He appeared to sense that the gravity of the situation was slowly sinking in. His view of the world was simple: it consisted of opposites, which he mockingly referred to as "the real Yin and Yang". There were police officers and non-police officers, men and women, Germans and foreigners, healthy people and sick people. Where there were combinations of these he stuck rigidly to a hierarchy. Right at the top of this list was "Police". If someone was a police officer they could have as many negative attributes as you like – female, half Turkish and on maternity leave, for example – but for Bermann they were first and foremost a police officer. One of the family. Family members could be shouted down, ridiculed, double-crossed, despised and punished, but ultimately you had a duty to them. If they collapsed you looked after them. For even if they were wallowing in their own excrement and only grunting, they were still police officers.

This was an advantage of sorts of Bermann's real Yin and Yang. A distinct disadvantage was that one thing could never be the other. If Bermann thought she was sick, nothing and nobody could convince him of the opposite. He would not relent in his determination to ensure that she went the way of all patients, removed from the set of healthy people and placed with the sick ones.

"Do you remember Calambert?" she said.

"The fucking French paedo."

"The man I shot. You went one way; I went the other. Calambert was there and I shot him dead."

Bermann misunderstood her. "Even a blind chicken finds the odd bit of corn," he said gently. An affectionate joke. In his own way, she thought, Bermann could be sweet.

"That's when it began. You . . . you know that."

"No," Bermann said.

"What do you mean, 'No'?"

"It began earlier, Luis. You started boozing when your husband dumped you."

She leaped up. "I don't *booze*, for Christ's sake!" The sentence resonated in her head, just as the footsteps crunching in the snow had echoed the night before. *I don't booze.* She almost laughed when she realised that she was exhibiting typical alcoholic behaviour: denial. Bermann had Louise where he wanted her, in the set of sick people. So she refrained from pointing out the differences between herself and an alcoholic, which lay mainly in causes and volumes.

"Come here," Bermann said.

She went to him. Carefully he took her hand and pulled her right up to him. His knees were touching the outside of her thighs.

"If I were the person you'd like me to be," she said, "I'd think you wanted to kiss me and I'd throw myself into your strong arms."

Bermann hesitated. The idea didn't seem to appeal to him. "Open your mouth," he muttered.

"Listen, Rolf, I'm not saying I don't have the odd drink, and I'll freely admit that sometimes I have a bit too much. Yes, I did have a sip or two earlier on and I probably smell of alcohol. I spent the whole night in the forest waiting for us to be attacked . . . In any case, *you* stink of bacon and scrambled eggs." She broke away. "Now can we get things moving and request back-up and a helicopter?"

Bermann slid off the table. "We're not going to request anything. Let me put it this way: Just because a pisshead has night-time hallucinations in the forest and a nutty Jap is wandering around half naked, I'm not sending anyone else out. Do you understand?"

Louise nodded; she'd been expecting that. This was the Bermann she knew, and she preferred him like this to when he wanted to "talk". When people overstepped the invisible line between the real Yin and the real Yang they became dangerous.

Smiling, she went and opened the door. She could see in Niksch's eyes that he'd heard too much. But then he looked at Bermann and she understood that he wasn't going to stab her in the back. She sent Niksch into the next room to use the database and internet to find a Japanese translator and get an overview of Buddhist institutions in southern Baden.

"And call Hollerer," she said, "to see if everything's O.K."

"Alright boss," Niksch said.

"I don't believe it," she heard Bermann say behind her.

She closed the door. "Believe what you want, Rolf. Am I going to get my back-up?"

"No."

"So what's going to happen now?"

"You're going home, you're off today anyway. And if Almenbroich comes tomorrow you'll be on sick leave." Bermann's voice had softened again. In his eyes was that anxious sort of anger you feel towards children, patients and dogs. It was how Bonì looked at dried-out plants on balconies. She held his gaze even though she found it sinister. Once again he had overstepped the line.

Bermann remained silent and did not move as she sat at her computer and tried to concentrate. Even if she didn't know where the monk was heading, she might be able to find out where he'd come from. She'd look through press agency reports, ring the police stations to the south, west and east of Freiburg, ask the radio stations.

She looked at her watch. One o'clock. It occurred to her that she had eaten nothing since Hollerer's rolls. She felt a sudden voracious hunger. A voracious hunger, a thirst and an indefinable sexual desire.

She sighed. "Fine," she said to Bermann. "Let's compromise."

Today Bermann would leave her in peace. If by tomorrow it transpired that the men in the forest and the danger facing the monk had all been in her head, she would voluntarily go with him to Almenbroich, the head of Kripo, the criminal police, and agree to whatever they decided. Sick leave, rehab, desk work.

When Bermann finally left, she wondered whether this was the abyss she'd foreseen the day before.

4

Niksch had been on the phone to a number of Japanese translators, now whittled down to a shortlist of three. "Three?" Louise said when they got into the car. "We only need one."

Niksch hummed and hawed. He hadn't been able to bring himself to choose one, had said he'd get back to them. "I don't know," he said, wiggling his fingers. "You'd be better at this. I'd go for the wrong woman."

"Woman?"

All three were women.

Bonì picked out a name and called the number. The voice at the other end sounded cheerful and savvy. Louise didn't consider her a good fit for the monk, but that was probably irrelevant. She agreed to an exorbitant fee and arranged for them both to meet the woman at 3.30.

They ate döners and drank mocha at a Turkish joint near the station. Niksch's eyes shone. For him, a döner kebab and mocha were synonymous with the big, wide world. "Döner was always a hit in our house, but there aren't any Turks in Liebau," he said, his elbows leaning on the high table. "There's an Italian, but he doesn't make döners either because he's a hairdresser."

She nodded mechanically while leafing through the printouts Niksch had given her. When he stopped talking she read out: "Buddhist Union, Buddhist Centre, Dharma Sah, Kum Nye Group, Mamaki Centre, Rangring Sangha, Rigpa, Rinzai Zen Association open brackets Kannon Dojo close brackets, Shambla Centre, Thich Nhat Hanh

Sangha, Urasenke Foundation, Kagyu House, Zen Academy, Zen Dojo Ho Un Do . . . And they're all in Freiburg." She took a deep breath. "Heavens. And what's Vajrayana, the Karma Kagyu tradition and Nyingma? Or Theravada? How about this? Tantra, Tibetan Buddhism, Soto School . . . I thought there was only *one* kind of Buddhism and that was that."

"Hmm," Niksch said with his mouth full.

"I mean, there's only one Christianity, isn't there?"

With his kebab Niksch made a movement that could have been a Yes or a skilful attempt to hide his ignorance.

Her eyes followed the döner to Niksch's mouth. "I know nothing about Buddhism," she said. Bread, meat and tomatoes vanished into Niksch's mouth. His jaws ground with relish. She emptied her glass of raki and said, "I don't know anything about Christianity either, or not much. All I know is that I don't believe in God and I certainly don't believe in Buddha. Which means I don't believe in anything I know nothing about. Interesting, don't you think?"

Niksch went on chewing for a while before wiping his mouth with a napkin. "Hollerer says there's an external faith and an int . . . Do you say internal or inner?"

"No idea, Nikki."

Niksch laughed and they went to the door. "Well, he says there's an external faith and an inner one. The external faith is like going to church on a Sunday, singing the hymns, praying, and during the sermon saying the Bible's right, so loud that everyone can hear. Your inner faith is doing everything God conceives. Hollerer says both are O.K."

Louise could find no fault with this theory either. "Talking of Hollerer . . ." she said.

This time she called Lederle.

"Ah, Bonì," Lederle mumbled and then yawned. Classical music was playing in the background. In her imagination Hollerer was sitting bunched up in the passenger seat, trying his best not to dirty Lederle's

Daimler, the interior of which was cleaned twice a week. She laughed silently to herself.

Everything was alright with Lederle and Hollerer.

"What about the monk?"

"He just keeps going."

"Stay as close to him as you can."

"Of course."

Outside the kebab shop the pavements had been cleared and melted snow dripped from the roofs. Milder temperatures and sunshine were forecast for the next few days. The worst was over, she thought, meteorologically at least.

The Kagyu House was nearest, so that's where they decided to begin.

During the short drive she told Niksch that the monk had been spotted in Badenweiler on Thursday morning. The postman there had called Freiburg police H.Q., which had sent a car to take a look, but the monk had already moved on. The officers drove for half an hour around the main roads out of town, but came back empty-handed. They drafted a report and oddly sent a copy to the foreign ministry in Berlin.

Louise had also had a copy of the report sent to her. It was as short as only a report could be. She'd chat to the postman tomorrow and ask him about the monk's head injuries.

From Badenweiler the monk had headed towards Kirchzarten – a good thirty kilometres as the crow flies, Niksch guessed. Thirty kilometres through snow, cold and darkness. Niksch was impressed. "In his sandals he can't be doing more than two and a half kilometres per hour."

To the west of Kirchzarten a farmer from Unterbirken had seen the monk. The farmer's wife had informed the Catholic priest – in the Unterbirken church confessional. With the woman beside him, the priest called the police station at Kirchzarten and another patrol car was dispatched. Again it came back unsuccessful; in the gathering dusk they hadn't been able to locate the monk.

The Kirchzarten postman hadn't made a statement and Louise wasn't able to get through to the Catholic priest. She found herself wondering, bizarrely, to what sins the farmer's wife had been confessing.

And then the monk had wandered in the driving snow past Hollerer's window in Liebau on Saturday morning. "Eight kilometres," Niksch said. "He's getting slower. The poor guy's going to pop his clogs at some point."

She thought of the warmth the monk's body had radiated and the strength of his hand.

Badenweiler, Kirchzarten, Liebau – he'd come from the southwest. From Badenweiler to the French border it was ten kilometres, perhaps thirty to the Swiss border. Had he come from a different country?

They were sitting in the car by a community centre covered in leafless ivy. From the outside, the four-storey building looked like all the others in the street. Bonì was curious; she didn't have the faintest idea of what went on inside. Niksch had already examined the doorbell nameplates, one of which read JULIANE VON GANDLER – KAGYU HOUSE. He said there was a "strange" smell by the front entrance.

What went on in a Kagyu House?

When they stepped onto the pavement she looked up. On both corners of a large stone balcony on the third floor sat two sturdy, grey Buddha figures, around forty centimetres high, like guards.

Juliane von Gandler was with Lama Tsogyal in India. Kagyu House was being looked after by a punk with piercings, sixteen years old at most. From inside came angry keyboard chords and deep laughter. "Are you her daughter?" Louise said.

The girl nodded apologetically. She was holding a lit cigarette, but there was also a strong whiff of incense. "Has she done anything wrong?"

"No. We just need someone who knows about Buddhism."

"Rich," the girl said. "He knows everything. He's at the university and his wife's from Japan. Richard Landen." The girl gave them an address in Günterstal, which Niksch jotted down.

Bonì thanked her, then noticed the can of beer in the girl's other hand. "Get rid of the fag butts and tins before your mum comes back."

The girl grinned. "That's not for another two months."

"What's she doing in India?"

"Contortions. Then she's going to organise a demo against China."

"Against China?" Niksch said.

"China's occupying Tibet," the girl said with a gentle smile. "The Dalai Lama can't go home."

In the car Louise scanned the list of Buddhist institutions in Freiburg. Richard Landen's name didn't crop up. Niksch sneezed twice, then suggested she give him a call. "Maybe he's with Lama Tsogyal in India too," he said. "If so, we're driving to Günterstal for nothing."

"Günterstal's really close, Niksch. It just sounds like it's far away." All the same she took out her mobile, called directory enquiries, then Richard Landen. Engaged.

"I prefer it when you say 'Nikki'," Niksch said, blushing.

"When did I call you 'Nikki'?"

"When we were having our kebabs."

"Oh, O.K. then, *bel ami.*"

She put away her mobile and tried to remember what connection she had to Günterstal. When the first houses appeared in the grey sunlight it came to her: Lederle had told her that Hans Filbinger lived in Günterstal.

Richard Landen's small house was surrounded by a wooden fence and stood beneath the bare boughs of a willow. To Bonì it looked as if the willow with its long fingers were making a grab for the roof to lift the house in the air and send it spinning away. In the garden to the side of the building she could see a shed amongst more trees, and in front of it stood some sort of fountain. The grass had a fine covering of snow. Only the stepping stones that led to the shed and the gravel path to the garden gate had been swept.

"Someone's at home," Niksch said.

She nodded. Lights were on in two rooms, to the left on the ground floor and to the right upstairs.

They went to the garden gate. The letterbox read TOMMO/LANDEN. Bonì pressed the bell, but heard no sound.

Niksch suddenly grew nervous. His right hand fidgeted with his thigh, his arm slightly crooked. "Funny names," he whispered.

"Quiet, Nikki."

From the corner of her eye she saw a curtain twitch at the downstairs window on the left. Nothing moved upstairs. She wondered what it was the willow didn't like about this house or its inhabitants.

The front door opened, revealing a tall, slim man of about forty. "Come in," he said. "The tea's just ready."

Niksch's mistrust was visibly aroused once more when the tall man – Richard Landen – placed what must have been a Japanese cup containing a steaming liquid in front of him. The tea was green. He cleared his throat.

Landen had taken them into a small, maize-coloured kitchen. The table, chairs and fitted cupboards were made of light wood. Bonì noted with awe how immaculately clean and tidy everything was. No dirty dishes in the sink, no crumbs of bread, no stains. The towels hanging on hooks beside the window were freshly ironed. On the windowsill sat a shiny black china cat, which stared at her implacably.

Only on the dining table was there any hint of disorder: a plugged-in laptop, beside it books, photocopied pages and pens.

She felt the urge to get out of this kitchen and house as quickly as possible. The orderliness, the cat and Richard Landen all made her feel uneasy. Why, she couldn't say. She considered asking Landen for a

dash of rum in her tea. An old habit, she could tell him, English ancestors. Instead she said, "We don't have much time."

"Selly said you were looking for someone who knows about
Buddhism." In Richard Landen's voice was a friendly, weary calm.
She found his expression distant, but open. His right eyebrow was
interrupted by a square-centimetre of grey hair.

"Selly?" Niksch said.

"The punk girl." Bonì moved her right hand towards the filigree
teacup in front of her. It trembled faintly and looked like a clumsy
paw next to the cup. She thought of all the things this hand had held
and done. Stolen, pleasured, hit, and two years ago even killed. Not
the ideal hand for such a pretty little cup.

"Tibetan Buddhism?"

"More likely Japanese."

He nodded. "Go on."

She withdrew her hand and told him about the monk and his
hike from Badenweiler to Liebau and beyond. She described his staff,
his bowl, his robe. She didn't mention his wounds or the figures in
the forest, nor the night in the hollow behind the rocks.

Landen didn't take his eyes off her as she spoke. His face was lightly
tanned, as if he'd just been skiing – or meditating in the mountains.
She thought again of the rum. If not rum, then maybe sake. Did the
Japanese put sake in their tea? Her gaze kept straying to the grey patch
in the centre of his right eyebrow. It bothered her. A haven of turmoil
in a narrow, peaceful, attentive face with slightly reddened eyes.

When she'd finished there was a moment's silence. Then Landen
said, "What would you like to know?"

She looked at the cat and concentrated. "Very generally, I'd like
to know how to deal with someone like that. What he believes in,
what he's thinking. If you've got any idea where he might have come
from."

Landen took a sip from his cup and then put it back down in a
graceful movement. He pursed his lips. "It's tricky, I mean, I know

practically nothing about the man." His uncertainty made him sombre, and fleetingly Louise found Landen incredibly attractive. "I'll speak to him, if you like."

"Yes," she said. "I would like that."

Landen had gone upstairs; Bonì and Niksch waited in the small hallway. She took her mobile from her pocket. The translator sounded just as cheerful and slick, even though the job had fallen through. "Oh well, perhaps another time," she said. "And thanks for thinking of me."

"*Sayonara*," Louise said, cutting her off. She closed her eyes. She was seriously regretting not having asked Landen for a dash of something in her tea.

"Look," Niksch said. He was staring at two narrow, parchment-like scrolls on the wall, an oriental symbol painted on each. "Mad, isn't it? And it *means* something, too."

She opened the front door and looked at the gravel path, the fence, the little street with mostly affluent-looking detached houses. Filbinger lived here somewhere. There weren't that many options; Günterstal was a small place. Filbinger used to be a menacing name, a politician's face on television, a bad feeling. Now, thirty years on, he'd become a person who lived, slept and ate somewhere. Had her parents known that Filbinger was just a man? Probably not.

"It could be saying anything," Niksch said.

"Such as?"

"Such as, you have to take your shoes off, and if you don't you'll drop dead. Or that every visitor has to leave a bit of their little finger here. Or how to manufacture poison gas, or build a bomb."

She sighed. "Call Hollerer, Nikki."

Hollerer was fine but his feet were frozen. Lederle and he were hungry and demanding cherry cake. The monk had just walked across a little wood; they had watched him through the trees. Sometimes the distance between him and the Daimler was twenty metres, sometimes a hundred.

A shiver ran down Boni's spine. One hundred metres. How could you protect someone that far away?

Niksch had turned back to the scrolls. "It's making me nervous, not being able to understand this."

"Call Amelie and ask her to bake a cherry cake."

At that moment Landen came down the stairs. He put on a roll-neck jumper then gestured to the scrolls with his chin. "The left-hand one is 'Happiness', the one on the right 'Friendship'."

Louise stepped out onto the path, chuckling. Landen and Niksch followed. When she got to the garden gate she turned. Now only the upstairs light was on. She shuddered.

Niksch opened the gate for her. "Amelie's dead," he said.

Amelie accompanied her through the northern part of Günterstal, through the narrow arch of the former Cistercian convent on Schau-inslandstrasse. Amelie's pasta parcels, Amelie's underwear, the ruck-sack. She wanted to warn Landen that what they were going to do might be dangerous, but Amelie wouldn't let her.

As they crossed the Dreisam, she pictured Hollerer and Lederle. They were sitting in the Daimler, observing the monk and talking about what happened when your wife died. As it turned out they weren't a bad match.

What must Hollerer have thought yesterday when she told him to say Hi to Amelie?

"Nikki," she gasped. "Stop!"

She got out. Filbinger, Amelie and Bermann – all a bit much for one day, she thought angrily. She felt like throwing up, but not in front of Richard Landen. In the pockets of her anorak she found only her mobile, purse and house keys.

She slumped back into the passenger seat. Niksch drove on in silence. Landen was quiet too, and yet she felt his presence behind her. She felt him and now and then she felt the house too, and the upstairs light and the willow.

She turned her head halfway. "I'd like you to know that this might be dangerous." Her voice sounded gruff and sour. She tried to be polite: "Something's not right, someone's following the monk, someone who might turn violent . . . Do you still want to come with us?" Landen went pale, but he nodded.

Beside her Niksch mumbled something incomprehensible, then wrenched the steering wheel to the right and stopped. They were outside the shop of a petrol station. Louise felt for the handle and thought how fortunate it was that she'd never been here before.

From a distance it appeared as if the monk was stationary. It was only when they got to Lederle and Hollerer, who had climbed out of the car, that Louise saw he was going resolutely on his way. The dusk appeared to be sucking up the black dot. Another few minutes and the monk would vanish into the gloom. Glass clanked against glass as they got out.

Richard Landen nodded briefly when she introduced him to Hollerer and Lederle. Then he set off in pursuit of the monk. She was about to follow him, but Hollerer asked, "What about the cake?"

There she was again, Amelie. She shook her head.

"Bonì, can I have a quick word?" Lederle took her to one side. "Nothing, nothing at all," he said. "Are you sure that . . .?"

Lederle's scepticism reminded her of her deal with Bermann. The abyss. Sick leave, rehab, desk job. For a moment she felt panic. "Have you spoken to Rolf?"

"Today? No."

She nodded and said, "Reiner, I *am* sure." But then she asked herself if it was true. She turned to Hollerer, who smiled wearily. He looked at a loss. But she felt that he trusted her, for whatever reason.

She looked at Niksch.

Yes, she was sure. She'd seen the figures and heard the voices. But more importantly she'd seen the monk's fear.

"So what's happening now?" Hollerer said.

"Niksch and you are going to stay, Reiner's going to drive me back to Freiburg. I'll come back at eight to relieve you."

Lederle looked doubtful; Hollerer nodded. "And we'll check in with you now and then," he said.

"Yes we will," Niksch said.

"O.K., thanks." She looked over towards Landen and the monk. The monk had stopped and turned. At that moment the two men put their hands together and bowed their heads. They were standing close to one another. The monk said something before turning his head away and coughing.

"Bonì, I don't know, perhaps I should come back with . . ." Lederle began.

"You go home, you're needed more there."

Lederle held his breath and blinked. "I'll have a chat with Rolf, he can't let you hang around here," he said.

"I'd rather you didn't. He doesn't know I called you."

Lederle rubbed his eyes with his index finger and thumb. "Which I suppose means I can't claim the day as overtime." He looked at her again, but didn't appear to be expecting an answer. Sometimes he said things that were typical of the Lederle she knew before his wife's diagnosis. The complaint about overtime was one. Not a week would go by without a grumble about unpaid hours. Now these things weren't so important anymore, and sometimes he said them out of habit, probably without even realising. "I'll relieve you around four tomorrow morning," he said.

"Stay at home, Reiner."

"Then you could have three or four hours' sleep. Come on, three or four hours' kip is better than nothing."

She nodded and set off after Landen.

Ten minutes passed before Bonì realised that the monk wasn't going to tell Landen anything of substance either. But at least now they had his name: Taro. She looked at him and wondered why she was so disappointed.

"Try again," she said.

Landen asked the key questions once more: where the monk came from, where he was going, how he'd been injured, who he was fleeing and why he wouldn't go with them to Freiburg.

The monk smiled and said nothing. The smile was mechanical; his eyes remained black and lifeless, drained of all softness and sensitivity. They reminded Louise of the eyes of Landen's china cat.

Since that morning Taro seemed to have crossed an invisible boundary. He no longer took an interest in what was happening to him. Essentially he'd stopped running away. He appeared to have retreated into another world, an intermediate realm. They'd lost him altogether.

"Shit," she cursed.

"Please be polite," Landen said.

"Fucking shit. Try again."

"He's not going to talk to us. You have to accept that."

She came close to the monk. That familiar tang tickled her nostrils again, stirring memories: their trek through the forest, the warmth in the cavity behind the rocks, the feeling of inner peace. "Would you like me to look after you tonight? Would you like me to be here in case they come back? Would you like that?"

Landen translated.

The monk looked at her and shook his head.

"*Sayonara*," she said, moving away. She heard Landen speak, then the monk, then Landen again. Then shoes crunched in the snow.

Landen caught up with her. "There's one thing you have to grasp," he said. "He's *different* from you. Completely different. He thinks differently, believes differently, feels differently and lives differently."

"What's that supposed to mean?"

"That you'll never understand what he does or says. And certainly not *why* he does or says it, or even doesn't say it."

They stopped. The grey patch in Landen's eyebrow was crimped downwards. "You'd never *really* understand him even if you knew more about him."

"I see it differently."

"I know. That's how most people think. Nobody wants to accept that you can never really understand another human being. Especially not someone from a different culture."

Bonì looked back. The monk had plunged deep into the greyness. A dozen metres further on, dusk ended in a wall of black. Soon the forest would swallow him up.

In the other direction, Niksch was kneeling by the patrol car putting on snow chains. Hollerer and Lederle were looking towards her. Voluminous clouds of vapour formed in front of Hollerer's face; barely visible cotton-wool balls flew from Lederle's mouth.

She looked at Landen. "I still don't get what you're trying to say. What am I supposed to do with someone I'm apparently never going to understand? Do I simply abandon him to his fate? Is that what you're saying? Just because he's different? What kind of crap is that?"

"Please calm down," Landen said.

"Oh, you're good."

"You don't need to abandon him to his fate, you just need to respect him . . ."

". . . and *then* abandon him."

"Let me finish." Landen had raised his voice, but he went on more softly. "You have to respect him, and that's really hard. It would be the *tour de force* of the enlightened individual, because to respect some-body you don't understand is the most difficult thing imaginable." The kink in his eyebrow evened out and he looked at her warily. It was the caginess you saw in the eyes of suspects when they feared they'd given themselves away. What was going through his mind?

She decided not to ask. Not now, at least. She grinned. "Under-standing, respect . . . are you a moral apostle, or what?"

Landen smiled. "Let's just say the term 'apostle' comes from the wrong religion."

As they walked on he said, "Don't give up on him."

"I'm not. I'm just infuriated by him."

"That's something *he* would never understand." Landen stopped again. The fleck of grey shot up and for a few seconds something flickered in his eyes. He told her she must never forget that behind the faces of strangers, behind the otherness, lay an infinite and fascinating universe of thoughts, feelings and experiences. Thousands of questions and answers that weren't so different from her own; it was just that they'd emerged from a different perspective, which would make *her* questions and answers appear in a new light, if she ever allowed it.

Bonì struggled to listen. Her eyes were focused on the eyebrow, this strangely animated patch of grey that both irritated and attracted her. All of a sudden a flux of mysterious things was set in motion inside her. Warmth flowed through her body, her skin tingled, her throat constricted.

Not that too, she thought.

The eyebrow stretched as if its work was now done and it could relax.

Disgruntled, she walked away.

The monk was no longer visible from where the cars were parked. For a moment Bonì panicked, but Niksch reassured her. It was a narrow strip of woodland and a dirt track ran around it to the south – no problem with snow chains. He cracked his knuckles confidently. His face was red and steam rose from his shoulders. He sneezed into his hand. "I'd love another döner later," he said with a grin. "Any chance?"

She smiled. "What about you, Hollerer?"

"A four seasons, if it's no trouble."

"It's got mushrooms, boss."

"I like mushrooms."

"Yes, but by the time you get home the pizza's cold and you have to put it in the oven."

"I think I can probably manage that," Hollerer growled.

"Mushrooms . . ."

"Shut up, Niksch."

"You're not supposed to heat up mushrooms," Louise said.

Hollerer rolled his eyes. "Then make it a four seasons *without* mushrooms."

"But then it's only three seasons," Niksch said.

The blanket of snow had broken up all around, exposing tar and gravel. Lederle steered the Daimler along narrow roads, Bonì navigating through the darkness to the place where he'd joined them that morning. In the past – *before* – he had been able to find his way anywhere blindfolded, but since the diagnosis, he'd increasingly lost his sense of direction. Lederle's anxiety about his wife seemed to have corroded vital areas of his brain.

"Up there on the right, Reiner."

"O.K." Lederle turned, then looked into his rear-view mirror and asked, "What do you actually do?"

Landen seemed reluctant to talk about himself. But gradually they learned that he taught at the South Asia Institute at Heidelberg University, lecturing on Tibetan and Zen Buddhism, and that he wrote the occasional article for academic journals and websites. "My wife," he said eventually, "earns the money."

Nobody laughed. It sounded too rehearsed. "So what topics are you teaching?" Lederle said.

"At the moment it's 'Shakyamuni's first speech at Vulture Peak'. Last semester it was 'The political role of the Gozan'."

"Well, well, who'd have thought it?" Lederle said.

"Indeed," Landen said.

For a while nobody spoke. Lederle slowed a little. Outside it had become dark and they could see tiny lights glittering in the distance –

sitting rooms lit up in Liebau, probably, Louise thought. Couples, families, friends, people like Niksch and his sisters and Theres, like Hollerer and Amelie, sitting in their Sunday best in small, cosy living rooms. A hill edged its way between the car and the lights. "What is a Kagyu House?" she said.

"A meeting house for Tibetan culture. Kagyu is one of the principal schools of Tibetan Buddhism." Landen's voice was that of someone well versed in patience. She wondered whether he was an engaging lecturer or a passive one. Whether the calm he exuded was in fact detachment.

She adjusted the rear-view mirror so she could see him in the gloom of the back seat. "What do you think about Taro?"

"Sorry," Lederle said, moving the mirror back.

"He's young," Landen said. "Early twenties at most. And he's a Zensu, a 'Zen child'. That's what they call Zen novices in Japan." He pronounced the word "Zen" softly and deeply – "Zzzenn". Judging by his dialect, the monk came from southern Japan, from Kyushu island, but Landen wouldn't swear by it.

"Have you ever lived in Japan?"

"A few years – in Tokyo and Kyoto."

Unintentionally, Bonì thought of Landen's wife, the Japanese woman who earned the money and whose surname was Tommo. "From Japan to southern Baden," she said.

Landen said nothing.

"Maybe there's a Zen monastery or something around here," Lederle said. "Where he's come from, or where he's going."

"Do you know where he's come from?" Landen said.

"He was seen in Badenweiler, then in Kirchzarten, and yesterday in Liebau," Louise said.

"Badenweiler," Landen repeated thoughtfully. "In Weiterswiller in Alsace there's the Ko San Ryu Mon Ji, and near Mulhouse the Kanzan-an."

"Weiterswiller is too far north. Mulhouse is possible."

"South of Zillisheim," Landen said. "I haven't been there myself, but I've seen photos. A place in the middle of the woods, if I remember rightly, set up in the 1970s. The 'an' at the end means 'hermitage'; in Japanese, temples and monasteries usually have the suffix '-ji'. Kanzan was a lay Buddhist from China, a poet and hermit – a 'freethinker', if you like. He commands huge respect in Zen because contemporary masters testified that he'd reached a high level of enlightenment."

"Do you believe in all this occult stuff?" Lederle said.

"You think of Buddhism as 'occult stuff'?"

"No," Louise said. "Just different."

A few seconds passed before Landen said, right into her ear, "I'd like to tell you a story if you'd be happy to hear it."

The warmth of his breath on her skin vanished all too quickly. She nodded. "Right again, Reiner," she said.

Landen waited until Lederle had made the turning. Then, in his soft voice, he said, "At the beginning of the sixth century A.D. a scholar came to Shaolin Monastery on Mount Song in northern China. His name was Huike. When Bodhidharma, the first Zen patriarch in China, received him, Huike requested to be taken in as a pupil at the monastery. Despite many years of study he hadn't found inner peace. But Bodhidharma sent him away again, saying that only those who never gave up teaching themselves could attain the state of inner peace. Huike withdrew to outside the gates of the monastery, where he sat it out for weeks in the snow, hoping that Bodhidharma would eventually agree to his request. But Bodhidharma was unrelenting. To prove that his determination to follow Buddhism was unwavering, Huike cut off his left hand."

Landen stopped talking. She sensed that he had leaned back.

Lederle had stopped the car. In the headlights she could make out the tyre marks of the Daimler and the patrol car from this morning.

"Why are we here, Louise?" he said.

"Because of the footprints."

Lederle switched off the engine, but nobody got out. They stared at the white of the snow broken up by dark patches in the beam of the

69

headlights. After a while Lederle turned his head and asked, "So how does the story go on?"

"It's not important," Landen said.

With the help of a torch and the headlights Bonì followed the footprints towards the hill. She thought of Huike. She had given him Taro's face and he was sitting in the snow, in the middle of an expanding pool of beautiful, bright-red crystals.

For about fifty metres the footprints formed a narrow line; the strangers had walked behind each other. Then they dispersed to become three parallel tracks in the snow. Side by side, they led up the gentle slope. Every so often there were small circles in the snow. The men – she was certain these were men's footprints – must have stopped and turned around. Were they being followed too? Or were they looking for someone?

At the top of the hill the tracks fanned out at acute angles to one another. The footprints on the left pointed directly to a pair of static headlights in the distance – probably Niksch's car.

She followed them a few metres down the hill. When the Daimler vanished over the summit behind her, she grasped inside the right pocket of her anorak.

Then she sat cross-legged with Calambert and Huike in the snow. What was Buddhism's view on killing? Did it accept it as inevitable on some occasions? She made a mental note to ask Landen when the two of them were alone together, and she would make sure that happened soon.

The headlights seemed to be moving slowly. Jägermeister movements, she thought. But then the light painstakingly peeled a bit of forest from the darkness.

She recalled what Niksch had said: Nothing, nothing at all. Had she been mistaken? Was Bermann right? Her inner voice fell silent.

Hollerer, Niksch, then Lederle and now Richard Landen. She'd mobilised four people, ruined their Sundays, set herself a ridiculous ultimatum and now nothing was happening. Apart from an injured and frightened Japanese monk roaming the snowy landscape of southern Baden. And her having spied shapes between trees in the dim light of daybreak.

Shapes that might have been trees.

She stood up. The beam from the headlights kept changing shape. All these questions merged into one: when, she thought, was something finally going to happen?

5

Bermann was not at H.Q. A message had been left on Bonì's desk: *We have a meeting with Almenbroich at 8 on Monday morning.* She considered it an unusually polite note; in other circumstances Bermann would have written: *Mon, 8 – Almenbr.* But he was gentler with sick officers.

Louise took a pair of scissors and cut the message into millimetre-wide strips, then the strips into tiny squares. It gave her less satisfaction than she'd thought it might. With her hand she swept the squares into the wastepaper basket and reached for the telephone. While the person at directory enquiries searched for the number of Kanzan-an, she scraped the remaining Bermann strips from her hand.

The monastery office was apparently unmanned. She left a message on the answerphone, then called Richard Landen's number without knowing what she'd say if he picked up. To her annoyance she realised she was nervous. It rang six times, then a woman's voice said, "Yes, hello?"

Bonì waited. It occurred to her that she'd hoped Landen's wife would pick up. She wanted to get her down from the upstairs room, hear her voice. She wanted confirmation that the woman really did exist.

As she hung up Anne Wallmer appeared at the door. "Ah, Luis, you *are* here."

Wallmer was the only woman Bermann would tolerate at his side on operations. Having said that, he didn't regard her as a woman, and to some extent this was logical. Wallmer tried to be like Bermann. Her behaviour was laddish, her laugh loud and coarse, and she cultivated rippling biceps in the gym. Like Bermann she usually wore jeans and a black leather jacket. Schneider, Bermann's close friend, said she used the gents' when no-one was looking. Sometimes Bermann and Schneider would lie in wait for her there, but they hadn't caught her yet.

"I need the Thielmann file," Wallmer said. She was standing by Bonì's desk, her hands in her jacket pockets, and staring right at her. Bermann had wasted no time organising the handover; Louise had been in charge of the Thielmann investigation.

"You can have it tomorrow."

"I need to read up on it this evening, Luis."

Bonì's gaze drifted over to the Thielmann file on her desk. She looked up and shook her head. "Tomorrow." She wondered how far Wallmer would be prepared to go. Whether any sense of camaraderie or fairness had survived in her pumped-up chest.

At that moment Louise's mobile rang. She walked past Wallmer and over to her anorak. The number looked vaguely familiar. "Yes?" Nobody answered. "Hello?" Silence on the other end of the line. No breathing, no background noise, nothing. A strange thought raced through her mind: the silence of the snow.

She waited another second then cut the connection and turned around.

Wallmer had gone. The Thielmann file was still on the desk.

Louise sat down. The silence of the snow. She accessed the "Calls" menu. She jotted down a mobile number and called back. Engaged. She stared uneasily at the numbers in pencil. Did she know the number or not?

There was a knock at the door and a constable entered. "Visitor for you. Says you know him. Apparently Chief Inspector Bermann sent him." He stepped aside and flapped his hand lethargically. A Japanese teenager appeared.

"I didn't order sushi," she said.

"And I haven't got any. The chief inspector said you were looking for a translator."

She closed her eyes. From the darkness behind her lids Bermann's grinning face lunged at her.

"And someone who knows about Buddhism. He says it's about samurais and ritual murder."

She opened her eyes. The boy, Enni, wore a serious expression. He was sixteen at most. Whenever she went to eat at the sushi place a few streets away he was always behind the counter, looking exhausted. "I think he's been watching too much telly," he said.

She wanted to laugh, but then felt tears in her eyes. She let them run down her cheeks.

"Is everything alright, Inspector?"

The silence of the snow. She felt for her mobile and pressed call-back. Still engaged. She wiped away the tears with her hands and suppressed the urge to fling her arms on the desk, lay down her head and give up.

The boy was now beside her. "Stand up, Inspector." She hesitated before doing as he asked.

He was only a few centimetres taller than she was. He placed his right hand on her lower abdomen. She recoiled, but the hand went with her movement. Warmth spread out below her belly button and Bonì felt herself blushing. Without wanting to, she imagined him sliding his hand down further. She wondered how she would have reacted. Would she have shot the boy or taken him home?

"What's that?" the boy asked.

"My tummy."

"And?"

"And what?"

"What's that, Inspector?"

"No idea. Skin, muscle, guts."

"It's your centre. The seat of your energy. It's the centre of the universe."

"All I can feel at the moment is air."

"Me too," the boy said with a grin.

As soon as they started laughing she remembered where she knew the number from.

Hollerer's mobile.

She couldn't reach Hollerer and Niksch by radio. Niksch's mobile rang a few times before going to voicemail. Hollerer's was still engaged.

She requested three patrol cars over the loudspeaker. Five policemen and one woman hurried with her to the stairwell. "Where are we going?" the policewoman asked, a pale blonde girl called Lucie or Trudi or maybe even Susie.

Bonì stared at her. Where indeed? Where precisely should she send the cars? *Into the forest east of Liebau?* "Liebau police station. Wait for me there."

She remembered Bermann. As head of department he would have to be informed. Louise turned back and went to his office, but he wasn't there. She met him on her way downstairs. This time he was livid. "You have to stick to the rules too," he snapped. "The uniforms are staying here."

It took her a moment to realise that he'd heard her announcement. "Hollerer called; someone's out there," she said breathlessly.

"Such crap," Bermann said.

She moved closer to him. His mouth was half open and he smelled of beer, onions and garlic. She remembered Niksch's döner and Hollerer's three seasons. She felt tears running down her cheeks again – or still. Her great, mysterious sadness was back, the dark hole inside her, where Calambert and Mick and Germain sat alongside her parents and Filbinger, and now Huike too, as well as her unease about the monk, Hollerer and Niksch. All of a sudden she was glad she was going with Bermann to see Almenbroich, to be put on sick leave or suspended or chucked out. She would give up and leave it to Bermann and Almenbroich and whoever else to make the decisions about her future. Relief unfurled within her. Give up at long last. Forget Calambert.

"Crap!" Bermann screamed.

She put her arms around his neck and pulled him towards her. Bermann froze. For a moment he didn't even breathe. Deep inside her stirred a vague horror at the degree of revulsion she triggered in him. But that wasn't important now.

She brought her mouth to his ear. "But what if it's true, Rolf?" she whispered. "Then *you'll* be the one going to Almenbroich tomorrow and it'll be *your* career that's over. Have you thought about that?"

Bermann began to breathe again, but his muscles remained tense. Footsteps came and went, voices spoke, doors were opened and closed. Then silence.

Finally Bermann pushed her away with two fingers. "Just us two, Luis," he said. "The uniforms are staying here."

Bermann didn't say another word until they got to Liebau, his tension didn't appear to have eased. "Where now?" he barked at the exit to the village. She directed him into the darkness to the east. Shortly afterwards her mobile rang, but it was only Lederle asking whether she needed him earlier after all. Whether he shouldn't do the whole night shift. He couldn't sleep anyway, he told her. "Thanks," she said, "but please stay at home."

Then she thought of Landen, imagined him sitting in the back. She wished he'd told a different story, one she could have understood. One where the ending was important. Had Lederle found out how it went on during the drive to Günterstal?

She tried again to reach Hollerer or Niksch by radio and telephone. The only sign of life was the engaged staccato of Hollerer's mobile. Memories of Calambert welled inside her. She had driven in Bermann's car on that occasion too. They'd come back with one dead person, and another dying.

"Drive slowly, it's left up there."

"There's no road."

"*Slowly*, Rolf."

Cursing, Bermann made the turn.

When they arrived at the spot where they'd left Hollerer and Niksch late that afternoon, Bermann switched off the headlights. The sky was cloudless and the moon had not yet risen. They walked a while in the dark-grey snow. No lights, no sounds. Their anxiety grew. For the thousandth time in the past hour she pressed number recall and heard only the engaged tone.

On the way back to the car Bermann discovered the tyre prints of the patrol car, running straight across the virgin snow. "Quick," Louise said.

They followed the car's path driving in the furrows. The tracks kept making small swerves to the left or right. Niksch had been enjoying himself. When the ground sloped upwards, the wheels of Bermann's police Mercedes began to spin.

"Half an hour, Luis," Bermann said. "Then I'm heading back." He took a torch from the glove pocket.

"But keep it switched off," Louise said.

She went in front. The surface of the snow was slightly crusty, though soft beneath. Bermann was wearing trainers and having difficulty keeping up. She heard him slip several times.

It had been the same two years ago. They'd had to abandon the car and continue on foot in silence through the snow. Bermann had slipped time and again. Then Bermann, Lederle and the others had gone in the right direction and she'd taken the wrong one.

After ten minutes the ground sloped gently uphill. The tyre tracks approached a sparse wood and then ran parallel to it. She stopped to blow her nose.

Bermann came up next to her. "Wallmer rang me earlier," he said.

She nodded. "Things not moving quickly enough for you, eh?"

Bermann didn't respond. He looked perturbed, pensive. She got moving again.

Soon she spotted the footprints of a solitary individual, leading out of the wood. The tracks of the patrol car branched off, following the footprints away from the trees. Only now did she notice how small the monk's feet were.

Ten minutes later they spotted the car. It was twenty metres away in an open field. The engine and lights were off, the passenger door open. Bermann stopped. His gaze wandered back and forth between Louise and the car. He appeared confused. She took out her weapon and tried not to think of Hollerer and Niksch.

The car was empty. On the passenger tray she saw gloves and a thermos. She placed a hand on the bonnet – cold. She stopped beside the passenger door; the seat was full of crumbs.

A movement made her turn her head. Bermann was standing by the boot, now holding his pistol too. He was staring at her shoes. She glanced down and saw she was standing in a muddle of footprints. Slowly she crouched and looked around. Nothing was moving. Darkness, snow – and footprints that ran to and from the car in a number of directions.

Bermann knelt beside her. "I don't believe it," he said, pulling out his mobile. His cheeks were red, his eyes screwed up in concentration, his breathing strained. She could almost like him in moments such as this, when he gave her the feeling that the disruption of the system was merely temporary. That there were opportunities to restore it. Bermann had the unshakable belief that the system was intact again when you found the person who had put it into disarray.

She thought differently. Nothing would ever be the same as before the deed. No matter what it was, the deed changed the system for ever. It left scars, holes, puzzles. People had disappeared. Those that remained had changed.

She stood up while Bermann whispered his call for back-up. The various sets of footprints fanned out in a semi-circle. Two people had approached the car from the side and from behind, and walked away from it in the same direction. Parallel to these ran more footprints, also leading away from the car. They were broad, long and deep – Hollerer?

Two metres away she stumbled upon a fourth set, coming from the driver's side of the vehicle. Niksch.

She turned to Bermann. He'd stood up too and was coming over to her. She thought of the lights of Liebau, twinkling in the darkness beyond the wood and the hills. And of how Hollerer and Niksch would now be sitting at home if she'd prevailed over Bermann that afternoon.

Bermann returned her look but said nothing. At once she knew that he was thinking the same. And that he'd blame her for not having asserted herself.

But that wasn't important now.

With her gun she indicated the direction in which the four sets of footprints disappeared and he nodded. Bent low, they followed the tracks as quietly as possible.

A few minutes later they saw Hollerer. He was lying on his back in a dark, icy sea of blood. Bonì almost passed out. A chill ran across her scalp and her heart starting racing. She forced herself forwards.

Hollerer was alive. When she kneeled beside him she saw he was weeping silently. His round face glowed white against the shadowy night snow. She put her hands on his cheeks. "Hollerer..." No response. She stroked his face and whispered, "Hollerer."

She was vaguely aware that Bermann was on his mobile again as he came to join her. She dropped into the snow. The damp cold on her bare neck was almost painful. The sky was clear and infinite; she found it too big, frighteningly big.

Louise rolled onto her side. Bermann had begun buttoning up Hollerer's coat. How could she have trusted this fat, old, slow man with such a task? And where was Niksch? Had he managed to escape? Or was he also lying . . .

She resisted taking this thought to its conclusion. She wanted to close her eyes, lie there on the ground and go to sleep. Give up. But then she thought of the mother and the three sisters who needed a policeman in the family to make them feel more secure. She saw their faces before her, staring at her, pleading silently for Niksch.

Bonì scrambled clumsily to her feet. She took off her anorak and laid it over Hollerer's legs.

"Fuck, we're losing him!" Bermann said.

"In case you need alcohol, there's some in the pockets."

Bermann looked up. "What do you mean?" he barked.

Without really knowing why, she said, "There's a camera somewhere. Niksch was photographing the monk."

"For fuck's sake, Luis, stay here. There are at least two of them."

"Do *you* want to go?"

"No-one's fucking going!"

"Yes, they are," she said, walking away.

From the distance between his left and right footprints it was clear that Niksch hadn't been running. He'd walked. Which meant that at this point Hollerer must have been in the car still, he hadn't yet been shot. Maybe he'd been able to get himself to safety.

For a while the footprints of the two pursuers ran directly alongside Niksch's. Then one set moved to the other side. They'd trapped him in a vice.

And a few metres beside these, apparently unaffected by it all, the small, ephemeral sandal prints of the monk, at times so soft that she could barely make them out.

She continued uphill for a few minutes, then down towards some woodland. Here there was more snow, the ground beneath it was uneven and Bonì kept sinking into ploughed furrows. She made no effort to hide her presence. Occasionally she stopped to listen, but there was nothing to be heard.

Just before she got to the wood the moon rose.

The footprints came to a halt at a stream, and she dropped to her knees to recover her breath. The cold air rasped at her lungs; her head and ears were hurting. The rippling of the water sounded cheerful and heartening. Gasping, she tried to penetrate the pallid darkness with her gaze.

Nothing.

Just the faces of the girls and the mother. Nikki's alive, they said as Bonì struggled to her feet. Yes, she said, he's alive and I'm going to bring him back to you.

She leaped through the stream with huge strides, horrified to realise that she didn't feel the cold of the water.

Now the footprints merged, becoming a single track on the narrow path. There was a steep bank of about three or four metres. On the slope and at the bottom there was no snow. But she could clearly see the path they had taken. She ran on.

Next to a tree a little way off the path she saw a dark body on the ground. She froze when she recognised the green and beige of a police uniform. But it couldn't be Niksch, Niksch was slimmer and taller, and when she kneeled beside the dead body lying on its stomach, it struck her that Niksch's hands were more delicate and his hair lighter. Carefully, she lifted the corpse by the shoulder. For a moment she thought it really was Niksch, but the dead officer only looked like him: young too, and with a very narrow face. She brushed earth from his cheek, then gently let him back down.

The police jacket was saturated with blood. They had shot him from behind in the head and midriff, then dragged the body away from the path.

One man seriously injured, one dead . . . She knew what had been going through Bermann's mind: if you were a man, you'd have been more assertive. You'd have dispatched an armada. You'd have managed to convince me. You could have prevented all this.

Bonì stood up. Where now? Follow the path? She came back onto it and stood there. She sensed she had barely any energy left. Then her legs gave way. The forest floor was soft. Rolling onto her back she stared up at the half moon above her.

A short while later she laboured to her feet and ran on.

But there were no more footprints. Ten, fifteen minutes passed, maybe a few hours, Louise had lost all sense of time. She followed the path, went off to the left, rejoined the path, turned right. No more snow, no more tracks. She had to sit down more and more often. She could no longer feel her legs below the knee, a ball of ice bounced around in her lungs. She was shivering uncontrollably. She found herself standing on the edge of the forest, looking at a silent field with a thin mantle of snow, shimmering like wax in the moonlight. Tyre marks cut through the slush at the edge of the forest, from broad tyres, perhaps a 4×4. But she wouldn't have been able to say when they'd been made. On another day she might have had a guess, but not now.

The tracks vanished into the dark.

She headed back into the forest and went in the opposite direction. In the damp mud she noticed some tracks she had not seen before: children's footprints.

The child had been running. After a few metres the ground became firmer and these prints ended too. A child playing in the woods? So where were the footprints of other children, the parents, a dog?

In the distance she heard the deep, solitary humming of a helicopter. The noise remained constant and low. She sank to her knees, wrapped her arms around her torso and tucked her chin into her chest. They were taking Hollerer away.

Louise returned to the young policeman. For the first time she wondered who he might be and how he'd got there. Even though the policeman wasn't Niksch, she found herself feeling that it might be, and she was confused.

Carefully she turned him over. She sat against a tree trunk and pulled him towards her. He was so slim that she could put her arms around his stomach. The half moon hovered above. It looked wan and feeble, as if struggling to keep itself in the sky.

Bonì began talking to the body. She asked his name, what he'd been doing here and if he'd come across Niksch or the monk. She told him about Niksch and his rally driving, and about Theres who went too.

Some time later she heard people calling and dogs barking in the distance. Circles of light danced between the trees. Another helicopter hovered above her, its powerful searchlight slicing through the darkness.

Now, she told the corpse, we'll find them.

At that moment she realised that the faces of the mother and sisters hadn't come back. And it took another couple of seconds for her to understand what that meant.

6

Her period of sick leave began at six o'clock that morning. Almenbroich pulled her hand to his chest and wished her all the best. His words were stern, but heartfelt. She nodded and left H.Q. On the pavement frozen snow crackled beneath her shoes. She stopped and asked herself where she should go, what she was going to do. It seemed impossible to make decisions in a world without Niksch.

Bermann had waited a long time. She'd watched him in conversation with Almenbroich, who'd been hauled out of bed, in the middle of the silent Liebau task force – now ten strong – which had gathered around them and three pots of coffee. He was exhausted and tense but seemed more thoughtful than usual. He wasn't making the decision easy for himself. There seemed to be a weighty argument against it.

But finally he did it, he took Almenbroich aside for a serious talk. Almenbroich unconsciously stroked his high forehead as his gaze wandered through the room and rested on her. No surprise in his eyes, just resolve.

Carrying a jumper, Anne Wallmer stepped between her and Almenbroich's line of vision. It was a black V-neck. Bonì had difficulty removing her own, the front of which was heavy and wet with Niksch's blood. Wallmer gave her a sympathetic smile and took it away.

Later they called for her. She'd been expecting to see Prader, the addiction counsellor, but he wasn't there. In Almenbroich's office Bermann delicately finished what he'd begun the previous afternoon. Sick leave, rehab, a desk job. For a split second the abyss became her lifeline.

Almenbroich had needed no convincing. He too had long since noticed the "signs": bottles around the place, the smell, inexplicable mood swings and dips in energy, mind blanks, "certain, er, complexion issues". His elbows leaned on the arms of his chair, the tips of his fingers meeting in a fidgety triangle. He didn't take his eyes off Bonì for an instant, his gaze paternal and uncompromising. The triangle became an angular circle, then a triangle again. His disappointment was not visible, but she felt it through her entire being. Cold crept into every fibre of her body.

As the echo of his words resonated in her head, it dawned on her that he'd been describing an alcoholic. For a moment a weary anger flared inside her, but she refrained from explaining to him the difference. Almenbroich had long harboured a suspicion that had been easy to ignore. Now this had been joined by a witness and a terse admission, leaving no further room for subtle distinctions. There were definitions, codes of practice, there was healthy and sick, and they'd already decided that she was sick.

She wasn't even surprised that Bermann and Almenbroich had leapfrogged all the intermediate stages. No confidential conversations, no offers of help, no appointments with Prader, no period of grace, no written warnings. She was being discharged with immediate effect.

But that was no longer important. The only thing of any significance was that Niksch was no longer alive. And that Hollerer might be dead soon too.

She gave Bermann a little more time to shoulder her with the blame for what had happened. When he said nothing, she stood up.

"One other thing," Bermann said.

She turned to face him and felt a tingling behind her ears. The dark hole inside her opened and molten fury poured out, burying Almenbroich's disappointment that had settled inside her. "What's that?" She swallowed and waited for Bermann finally to give her a reason for thumping him.

He hesitated. "None of this should have happened . . .We lost a man and that should never have happened . . . whatever. What I wanted to say was: You've got balls, Luis, bloody great balls."

The hole closed, the fury retreated. Shattered, she turned away.

Almenbroich had got to his feet too. "'Whatever' isn't a good word just now," he said calmly.

"No, maybe not," Bermann conceded.

Almenbroich came to her. "I'm not going to blame you, Luis. Rolf has a different view, which of course he's entitled to, but as far as I'm concerned you acted correctly today. Don't try to convince yourself otherwise. Alright?"

She nodded.

Almenbroich took her hand. "Try to forget it."

"Has anybody informed the family?"

"Not yet. Would you like to do it?"

She thought of the faces of the mother and girls in the forest. "No."

She was back home at half past six. Ronescu was already awake, the lights on in his kitchen. But he didn't respond when she rang the bell.

She got herself something to drink and sat on the bed in her jeans and anorak. The sensation of Niksch in her arms, her holding him to her body, would not fade. She felt his hard head against her chin, his back against her belly and chest.

She wondered why she couldn't cry.

Crying didn't seem to be the appropriate reaction to Niksch's death. Killing Bermann and then crying – now that would have been more apt, she thought.

At seven she rang the hospital, then again at half-past and at eight o'clock. Hollerer was unconscious but stable.

Then she called Bermann's number and asked, "Are you alone?"

"No."

"Call me back when you are."

Bermann telephoned half an hour later. She was still sitting on her bed staring at her filthy, damp jeans and wondering whether it wouldn't be a bad idea to have a shower. "You want to hear me say it, don't you?" he said.

As earlier in Almenbroich's office he hesitated. Then he said, "You fucked up, Luis, and that's not a matter of perspective." He was slow in getting going, perhaps because he was tired or perhaps out of consideration for the sick. But maybe just because, in his eyes, she was already history.

The alcohol, her defiance, her inability to work in a team, her irritating lack of self-control, her mixing up of action and feeling, her dilettante-like behaviour at the crime scene in the forest – and the fact she was a woman; her thinking wasn't logical or structured, her analysis not rational and neutral. He, Schneider and Lederle – all male members of the department – and "even Wallmer" would have acted differently, with more *commitment*, more conviction, and most of all, with credibility.

She heard a loo flushing in the background. For a moment Bermann's voice faded in the roar of the water. Then it was clear again. "The fact that you spent the night with the Jap in the forest . . . I just can't believe it. How neurotic do you have to be to . . ." He broke off.

They were silent for a few seconds. Then Louise launched into a volley of insults.

When Katrin Rein, one of the two psychologists at the Baden-Württemberg Police Academy, called shortly afterwards, she was still sitting on the bed staring at her jeans, feeling the weight of Niksch's body on her arms, chest and belly. Although Rein sounded friendly she widened the abyss by another few grim metres. She wanted to see Bonì, straightaway if possible, and if that didn't work then she wanted at least to arrange some appointments for the coming weeks. "There's a lot to do, Louise, let's get cracking," she said softly.

"O.K."

"Shall we schedule a few appointments?"

"O.K.," Louise said, and hung up.

At around noon she forced herself into the shower. As she dried herself, Niksch's body seemed to have disappeared from her arms and body. But when she got dressed he returned, momentarily invading her space.

There was another message on the answerphone. Not Katrin Rein or Prader this time, but Lederle. "If you need me, for whatever reason, just give me a call," he said. He spoke clearly and slowly, and she realised that uttering these words had done him the world of good.

Hollerer's condition hadn't changed. They wouldn't be able to question him for two or three days at least. The nurse tried her best to remain patient, begging Bonì not to call every half hour. Louise gave her word and left her mobile number. "I'll be away for the next few days," she said.

When she hung up she stayed on the sofa and tried to remember when she'd decided to go away. And most of all, why she'd chosen to go *there*, of all places. Drawing the curtains, she swore she wouldn't open them again until the snow had completely melted.

In the stairwell she met a young woman. She was slim and blonde with a distinctly pretty, doll-like face. A Bermann woman. "I was worried," the Bermann woman said sheepishly. Bonì recognised the voice of Katrin Rein.

"Unnecessarily."

Katrin Rein tentatively blocked her way, but kept a respectable distance. She noticed the travel bag. "Louise, we . . ."

Bonì raised a hand in warning. They looked at each other for a moment, then Katrin nodded. "I'm sorry. Will you call me?"

"In a few days' time."

Katrin stepped aside. Her bashful smile appeared genuine.

When Louise was sitting in her Mégane in the underground car park, the events of Saturday seemed to repeat themselves, as if everything was starting again from the beginning. The ramp up ahead wobbled, the concrete pillars moved, a blurry Ronescu stepped out of the lift. Stooped, he shuffled past her in his skewed aura. The grey, fleshy canine face looked stony and melancholy. Silently she promised she'd make up for the țuică evening.

II

THE KANZAN-AN

7

The village was smaller than she remembered. All of a sudden the houses on either side of the little street receded and complete darkness enveloped the car. She turned around and drove at a walking pace back the way she'd come. Only a few houses still had lights on. She almost missed her mother's house for a second time; she could have sworn that last year it had been painted dark brown. Now it was yellow.

When she got out she shuddered. It may not have snowed in northern Provence, but the cold night wind smelled of snow.

It took a while for her mother to open the door. She was wearing pyjamas, her grey hair was down, her face tanned. She raised her eyebrows. "Well I never," she said. "The only people who turn up unannounced at night around here are cutthroats and the dead."

They embraced briefly.

"Did you repaint the house?"

"Only the front – then I lost interest."

Louise stepped into the little sitting room and put down her bag. Glowing embers crackled in the fireplace. There was a new period armchair and the sofa had been moved around, but otherwise nothing had changed since the previous January. Her gaze drifted across the few photographs on the small bureau in front of the window. As ever these were of unfamiliar faces, unfamiliar landscapes. None of the family, not in this room nor in any of the others.

She turned around. "You can shut the door. Mick's not with me."

They sat opposite each other at the kitchen table. On a plate in front of Louise were bread, cheese and ham, half a bottle of red wine and a glass within her reach. She tried to ignore the bottle.

Her mother had sat down with a brown woollen blanket around her shoulders and was now watching Louise eat. With the blanket, her loose hair and her dark skin, Louise thought she looked like an American Indian. And in some respects that's what she was: a warrior. Throughout her life she'd been waging war. Against society, against the patriarchy, against politics, against her husband.

"I was in Günterstal yesterday."

"And?"

"Filbinger lives there. I thought you knew that."

Her mother shook her head. "I stopped thinking about that man years ago. Him and all the others. Here," she said, raising her arms, "they're not so important."

"Then we ought to have moved here in the seventies, Papa, Germain, you and me."

"Yes, maybe," her mother said. She stood up. "You can tell me why you're here tomorrow. Tonight I'm too tired."

Her mother's day began during the night. At around five o'clock Louise heard her in the bathroom upstairs, then she came downstairs humming. In the kitchen, perhaps because of the empty wine bottle, she remembered that her daughter was sleeping on the sofa. She stopped humming and moved more circumspectly. The aroma of coffee drifted from the kitchen. A quarter of an hour later the front door closed.

Louise waited for a few minutes, but her mother didn't come back. She got up. A profound darkness lurked behind the small, square windows. Frozen, she put some wood in the fireplace and lit it. In the kitchen she drank lukewarm coffee, ate some dry bread and took two aspirin. The family had fallen apart because of Hans Filbinger, but he was no longer of any significance. Perhaps Calambert would stop being of any significance too one day.

She took her mobile from her anorak and sank onto the sofa.

A foreign nurse was on duty in Hollerer's ward. He said Hollerer had briefly regained consciousness during the night, but hadn't yet spoken. He was going to pull through, but they wouldn't be able to say for some weeks whether he'd ever be able to work again.

Hollerer had also been shot twice from behind. One bullet had shattered his right shoulder, the other had shredded his left kidney.

She dialled again. As the telephone rang she prayed she wouldn't wake Lederle's wife. Her prayer went unanswered.

"Louise, he's *asleep*," Antonia Lederle said crossly.

"I'm sorry to have woken you, I really am, but I *have* to speak to him."

"Call back at eight."

"Please, Antonia."

"*No.*"

Lederle's wife cut her off.

Louise stared at the time on her mobile. Two and a half hours until eight o'clock. She rang Bermann.

Bermann wasn't asleep. "Where the hell are you?" he said.

"At my mother's. Have you got anything?"

"You're in Provence?"

"Come on, Rolf."

Bermann paused, then said slowly, as if struggling to control himself, "You're off the case, Luis. Get used to it, otherwise you're never going to pull through. Forget the Jap and the dead boy and concentrate on getting off . . ."

"Rolf!" she shouted. "What have you got?"

Again Bermann paused. Then he took a big, noisy breath and said, "Nothing. A few ballistics details, some shoe and tyre markings. Other than that, nothing. Don't call again, Luis."

"What about the monk?"

Silence. Bermann was wrestling with the last vestiges of his patience. "Nothing there, either." The line went dead.

She let her mobile slide to the floor and crept under the blanket.

What had happened to the monk? Did he manage to escape? Or would they at some point find his body too?

Outside it was still pitch black, but the fire was burning and the living room gradually warmed up. Louise closed her eyes. She had barely slept; Niksch had been giving her a hard time.

The bakery where her mother worked was in the centre of the village. When Louise entered, a hectic chorus of bells rang out and she was surrounded by warm, yellow light.

Her mother was talking to an old man, occasionally casting a glance in her direction. The old man was talking about a dog. He thudded his stick against the floor and said the dog was a divine visitation. Her mother laughed and disagreed, but the man raised his voice as well as the stick, and repeated: a divine visitation. Then he took his paper bag and left.

"You look absolutely dreadful," her mother said in German.

"Your sofa's too soft; I didn't get a wink of sleep. What kind of dog is it?" Louise went to the counter and put her hands on the angled glass. It was warm and smeared with fingerprints. A fridge was humming away by the wall. The shelf next to it and the baskets beneath were almost empty.

"A wild Alsatian who's been ripping apart chickens and geese. They've been trying to shoot him for days, but he's too smart for them. He hides during the day and at night he comes out for food. You should see them with their shotguns, shooting holes in the sky and in the fields. They're scared shitless, and every day there's a meeting at the mayor's where they discuss 'strategies' as if they were conducting a war . . . You've got fat, my sweetheart, and as for your skin . . ."

"I may have put on a few kilos, but I haven't got *fat*."

"Are you drinking?"

Louise sighed. "Give me a baguette."

Her mother wrapped the baguette in paper and handed it to her.

When Louise tried to pay she refused. "Why have you come? Have you had a row with Mick?"

"There are some marriages that last longer than yours, Mama."

Her mother laughed. "That's an invention of the Catholic Church."

The bells rang as two elderly ladies came in. A chatter of voices, greetings exchanged, comments flew back and forth about the cold, the dog and the hunters. In the midst of all this her mother said in German, "I'm finished at one, will you come and get me?"

"Yes," Louise said. "Yes, Mama, I am drinking."

It took her an hour to search through the house. Still she could not find a single family photo. Of her brother Germain, her father, even of herself – none of them existed in her mother's new life. Nothing from their shared past seemed to have enough sentimental value for her mother to be able to stomach the bitter memories it might evoke. Not Germain's letters from north Africa, not the endless paintings she'd done as a girl, not the newspaper cuttings her mother had collected when they still lived together in Freiburg. Even her clothes, bedlinen and jewellery were from a new era.

She was on her way down the steep, narrow stairs when Lederle called. "Really sorry, but all hell's broken loose here." He sounded exhausted.

She sat on a step and nodded. A policeman had been murdered. The Liebau task force would soon comprise around forty colleagues from various police departments and the constabulary. Every two or three hours Almenbroich was being summoned to the head of the regional police. They were preparing for the first press conference, and an H.Q. for the task force was being set up on the ground in Liebau. All she could hear was Lederle's voice, short of breath, but she could sense the footsteps, conversations and activity beyond his office door.

"Who's in charge of the team?"

"Rolf."

"It's not his turn. It should be Alfons' turn, and after Alfons it's you."

"Almenbroich has declared an emergency. Alfons is heading the investigation team and I'm leading the back-room operation."

She nodded. Not fair, but sensible. Bermann owned situations like these. His energy and determination set the many-limbed machinery smoothly in motion. He was depressing proof of just how much dictators are able to achieve. And how first they create problems before solving them.

"Anything else come to light?"

Lederle hesitated. "No, nothing. We've got literally *nothing*."

"Talk to Landen."

"He was just here."

"And?"

"Well." Lederle sighed. "You know Bermann. He doesn't like intellectuals. At any rate, we haven't found out anything we didn't already know."

She went into the sitting room. It was cold; she'd forgotten to put more wood on. She sat on the sofa, pulled the blanket over her legs and placed her hand on her aching tummy, which would not release Niksch. Her gaze came to rest on the framed photographs of strangers on the windowsill. "How about the monastery?"

"Schneider and Anne are on their way, with a French colleague."

"Really? Why are the French being so cooperative all of a sudden?"

"They're not," Lederle said. "Schneider and Anne are allowed to go along, but they're not allowed to ask questions, take photos, carry weapons or take their own car. The usual rules."

"All the same, they're being allowed to visit."

"Only because Almenbroich grovelled to Mulhouse."

Bonì smiled. It was Almenbroich who had come up with the saying: Freiburg Kripo gets more support from Moscow than from Colmar.

She stroked the faces with her fingers. Portraits of two men and two women, all about sixty years of age. Secretive, weather-beaten faces that told you nothing except that these people had led a simple life in nature. And yet they had some connection to her mother. They were important to her.

"We'll see," Lederle said, clearing his throat. "How are you getting on, anyway?"

All of a sudden she realised that Lederle was keeping something from her – just as Bermann had. "Rolf thinks the monk's involved, doesn't he? Have you launched a manhunt for him, then?"

"Please don't get worked up, Bonì."

"I'm not getting worked up."

"It's a possibility, isn't it? He might have had accomplices . . ."

Of course it was a possibility. What's more, it *ought* to be one. Dictators didn't just create problems, but possibilities too. She could have laughed out loud. Bermann was so unimaginative. "Promise me you'll do your best to see it's not the only possibility," she said.

She waited outside the bakery. On the other side of the steamed-up windows two or three small dark figures were moving about in the yellow light. The door opened and a woman emerged. Louise recalled the faces on the photographs, but none matched. Then her mother left the bakery and tentatively linked arms with her.

At lunch they barely spoke. Louise thought of the photographs, of Filbinger, and of the fact that neither he nor the past were important anymore. "Is water O.K. with lunch?" her mother asked, and she gave a disgruntled nod.

The downfall of the family, or so her father claimed, had begun in 1968. That year gave "people like your mother – frustrated feminists, hippies and communists – ideas, comrades, forums, focal points". Those four digits pierced the body of the family, which began to haemorrhage in 1968 and collapsed completely ten years later.

In the interim there were discussions, followed by arguments, hysteria, fisticuffs, and finally an uncanny peace. Her mother became a "communist whore", a "man-eater" and "terrorist"; her father a "fascist" and a "collaborator". Germain dropped out of school and fled to north Africa. Louise stayed and hoped things would improve.

One night legions of uniformed officers turned up to arrest her mother. The reason? She was alleged to be close to the Baader-Meinhof gang, or at least a sympathiser. It took weeks for her lawyer to disprove the charges.

It never came to light who had denounced her mother. But soon it became clear who she suspected. She never went home, and from that day on she never spoke another word to Louise's father.

Even then she had favoured simplistic solutions.

At the beginning, at least, it was more complicated. Louise remembered a photograph of a demonstration her father had been on too. In her mind she had a clear picture of him smiling hesitantly at the camera. Beside him her mother, with one arm raised. This photograph had vanished too.

I've *never* been on a demonstration in my *entire* life, her father claimed later. Conformists don't *demonstrate*, her mother had said.

After Filbinger's resignation in 1978 she expended her entire energy on individual battles: against Christian Socialist Franz-Josef Strauss, N.A.T.O., the arms industry, the Kohl government. New fronts opened up daily. But when Germain died in 1983, she gave up the war overnight.

"Did you have a boyfriend at the time?" Louise said with her mouth full.

"When?"

"At the beginning. In sixty-eight."

"Heavens . . . Is that what your father told you?"

"'You can imagine what they got up to in their communes,' is what he said."

"'What they got up to . . .'" Her mother broke off.

"Well?"

Her mother got up to put the plates in the sink. "Why is all this coming out now? It's more than thirty years ago."

"Did you have a boyfriend, Mama?"

"Are you holding *me* responsible for *your* problems?" Her mother put an Italian coffee pot on the stove. She didn't look rattled, just cross.

Louise smiled faintly. You can get rid of photographs, but not memories. At least not when other people keep them alive. "So why is Filbinger no longer important. For ten years everything revolved around him, and now he's unimportant."

Her mother turned around. "What I said was: He's not important *here*." For a moment they looked each other in the eye. Her mother's face was still smooth and beautiful, in its pinched way. Her eyes had a particular, intense life in them. Louise had never been able to work out what went on behind them.

Her mother filled two cups with espresso. The cups were more robust than Richard Landen's and showed signs of frequent use. They matched her hands. Louise tried to imagine Landen with the task force. But he was just a shape, a feeling, barely even an image. All she could remember vividly was his clear, detached voice. You can never really understand another person, the voice said.

Her mother sat down. "Why is all this so important for you?"

"Why this . . ." She paused, took a sip of coffee, closed her eyes.

No other name had become so branded on her mind as *Filbinger*. In her memory she'd got out of bed with this name and gone to school, she'd spent her evenings with the name and sometimes even dreamed of him. To begin with the name had sounded wonderful, representing a mysterious being her father and mother had long discussions about. These discussions had escalated into serious rows and the mysterious being had turned into a nightmare.

She opened her eyes and looked at her mother.

"Is that why you're here, Louise? To accuse me? To tell me I'm to blame for everything?"

She shook her head. "I'm here because two days ago someone died."

Later that afternoon they went out. It was raining softly; the bright-grey sky hung low over the village. They followed the road for a while, then turned onto a path at the edge of the village, which led up a small hill.

Her mother had barely said a word since Louise had told her about Niksch. She looked thoughtful, exhausted. When they reached the top she stopped and said, "Do you ever think about Germain?"

"Occasionally. Why?"

"He was only a few years older than the policeman."

Louise nodded. They went on. Her mother was wearing a simple, dark coat, a simple, checked scarf, walked with simple, small steps and had become a simple woman for whom a few square kilometres sufficed. Louise found it difficult to recognise in her the warrior from her childhood and adolescence. Like Landen's Japanese wife, she had travelled a long way.

"I rarely think of him. Never, in fact."

"Isn't *he* important here either?"

Her mother shrugged. "It's impossible to forget the bad things and only hold on to the good ones. *I* can't, at least. Somehow it's all connected. When I picture Germain I automatically have your father in my mind, and then I think of Filbinger and that unbearable male world of power, lies, greed, war . . . So I prefer not to think of Germain."

"Or of me," Louise said.

"Yes." Her mother shot her a glance. "It's appalling, I know, but that's how it is."

Beyond the hill lay a gently sloping meadow with yellowish grass, which after a couple of hundred metres became a barren, rocky land-scape. Wisps of fog hung between the hulking boulders and a muddy path led up to them. They followed it in silence. Louise thought of Landen and wondered how he coped with the knowledge that he'd never really understand his wife. And whether he had a way of making it bearable.

Her mobile rang. Lederle. Every other second the poor connection made his voice cut out. She swivelled around, but it made no difference. She did grasp, however, that Hollerer's condition was unchanged. She wanted to ask more, but Lederle was already talking about Schneider and Wallmer. They had been at the Kanzan-an with the French detective. The monk – "Taro", Lederle said – had indeed come from there.

"What else? . . . Reiner?"

Lederle's answer was incomprehensible.

She walked a few steps further. There was a roaring in her ear, and then Lederle's reedy voice again. Nobody at the monastery knew anything more, he said. "Bonì?"

"I can hear you."

Schneider and Wallmer had been allowed to take a look at Taro's cell, while the French detective had questioned the people at the monastery. As Richard Landen had suspected, Taro was from Kyushu. He was twenty-three and had been at the Kanzan-an for four months. He'd left the monastery some time on Wednesday night; his absence had gone unnoticed until the following morning. That was all they had been able to discover.

Louise wondered whether Schneider and Wallmer had primed their French colleague with the right questions. Questions you would ask based on the assumption that Taro was a victim, not a suspect. Questions that assumed other possibilities than the one Bermann had served up.

"What about at your end?" Lederle said. "Everything alright? Anything I can do for you?"

"Who's the French guy they went with?"

"Your father rang, by the way. He says he can't get you at home anymore. Doesn't he have your mobile number? Shall I give it to him?"

"Please don't. Reiner, who were they there with?"

Lederle said nothing for a moment. Then he said, "Bonì? I can barely hear you . . ."

"I can hear you loud and clear."

"Bonì? Hello? . . ."

"Cut the crap, Reiner."

"Bonì, I'm going to hang up now, O.K.?"

"Christ, you're such a coward."

Lederle sighed. "Muller," he said. "But *please* keep out of it."

"Thanks." She put her phone away.

Justin Muller. She grinned. One of the few French colleagues of theirs who assessed requests from Germany according to their urgency rather than by any other criteria. An honest, likeable chap with curly hair, a bit tubby, paternal in a nice way. Two sons, divorced – or at least he was. A great kisser. A year ago she'd almost got him into bed. Or was it the other way around? We shouldn't be doing this, we're colleagues, one of them had said at some point. She? Muller?

She instinctively felt in her anorak pocket. Car keys, tissues, four packets of chewing gum, mobile. Nothing else.

"Louise?"

She looked up. A grim smile sat on her mother's lips. Although it was raining more heavily now, she'd untied her headscarf and pushed it over her head. *We shouldn't be doing this, we're colleagues.* She'd never say anything like that.

Louise slowly came back to her mother.

"What happened to you?" Taking her arm, her mother pulled her onwards. Louise felt how much strength she still had.

A gentle, damp wind was stirring. The path wound between the head-high rocks. Once more she thought she could smell snow hanging in the air. It occurred to Louise that in the last few years she had always visited her mother in winter. After her hurried separation from Mick three years ago, after Calambert's death two years ago, and in January last year, having spent Christmas and New Year alone, and then taken half the night to quietly dispose of the empty bottles.

"Do you remember Calambert?"

"The man who . . . that girl? . . . Yes."

She nodded. She'd driven here a few days after the case had been wrapped up, after Annetta had died. There were no photos on the windowsill then, the sofa was in front of the fireplace. Sitting bolt upright on a kitchen chair, her mother had said, "That poor girl. That poor, poor girl."

"I can't come to terms with it."

"With what?"

"That I'm responsible for his death."

Her mother stopped and looked at her. "It made me *proud*. For the first time in my life I was *proud* of something." Her eyes were full of resolve, vaguely reminding Louise of the warrior her mother had once been.

"He was married with a young daughter, Mama."

"He killed a girl. He *raped* and killed her."

"Still."

"I was proud of you, Louise." Her mother's voice had gone cold. But her grip around Louise's wrist remained firm.

They turned and went back along the path. Beyond the meadow and the hill a handful of dark houses had come into view. Smoke rose from chimneys. A weary, warm yellow shimmered through a few windows. Louise imagined tidy kitchens, simple wooden tables, old people drinking coffee. Niksch, staring at a tiny cup with green liquid. A black china cat on a windowsill.

Landen, she thought. He would have asked the right questions.

"How bad is it, your drinking?"

"What do you mean?"

"Well, can you stop?"

Louise raised her eyebrows. She thought of Calambert and of Mick. Those long, free weekends. The winter, the snow. Of the fact that she now had a fourth snowman: Niksch. "Of course I can," she said.

Her mother nodded. "You started before, before Calambert," she said. "You started because you didn't have any children, because you weren't happy in your marriage, but you don't want to admit this because then you'd have to admit that I was right, that your husband couldn't be trusted for five minutes."

Red-hot anger shot into her limbs. But she was tight-lipped. She could hardly complain that her mother was reinventing her past if she withheld essential information from her.

"It's not meant to be a criticism, Louise. I mean, women fall in love with words, not values."

"Can we just drop this, O.K.? I'd rather you told me if you had a boyfriend back then."

Her mother let out an irate laugh and snatched her arm away. "Whether I did or didn't, it's irrelevant – *that's* not why our marriage failed, Louise."

"Correct. It failed because of Filbinger."

"No, it failed because I married a Frenchman who suddenly became a German. Sometimes things really are that simple."

"*Here*, they're simple."

"Yes," her mother said, taking Louise's arm again.

While her mother prepared dinner Louise sat on the sofa wondering why her own marriage had gone down the pan. There was a simple answer to this one. In the space of five years Mick had cheated on her with half of southern Baden.

There were probably more complicated answers too. Answers that were more insightful, that contained a higher degree of qualitative information. But to get there you had to take a path through a jungle of awkward questions. Was she boring in bed? Had he ever loved her? Why hadn't he wanted children? Was it just that he didn't want children with her? As a policewoman, was she unsuited to marriage and a family?

With a groan she reached for her mobile.

Hollerer had woken up, asked about Niksch, then fallen straight back to sleep. She picked up the wine glass from the floor by the sofa and thought: Niksch is here, Hollerer. Here, where everything's simple.

Her eyes locked onto the strangers' faces on the windowsill. Friends from the village, her mother had said, giving names that she'd immediately forgotten. Stranger–friends. She tapped in Richard Landen's number. Once again the Japanese woman by the name of Tommo answered, and once again she hung up. She crawled under the blanket and imagined that Landen and Tommo had complicated questions for each other, and were on the hunt for complicated answers. Answers that helped them achieve mutual respect without actually understanding each other.

Then she fell asleep.

It was dark in the sitting room when she woke, and there was no light coming from the kitchen either. Just a reddish glimmer from the hissing embers. Her phone read 21.54. She felt for the wine glass. It was gone.

On the stove was a covered pot of pasta with meat sauce. She wasn't hungry, but she knew that her body needed something to eat. Half-heartedly she lit the gas beneath the pot. Her hands were shaking, her palms wet. In a metal breadbasket she found the remains of a baguette. She broke off half. For a second or two she could see Niksch before her, döner in hand. His beautiful, friendly lips, closing with relish on bread, meat and tomatoes.

When she sat down at the table she heard footsteps in the room above.

A few minutes later her mother appeared in the kitchen in her pyjamas and said, "I didn't want to wake you." She went to the cooker and turned down the flame. Then she removed the lid, stirred the pasta and added a pinch of salt.

"I want something to drink, Mama."

"In the cupboard behind you is red wine and pastis. If you want anything else, we'll have to . . ."

"No, that's fine."

"Would you pour me a glass too?"

Louise put the wine and pastis on the table. "Have you already eaten?"

"Yes."

While her mother was serving some pasta onto a plate, she drank half a glass of pastis and quietly gave herself a top-up.

"Did they chuck you out?"

"I'm on sick leave."

Her mother put the plate in front of Louise and gave her a cursory stroke on the arm before sitting down. Louise stared at the pasta, the light-brown sauce. It was so familiar, her mother's spaghetti bolognese had looked the same for forty years.

As she ate she talked about Almenbroich, Bermann, Katrin Rein and the abyss.

At around eleven that evening her mother revived the warrior in her. She could not understand, she said hoarsely, how Louise had simply surrendered. Her cheeks were red, her mouth a tense, narrow line. She half stood up, as if about to launch herself at an invisible enemy. "Sue them," she said, slamming her hand onto the table.

"Sit down, Mama," Louise said. The wine was finished, the pastis almost gone too. She drained the last few centimetres into her glass.

Her mother slumped back into her chair. The blanket slid from her shoulders to the floor. She bent to retrieve it, and when she came up again her eyes looked shattered, a sign that she'd drunk too much.

"I haven't surrendered, Mama."

"Why are you here, then?"

"Because I need some time out."

"And while you're taking time out, they're sorting out the facts." Her mother's voice now sounded exhausted, dark from drinking and from tiredness. Louise wondered who she meant by "they". Her colleagues? The authorities? The men? "Sue them, Louise," her mother said. "*Fight!*"

Both were silent for a while. The occasional crackling of wood drifted in from the sitting room. Otherwise it was eerily quiet in the kitchen. She looked at her mother, then at the two empty bottles, the two empty glasses. In her consciousness a single word reverberated: Fight. "Against what, Mama? For what?"

"What a question, Louise!"

She shrugged. "It can't be done by fighting alone. There has to be something else."

Her mother's anger flared again. "Of course," she said. "Capitulation."

From a distance she became aware of the muffled ringing of her mobile. "That might be right for you, Mama, but not for me. I live *today*. There must be something else for me."

Her mobile was on the sofa beneath her duvet. She recognised the number instantly. What now?

As she sank onto the duvet, the down feathers gave a soft sigh. She wished her mother wasn't in earshot. But she didn't seem to be taking any notice of her daughter. She sat huddled at the kitchen table, frowning, perhaps thinking of a time when it *was* all about fighting or submission.

Louise cleared her throat twice. "Hello? Louise Bonì here."

"Ah, Inspector," Landen said. There was surprise in his voice. He mumbled a few words in Japanese, and in the background his wife replied. "I'm sorry to call so late," he said. Two calls on two consecutive days in which the caller hadn't said anything. They had, he explained with a cheerless laugh, thought it might be a pervert who wasn't *au fait* with the latest technology. He paused, apparently waiting for an explanation.

But Louise had no desire to explain anything. She thought of all the things she wanted to ask Landen, and say to him. The things she wanted to do with him.

Then she thought of the filigree teacups and felt ashamed of her hands, her bloated body, the smell it gave off. Of the increasingly regular stolen moments in the loos at work, the lies at parties, the many other lies, the weekends in bed. The increasing gaps in her memory. Of her craving *beforehand* and her contentment *afterwards.*

Fight, her mother's voice had said. But she sensed this wouldn't be enough. If you didn't know what to do with the territory you conquered, you didn't start a war.

"Are you still there?" Landen said.

"Yes. I need your help again."

"I thought you were on holiday?"

"I'm on holiday nearby. Will you help me?"

"This morning I didn't get the impression that my help was welcome."

"Drive with me to the Kanzan-an." All at once she felt incredibly tired. She closed her eyes and leaned her head on the back of the sofa.

"Weren't your colleagues—"

"Let's leave that, O.K.? Do you have a car?"

Landen hesitated before answering. "Yes."

"Great. Two o'clock tomorrow, at the monastery. Does that work for you?"

"No, it would have to be three at the earliest."

"Alright, three then. Thanks."

After hanging up she stayed for a moment on the sofa with her eyes closed. When she opened them again, almost instinctively her gaze sought out the pictures on the windowsill. One of the frames reflected light from the kitchen lamp. In the dark she couldn't make out the faces.

She was happy that there were no photos from the past in her mother's house. No photos to show how much she had changed.

Her mother had started to clear the table. "Well then," she said when Louise came into the kitchen. "You're going back . . . You're not just going to give up . . . You're *fighting* . . ." Her movements were heavy and sluggish. Her breath smelled of wine.

"I'll do that," Louise said. "Come on."

Putting her arm around her mother, she helped her through the sitting room. She climbed the narrow stairs behind her, but kept her hand on her mother's hip. It felt warm and thin and alien.

She wondered whether she was right. Was she going to the Kanzan-an to fight? Or was there an essential difference between fighting and not giving up? Fighting for something meant excluding all other possibilities. Not giving up meant – in her case at least – *finding* other possibilities.

It was ice cold in the tiny bedroom. She switched on the bedside light. The window was tilted open. "Leave it," her mother said when Louise went to close the window.

She plumped up the duvet and held her mother until she sat on the bed. Only now did she notice tears running down the tanned cheeks. "I can't begin to imagine what you must have gone through," her mother said. "In the forest, with your dead colleague."

Louise didn't reply. Her mother lay down and she pulled the duvet over her. "It's not over yet, Louise. Don't believe it, even if it looks that way. So long as women and children have to suffer, it's not over."

"Niksch wasn't a child, Mama."

"Of course he was."

"Go to sleep now, O.K.?"

Her mother took her hand. "I was proud of you, Louise. I thought you'd go on fighting for me."

"Night, Mama."

"Do you know what I'm talking about Louise?"

"Yes."

"About men's greed."

"I know, Mama."

"Good. That's . . . important." Her mother let go of her hand with a distant smile. "Will you come past the bakery before you go?"

"Of course. Good night."

She shut the door quietly. On her way down the stairs Louise turned. There was no light coming through the crack in the door.

As she washed up in the kitchen she thought about how her mother had failed in all her ideals. None of her hopes had been fulfilled, or at least not those she knew of. Neither the political, nor social, nor the ones for her family. Did she still harbour ideals? Hopes? *Simple* hopes? Or was she now merely intent on healing her old war wounds? Who was her mother, in fact? What did she want, think, feel?

And Louise herself? What did *she* want and feel? Who was *she*?

She laughed softly when it struck her that she was asking all these questions while washing up.

That night she dreamed of Calambert. He was lying in the snow and she was standing over him. His eyes were open. He wouldn't die, even though she was firing bullet after bullet into his stomach.

She woke and sat up.

The images from her dream had gone, but the anger she had felt remained. Uncontrollable anger.

In the past, her mother would have felt this kind of anger.

She left at around nine. The sun was shining, it was going to be a mild day. There might be snow fifty or sixty kilometres to the north, but not here. A small world without snow.

When she stopped her car by the bakery, her mother came outside. They embraced briefly.

"Come some time in spring or summer, not always in winter."

"We'll finish painting your house."

Her mother nodded and stepped back. "Say Hi to Mick."

Louise looked at her. In her head a sentence began to form that was both simple and complex. Before it could be articulated she got back into her car and drove off.

8

Justin Muller looked just the same as last year, he spoke the same and smiled the same. It seemed as if it were only yesterday that she'd left Mulhouse after their last meeting. If she remembered right, he'd even been wearing the same checked jacket. A rock in the tempestuous swell of time. Unimpeded by the worries, failures and setbacks of a police officer's year and the potential minor ailments of a fifty-year-old. His gaze wandered nervously over her body. "You look good," he lied in French.

They were standing in his office. It was 2.15. There was barely any snow left in Mulhouse; the thaw had begun, moving from west to east. It must have reached southern Baden too. Landen would have no difficulty getting here. She pictured him crossing the bridge over the Rhine in a Mitsubishi or a Honda or a Mazda. An unpleasantly warm shiver ran down her spine.

"You really do," Muller said.

His holster and pistol were hanging from the coat stand behind him. On his desk was the same photograph from last year, of him with his ex-wife and two sons. Streaks of light in their hair. A light-blue background. They smiled as if they were in a photographic studio.

"Thanks," she said, also in French. "And how are you?"

"Fine."

"Good. Listen, Justin, I've got to talk to you."

He shook his head in dismay. "I'm sorry, but I haven't got time." He stretched out his arms, as if to encompass all the documents, files, notes, computers and telephones in the room. From his expression one might think that the *entire backlog of things to do* was about to collapse on top of him.

She waited. Nothing happened. "Let's go for a little walk."

"But I *can't*. I've got a meeting with Chervel, and in half an hour I have to be in . . ." He broke off. He was frowning, but not looking at her.

All of a sudden she understood. Something *had* changed since last year. Muller was now on the other side. "What have they been saying about me?"

He looked up. "Who?"

"Well, Wallmer, Schneider, Bermann."

"We haven't spoken about you."

"So what *have* you spoken about?"

"I've got to go now, Louise. Chervel . . ." Again he left his sentence unfinished.

She followed him to the door. "Of course you spoke about me. Bermann told you that I . . . that . . ."

They stopped and looked at each other. The corners of Muller's mouth crept downwards as if in slow motion. The tension vanished from his facial muscles. He blinked slowly, as if afraid that any rapid movement might encourage Bonì to continue talking.

"Why are you asking if you already know?" he said.

He went back to his desk, eyeing the photograph as he sat down. A ritual. A glance at the photograph each time he sat down. He'd done that last year too. Crossing his arms, he looked at her.

She pointed to the door behind her. "What about Chervel?" Louise sounded scornful. She realised too late that she ought not to have asked this question.

Muller blushed perceptibly, but said nothing.

"Sorry," she said. "I'd hoped . . ." She went over and leaned on the table. She was grateful that he hadn't forced her to say: Bermann told you I'm a drinker. He hadn't wanted to hear it; she hadn't wanted to say it. At least they had something in common.

Bonì lowered her voice. "I need a gun."

He swallowed. "You're in France!"

"Justin, I'm going to the monastery; there *must* be answers there. Bermann and the others . . . Did they tell you about the monk who's disappeared?"

Muller hesitated a moment before giving the faintest of nods. He was remarkably pale. He put his hands on the desk and interlaced his fingers.

"They think he's in on it. But he isn't."

"You ought to go now . . . Please, I'm asking you to leave."

Louise smiled patiently. She'd known it would be difficult. Muller had a different attitude towards regulations, but he was also reasonable and understanding. He knew what was important and what was not.

So she tried to explain the situation. She had no idea what to expect at the Kanzan-an. One colleague was dead, another in intensive care. She wouldn't be alone, she was meeting a Buddhist expert at the monastery. He was her responsibility, so she *couldn't* go there without a weapon.

Muller said nothing. His helpless gaze strayed across the wall beside her to the holster, then to the photograph. Last year, with a jittery hand on her breast, he'd said, "We shouldn't be doing this, we're colleagues." He'd been panting with excitement, but ultimately had succumbed to outdated bureaucratic rules. Now there was no prospect of an expectant vagina as a reward for his bad conscience.

She sat on the chair by the desk. Muller stared at her, helpless, speechless, spineless. She could see from his face how disappointed he was in her, and in himself. In a world that expected him to deal with these situations, but had not taught him how. She placed a hand on his. His fingers were cold and tense.

When the tension relaxed, she gave him a smile. Then she stood up and left.

On her map no roads were marked in the triangle of countryside between Zillisheim, Illfurth and Steinbrunn-le-Bas. She couldn't see any signs. It was 2.50 p.m. She was heading towards Illfurth and decided to ask someone when she got there, but then she came across a narrow strip of asphalt that led into the forest on the left. She turned off the main road.

The trees were bare but densely packed. Immediately it grew darker. The forest floor was sprinkled with innumerable untouched patches of snow. All of a sudden the memory returned: the snow, the cold, Hollerer's vacant stare. Niksch, his back lying against her, turning hypothermic with terrifying rapidity. His hair, still smelling of the cold and the dew. Niksch, the child. She thought she remembered wanting to kiss him after their kebab dinner. Now he would be buried.

Bonì stopped the car. The asphalt track led to a narrow gate of white light five or six hundred metres away. In her glove compartment there were small bottles and one large one, all carefully wrapped in newspaper. Half of the weekend edition of the *Badische Zeitung* nicked from Ronescu's letterbox. The first miniature was empty. As was the second. But not the third.

Mild temperatures of between 5 and 8 degrees were forecast for the next couple of days.

They'd all be there: Almenbroich, Bermann, Wallmer, Lederle. The entire department, probably half of Baden-Württemberg's police H.Q.

The chief of police.

There would be a speech or two. A policeman had been murdered.

Only Lederle had met Niksch. The others didn't know him. They'd be putting a stranger in the ground.

Cry, damn it, she thought. But she couldn't.

She rang the hospital. Engaged. She tried again and got a community service assistant. Hollerer was over the worst. He was rarely conscious, but over the worst, at least. The assistant seemed glad to be able to give her information. He said his name was Roman and she should ask for him when she called again.

Lederle was not engaged; he answered at once. "Oh, it's you," he muttered frostily. She apologised for yesterday. In a friendlier tone he said, "Well, the main thing is that you stay out of it."

"Of course."

"How's Provence?"

"Beautiful. We're doing a lot of walking."

There were raised voices in the background. She heard hurried steps. Someone knocked at a door and called out something. Then there was a rustling, a squeaking and creaking. "I've got to go," Lederle said.

"Wait, Reiner. When's the funeral?"

"What funeral?"

"Niksch's."

Silence. Then Lederle said, "Don't do it to yourself, Bonì."

She heard him pacing around the room. More rustling. It sounded as if he was putting on his coat. "Has the body been released yet?"

"No, it's going to take a few days."

"Call me when you know more details."

"Don't do it to yourself, Bonì," Lederle repeated and hung up.

She put her mobile on the passenger seat and closed the glove box. Then she drove through the gate of light.

Beyond the forest the road ran down a hill, then climbed again soon afterwards. In three or four places a dirt track branched off, but as they were not signposted she stayed on the asphalt. She couldn't see any houses or farms, not even a fence. No walkers, no farmers, no traffic. No cows. Just black birds and a light-grey cat on a rock near the side of the road, which kept its eyes fixed on the car as it drove past.

In a dip the road curved to the right. A weather-worn sign pointed to the left. Beneath Japanese or Chinese characters it read: KANZAN-AN.

Bonì followed a dead-straight dirt track with large potholes and scraps of snow. Stones rattled against the underside of her car. She forced herself to drive more slowly. It was 3.15. She wondered whether Landen would wait for her.

Five minutes later she caught sight of three cars parked in a row. Although she couldn't see the Kanzan-an, the track ended here. She parked the Mégane beside a black Volvo and got out. The air was cold and damp. Just as in Provence, here too it smelled of snow.

The Volvo bore a Freiburg number plate. The bonnet was still warm. Inside the car she could recognise Landen's fastidious tidiness. Did he ever leave traces that said anything about him? If not, she'd have to keep on drawing conclusions from the absence of things: dark windows, a faceless woman's voice, Landen's silence. Unfinished stories.

From the car park a straight, narrow path led into the forest. Flat stones had been sunk into the ground roughly a pace apart. Apart from the wooden sign these stepping stones were the first indication that visitors were not entirely unwelcome at the Kanzan-an.

She was freezing and soon felt out of breath. Once again images from Sunday evening reared in her mind. The sickly moon, the pale snow. Her hands covered in blood. Niksch's dirty, lifeless face that could not have been Niksch.

The path led to a broad, hilly clearing, in the centre of which stood a gloomy building with stone front steps. Scattered throughout the clearing were a handful of flat-roofed wooden houses. There was not a soul in sight. It was deathly quiet. No sound, no movement. Nothing to suggest that the Kanzan-an was inhabited.

Then Landen stepped out of the entrance to the main building.

They shook hands. Landen didn't smile, but he wasn't unfriendly either. The grey fleck on his eyebrow didn't move. He was wearing a black roll-neck jumper, a brown corduroy suit and a black over-coat. This was how she imagined men looked in existentialists' cafés in the '50s. She suppressed a smirk. Her mother would have liked this man.

"My deepest condolences," he said.

"What?" She looked at him in surprise. She was still trying to work out what he was referring to when the tears came. Furious, she let them run.

Landen narrowed his eyes and cleared his throat. One wrong word, she thought, and I will kill you. But he just watched her and said nothing, his hands in his coat pockets.

Then it passed. She blew her nose, dried her cheeks and said, "Let's go in."

"We have to wait; the monks are meditating."

"How long does that go on for?"

"Nine years, if we're unlucky." He smiled. "That's how long it took Bodhidharma." His ornamental eyebrow rose into an arc. Landen had tried to cheer her up. She smiled.

"Then let's take a look around." She brushed his arm lightly.

They walked along the front of the three-storey building. Nothing about the house gave it a Far-Eastern flavour. She thought it resembled the Freiburg Staatstheater after renovation – a slightly rounded façade, tall windows that were semi-circular at the top. It may have been beige a long time ago, but now it was brown. Cracks ran vertically down the render and the base of the building was covered in moss. The cold air carried the occasional whiff of mould.

She looked up. No balconies guarded by statues of Buddha like at the Kagyu House. But there was a child. At a window on the first floor stood a boy, she could see only his head and shoulders. He seemed to be staring down at them. She couldn't make out his features in any detail, but he appeared to be oriental. Louise guessed he was three or four, but she had no experience of children from that part of the world.

Landen had noticed the boy too and had stopped. He waved awkwardly. She wondered whether Tommo / Landen had children. Nothing in their tidy kitchen suggested it. But perhaps their children left no visible traces either.

The boy waved back.

They walked on. Muffled strokes of a gong sounded in the distance, the first noises she'd heard from the Kanzan-an. They appeared to rise from the ground, or radiate from the masonry. Always the same tone, soft and steady.

"Is there any hope for Taro?" Landen said.

She didn't answer immediately. Somewhere in her sub-conscious a thought was stirring. She tried to focus, but couldn't grasp it.

More and more holes in her memory.

Fear raced momentarily through her arteries. A perforated brain. A sieve that caught only the biggest grains of rice.

She pushed her fear aside. "There's always hope."

Landen didn't probe deeper. He seemed to have understood what she had wanted to imply: that Taro might already be dead. That she didn't want to talk about it anymore.

She looked at him. "What do the Japanese do when someone dies?"

"The Japanese, or Buddhists?"

"Buddhists."

"They mourn."

"What else?"

"That depends."

"On what?"

"On how far down the path of Buddha they have gone. The greater their degree of maturity, the more easily they find it to accept death as part of life – as part of the cycle of reincarnation. I'd like to tell you a story."

"Only if this one has an ending."

"It has," Landen said.

They stopped at the corner of the house. Another path of stepping stones led up the clearing to a simple wooden shelter, vaguely reminiscent of a home-made tram stop. Beside it was a garden gate, also of wood. Fifty metres beyond this, in the middle of trees, stood a shed with a low overhanging roof. Just in front of it she thought she could make out a fountain.

"*Sukiya*," Landen said. "The teahouse."

A stepping-stone path, a fountain, a wooden house. She wondered whether the barn in Landen's snowy garden was a sort of teahouse too. "What about your story?"

"On his travels the Buddha met a woman whose child had just died. In desperation she begged him to bring it back to life. The Buddha said: Alright, I will help you, but on one condition. Bring me a few grains of rice from a house in the area where nobody has ever died. Going from door to door the woman found only families who had already lost someone. She understood that death was inevitable and affected everybody. And so she learned to accept the death of her child and to let it go."

The sounds of the gong had faded away. They were still at the corner of the main building, looking towards the little teahouse.

"Nice story. Do you have children?"

Landen hesitated. "No," he said. "But soon we will."

"What do you mean? Is your wife pregnant?"

He nodded.

As if from nowhere a dozen monks and nuns now emerged between the raised mounds of the clearing. They wore black habits and their heads were shaven. Around half of them were from the Far East. Silently they dispersed without looking over at Boni and Landen.

Then the thought she hadn't been able to grasp was suddenly at the front of her mind: children's shoes. On the evening of Niksch's death she had discovered a child's footprints.

She turned around. The boy was gone.

"The roshi," Landen said, touching her arm.

"What?"

"The master."

An elderly Japanese monk came towards them, his arms folded over his belly. He was tall and walked slowly but with vigour. His cheeks were crossed with deep wrinkles which seemed to have been etched on the skin with a hard object and lent his face a terrifyingly stern expression. For a moment she expected him to expel them from the property. But then he gestured to himself and said in English, "Hello, Bukan," and gave a friendly nod.

But far more important was the fact that Landen's finger still rested on her arm.

Once again there was tea out of small, delicate bowls for people with a pure conscience. The tea was black, offering a distant reminder that this world contained dark abysses too. All the same she couldn't bring herself to pick up the little bowl.

They were sitting on raffia mats and cushions in a tall room on the ground floor of the main building. Even though they had kept their coats on it was freezing cold. Boní cupped her hands around the bowl without drinking. "No heater," the roshi said softly in his idiosyncratic English. "No heater China of Kanzan, no heater here."

She smiled. "Roshi . . ." she began.

"Wait," Landen said.

The roshi took a sip of tea, then said, "Kanzan-an founded thirty years back." He raised his right hand and pointed over his shoulder behind him. "Founded in memory of Chinese Buddhist layman name Kanzan." He smiled. "No electric light China of Kanzan, no electric light here. No car China of Kanzan, no car here." He raised his finger. "Kanzan poet, we poet. Kanzan beggar, we beggar. Kanzan laugh, we laugh. Understand?"

"Yes, roshi," Landen said.

"The tourist spiel," Louise mumbled.

Landen said something in Japanese and laughed. The roshi laughed too. For a second the harsh lines on his face assumed a cheerful expression.

"What's so funny?"

Landen looked at her. "Behave, or you won't learn anything. You're in a monastery. Irrespective of what you think of Zen, Japan or the roshi, he's a dignitary. And so he deserves respect."

The muffled gong strokes rang out, joined now by muted male voices. She turned to look at the window that gave onto the rear of the building. Two monks were kneeling at a stone fountain. The younger one looked Chinese, the elder was European. They were spreading mortar on the lower edge of the fountain and setting rectangular stones side by side. Next to them sat a light-grey cat, perhaps the same cat or maybe a different one.

She looked at Landen. Are you sure he warrants respect? she wanted to ask, but instead she said, "Why did you laugh?"

Before Landen could reply the roshi said, "Laugh important Kanzan. Kanzan hermit, Kanzan funny, Kanzan laugh. Taro no laugh. No laugh in Taro. In Taro doubt." His right hand pointed to Bonì. "Doubt. Understand? Many questions." He tapped his chest. "Soul inside man? Where is? What look like? Taro many questions. When Taro child, father die. Monks give rice and cake and fruit for sacrifice. Taro say: Father die, how can eat? Monks say: Soul of father eat. Taro say: Where soul? Soul in body of father?" The roshi rubbed his fingers together. "Taro say: Soul what made of? What look like? Many questions. Taro say: Buddha Shakyamuni say, everything emptiness. Shunyata. Everything nothing. But inside man something. Something can see, something can hear." The roshi raised his palms. "Taro come Kanzan-an find answer. Maybe now Taro leave find answer."

"No," Louise said. "Taro *hurt*."

The roshi leaned on one elbow. "You see Taro?"

She nodded. In German she explained the circumstances in which she'd met Taro. Then she described his wounds. Landen translated into Japanese. The roshi nodded as he listened, his strong hands that bore the signs of physical labour resting on his stomach.

As Landen spoke, Bonì's gaze was fixed on those hands. She couldn't help but think of Enni, the sushi boy. The warmth of his hand, the rumbling centre of her body beneath them. The idea, the hope, the apprehension that his hand might have intentions that went beyond the purely spiritual.

She gave a sombre grin. A sixteen-year-old. What weird path was she on?

Landen and the roshi looked at her. The roshi's eyes were half closed. The wrinkles on his face looked dark. She wondered whether there was a connection between the boy at the window and the small footprints in the sodden earth to the east of Liebau.

"Taro hurt," she said. "Old policeman hurt. Young policeman dead. Taro gone."

"Taro Zensu, scholar of Zen," the roshi said with sudden, barely restrained anger. "Zensu no harm people. Zensu look Buddha-nature. Look own-nature. Look shunyata."

"I know, Roshi Bukan. But someone did it and I need to know who. If we don't find out we may never see Taro again."

After Landen had translated, the roshi lowered his eyes. Both hands were now on one knee and he was frowning. Four or five minutes went past without a word.

Finally she turned to Landen and asked, "What does 'shunyata' mean?"

"In Japan language shunyata name ku," the roshi answered instead. "In English language shunyata name emptiness. Explain, please." He nodded to Landen.

"'Shunyata' is Sanskrit and means 'emptiness'. The Japanese term for that is 'ku'," Landen said.

"I got that."

Landen carefully reached for his bowl and took a sip. "Zen says that all living beings and things are merely ephemeral. They have no nature, no I; in this sense they are empty . . ."

Louise nodded. She watched in fascination the movements of the two-tone eyebrow, drifting up, drifting down, jack-knifing at the grey part. She found it hard to suppress the urge to stroke it with a finger.

". . . at the moment of enlightenment. The duality is eliminated, and by that we mean the division into subject and object – that which sees, and that which is seen. Now you perceive things as they are, you see their true nature."

Landen's voice once again conveyed the well-rehearsed patience she knew. He was lecturing. The passion had gone, the eyebrow had stopped moving. He said, "Insight into shunyata is essential in order to leave the painful experience of life and become a Buddha."

"Aha," she said.

"Buddha-nature inside every man," the roshi said.

"Also inside every woman?"

The roshi nodded with a laugh. "Also inside every woman. Buddha-nature own-nature. Understand? Own-nature."

"Own-nature?" she repeated, at a loss.

"Everyone has the Buddha-nature inside them. It's their own nature," Landen said.

The harsh staccato noise of hammer blows sounded from outside. The two monks were knocking the fountain stones into place. It was getting dark, and it was a moment before Bonì noticed that a light snow was falling. Watery, almost transparent flakes. Either the cat had gone or it had merged into the grey light of dusk.

A child near to the place where Niksch had been murdered and Taro was last seen. A child in the Kanzan-an, where Taro had lived.

Bermann would have laughed in her face if he'd known what she was thinking.

Bermann stuck to probabilities and logic, whereas she looked for connections, analogies, systems. Bermann was head of Section 11, she was on sick leave.

She looked at the roshi and he returned her gaze, nodding. In his eyes she could see toughness, severity and anger, but also wisdom and understanding.

Landen's comments about unfamiliarity filled her head. The idea that you could never really understand another person, particularly not someone from a different culture. She realised that she had no idea what the roshi was thinking, feeling or wanting just at that moment. What he was *seeing*.

She didn't know much about Landen either.

What about herself? She knew that in her handbag there were bottles wrapped in newspaper. That in Freiburg a very young psychologist was waiting for her call. That she was in the process of falling in love with a married intellectual whose wife was pregnant. That she desired the hand of an underage sushi-seller on parts of her body where it ought not to be.

With a tired smile she asked, "Are there young Zensus in Kanzan-an, roshi? Children?"

Landen translated.

"No," the roshi said in English. "No children in Kanzan-an."

9

Fifteen minutes later it was almost dark. Watery snow was still falling but didn't settle. The gong resounded and then fell silent. They stood at the entrance, watching the roshi as he led the monks and nuns across the clearing to the "dharma hall" for a *teisho*, a presentation.

"Don't rush to any conclusions," Landen said, close behind her.

"You saw the boy too."

"Yes, but unlike you I trust the roshi. These people are different. They're not interested in the things people lie about. They have overcome all human desire, which is the fundamental problem behind everything, do you understand? Without desire there would be no suffering. All that these people need and are looking for they can find within themselves."

A French novice had been given the job of showing them around the monastery. His shaved head was covered in a fuzz of blond hair. His nose was running.

It was dark in the corridors. *No electric light China of Kanzan, no electric light here.* The novice was carrying an oil lamp. Candlesticks were screwed to the walls, but only a few candles were alight. The further they went into the Kanzan-an, the less hospitable, the quieter, the eerier it became. If it was only in places like this that you found the things inside you, she would rather do without.

The novice opened a door. A large kitchen. Candles flickered in holders on the walls. No cooker, but a fireplace in the middle of the room, open on all sides. Here it was almost warm. As far as she could make out, the simple wooden shelves were perfectly clean.

"This is where we cook," the novice said, wiping his nose on the sleeve of his habit.

Landen asked Louise to translate as he spoke no French. He knew Japanese, Sanskrit and possibly Tibetan, but not the language of the country he lived barely thirty kilometres from. She resisted making a comment. "This is the kitchen," she said amicably.

"Aha."

"Why did you and the roshi laugh earlier on?"

Landen smiled but didn't reply.

They continued with their tour. A common room with raffia mats and cushions to sit on. A study with a desk, an old-fashioned dial telephone and white folders on a tall shelf. She remembered that on Sunday she'd left a message on the Kanzan-an answerphone. She'd asked to be called back. Nobody had.

By then Niksch was probably already dead.

Then Anne Wallmer had come into her office and Hollerer had called without saying anything, because he couldn't.

"Ask about the boy," Landen said.

"Later."

"The visitors' lavatory," the novice said, pointing to a door as they walked past.

She excused herself and entered the loo, where she was hit by a damp chill. An oil lamp gave off a weak light. Beside the door was a wash basin and the toilet stood in darkness at the end of a five-metre-long narrow room.

She felt her way along the wall. The window above the toilet was open. She covered the seat in loo paper, overcame her dread of the cold and sat down. A cool draught blew around her head. At least it's not an outhouse, she thought, urinating noisily.

At the basin she let glacial water run over the tips of her fingers. The towel beside it was wet and clammy. Thank God she had something to warm herself with.

*

As they walked on Bonì asked the novice where the money came from to maintain the Kanzan-an and those living here. He was coy in his response, explaining that he hadn't been in the monastery long. There were some things he didn't know, in particular which information he was allowed to impart and which not.

"Can you say what your name is?"

He laughed. "Of course. My real name is Georges Lazare, but as a monk I'll be called Ikku."

"How should I address you?"

"As Georges."

"Because you're not a monk yet?"

"Exactly."

"And what's your opinion on the murder of police officers, Georges? As a person, as a novice and as a future monk?"

Georges said nothing.

"Good," she said, satisfied.

At nearby markets the monks and nuns sold fruit and vegetables they grew themselves, as well as small objects they crafted. Apart from that the monastery relied on donations. Sometimes guests came to the Kanzan-an for a few days, a week or a month. They paid what they wanted to pay. The first floor was reserved for these guests, above that were the monks' cells. The nuns lived on the ground floor.

She translated for Landen. Impatience lurked in his eyes. Bonì raised a finger as a warning. "And Roshi Bukan?" she asked. "Where does he live?"

"Where he spends his time."

"And where does he spend his time at night?"

"In a cave in the forest."

"Like Kanzan?"

In the diffuse light of the oil lamp she could only surmise that Georges was nodding. *Kanzan cave, Bukan cave*, the roshi said in her head.

They went up a wide staircase. On the first floor a corridor ran alongside the windows at the front of the building, its shape following the gentle curvature of the façade. The corridor appeared to be empty. Wooden doors led to the guest rooms. Candle holders were fixed to the walls between the windows. Georges lit the first one and was about to head up to the second floor.

She pointed at one of the doors. "May I?"

Georges nodded uncertainly and passed her the lamp. She hesitated for a moment, then opened the door. This was more like a prison cell than a guest room: a small, stone rectangle with a mattress, a duvet, candle holder, candles. A tiny window with no glass gave onto the rear of the Kanzan-an.

"Is this what your rooms are like too?" She shut the door and picked up the lamp.

Georges' face was pinched and anxious. His eyes looked pensive, as if he didn't yet know whether his retreat to the Kanzan-an had been the right decision. His expression conveyed hope and worry. Courage and feebleness. He put his hands together in front of his stomach, in the Christian way with his fingers crossed. "Yes. We need nothing more."

She took a few steps along the windows. Georges and Landen did not follow. In the darkness outside there shone a yellow eye: the dharma hall. She thought she could make out the shadows of people sitting. But no movement.

She stopped at the window at which she had caught sight of the boy. A child in the forest to the east of Liebau, where Taro had vanished; a child in the Kanzan-an, where Taro had lived.

She wondered how many children must be living in the Mulhouse–Freiburg area. Tens of thousands. She pictured Bermann putting his head in his hands.

No children in Kanzan-an.

She went back to Georges and Landen. "Are there visitors staying here at the moment?"

"Yes."

"Visitors with children?"

Georges laughed again. His laugh was gentle and spontaneous. She liked this, for a while it made up for his indecision. "I'd be more inclined to say: visitors with adults. Currently we have eight children visiting with three carers."

"What sort of children?"

Georges didn't know the details. He'd heard that they were orphans from the Far East. Children who'd been rescued from miserable existences to begin a new life here.

"Here? At the Kanzan-an?"

"In Europe." Charitable organisations such as U.N.I.C.E.F. and Terre des hommes were picking up children from the streets of large cities in the Far East and accommodating them in Buddhist or Christian children's homes. For some they had managed to find European adoptive parents, for the children at the Kanzan-an, for example. They were recuperating from the strain of the trip before being taken on to their new families.

"Who would have thought it?" Bonì said to Landen. "A refuge of humanity in a tomb like this." She gave the lamp back to Georges.

As they made their way up to the second floor she summarised for Landen what she'd found out. Then she asked him to repeat in German the exact words he'd used when enquiring about young pupils at the Kanzan-an. Landen said he'd asked whether there were children amongst the Zen pupils.

She sighed. *No. No children in Kanzan-an.*

Taro's cell resembled the one they'd seen on the first floor, the only difference being that a dark habit hung on the wall. This room didn't look lived in either. For several minutes she stared at the mattress, the window and habit, waiting for the intuitive certainty that one day Taro would return here. It did not come.

She closed the door softly, walked to the windows and looked once more towards the invisible clearing. In the darkness she saw the little yellow eye.

She was still at the beginning. The Kanzan-an hadn't yet imparted its secret.

They went down the stairs in silence. Ahead of them, Georges didn't hide the fact that he was in a hurry. His sandals slapped hectically on the steps, his indecision now apparently joined by unease. Did he think he'd said too much? Was he afraid of the roshi's anger? Or perhaps he was simply keen to make it over to the little yellow eye.

On the first-floor landing he stopped and lifted the lamp. The soft light fell onto the alert, round face of a child. At a window stood the boy.

"Well, well," Landen said, bending over as the boy came to him.

The boy began to speak. He pointed to Louise and looked at her briefly, before turning back to Landen and pointing at him. Then he was silent.

Landen cleared his throat. "He's from Vietnam."

"What's he saying?"

"I'm afraid I don't . . ." He paused. There were noises in the darkness. A door had been opened and dull footsteps could be heard. Bonì, Landen and the young novice peered into the corridor but could see nothing. Only the boy was completely still.

The footsteps hurried closer. A woman who looked central European came into the light. "Please forgive me," she said in German. "Pham?"

She spoke with the boy in Vietnamese for a while. Her voice was soft and comforting. Then she looked at Landen, now upright again. "He thought you were his new parents." She smiled ruefully. "But he's going to have to wait a few more days."

Louise guessed the woman was in her mid-forties. She was wearing a puffa jacket, jeans and walking boots. Her expression and bearing were confident. "Annegret Schelling," she said, offering her hand.

The boy had put an arm around her left leg. Annegret stroked his head. "Eight more sleeps," she said in German. "Then it's time. Make a wish that he gets good parents. Goodbye." A wink, a smile, and then she vanished into the dark corridor, holding the boy's hand.

Georges escorted them outside. Louise thought feverishly of more questions she might ask him. Questions Muller, Schneider and Wallmer hadn't asked. Questions leading to answers to other questions. Why had Taro left here in the middle of the night? How had he been injured? Why hadn't he wanted to open up to Landen, or to anybody else? Why had he been followed by men who didn't shy away from killing police officers?

Georges gave them the lamp to find their way back to the car park and folded his hands over his chest. Then he hurried off to the dharma hall.

"So what now?" Landen said. "Back to your holiday?"

"Exactly." She took the lamp from his hand and led the way.

It struck her only when she was back in the forest that Taro's cell had not just been free of all personal items, but of religious ones too. No Buddhist texts, no images of the Buddha or other holy people. She asked Landen why. He told her that there were different schools of Buddhism, and in some of them sutras, devotional objects and Buddhist iconography played little or no role. How lonely and unsafe she would feel with a religion like that, she thought. No sacred books, no gods, no objects. Subject only to what might come from outside or from within.

Landen was still talking. She listened to the tone of his beautiful, boring voice and wondered whether to turn and kiss him. Whether to rip the clothes from his body, to see just how exciting he could be.

But then he would have tasted the alcohol on her breath.

Their two vehicles were the only ones left in the car park. She extinguished the lamp and placed it at the end of the path. "Will you keep me up to date with developments?" Landen said. She nodded, and they got into their cars.

Landen turned his car. When the rear of the Volvo was briefly higher than the bonnet, its headlights lit up the ground immediately in front. Deep, broad tyre marks were visible in the muddy earth.

Images came flooding back. She saw a snowy field, glistening and waxen in the moonlight. Impressions of broad tyres in the slush alongside the forest. Niksch's dead body.

Cursing, she leaped out of the car and waved at Landen to stop. She could hear him putting on the handbrake.

"Don't ask," she said.

For several seconds she stared at the marks on the ground. There was a similarity, at least. But what did that mean?

Louise angrily kneaded her anorak pockets. Children's footprints, tyre marks – her thought processes grew more and more abstruse, her attempts to make connections ever more helpless. How many off-road vehicles were there in the Mulhouse–Freiburg area?

Probably fewer than there were children, at least. But still the number must run into the hundreds. She cursed again.

"What's wrong?" Landen said.

She gestured to him to be quiet.

What make of car had been parked beside Landen's Volvo? She hadn't really looked at it because the Volvo was in front. She'd seen the Freiburg number plate, put her hand on the bonnet of the Volvo, peered in and thought only of Landen's tidiness.

"Do you remember the car that was parked next to yours?"

"No, I don't pay attention to cars. I mean, I'm not *interested* in cars."

"Small, big? Dark, light? Low, high?"

Landen sighed. "Something . . . big, light."

"What do you mean 'light'?"

"Light brown, beige, maybe grey. Light blue. Dark yellow. Something in that direction."

"What sort of direction is that, then?"

Landen shrugged and grinned.

"Got a camera with you?"

He shook his head.

"Can you draw?"

"Not especially well."

"Christ, what *can* you do? I mean, can you do anything *useful?*"

"Yes, I could drive myself home."

But he made no move to get back into his car.

She apologised reluctantly and kneeled beside the spot where the tyre tracks were most distinct. Tyre identification was Lederle's domain. Bermann used to say that Lederle could even tell you from the tyre marks what people in the car had been thinking.

Louise thought for a moment. In the car she had some hairspray to fix the marks, but no plaster. She fetched a measuring tape from the boot, took her notebook and pen from her pocket and kneeled down again. She measured the width of the tyres and tracks, and the depth of the impression. Where the car had been parked she managed to get an approximation of the wheel base. The tread was asymmetrical: circumferential grooves on the right, lateral on the left.

Landen watched her in silence and with evident interest in what she was doing.

Bonì turned in such a way that he couldn't watch over her shoulder and began to draw. She used four pieces of paper and then gave up, her left hand was trembling too much. She couldn't manage anything better than irregular jagged lines and unidentifiable shapes.

"O.K.," she said, sinking onto her bottom. "You might as well leave now; I'm going to be here a while longer."

Landen did not respond.

The cold and damp assailed her skin. She wished she'd kissed him earlier. She wished Roshi Bukan were here. She wished she had been in Niksch's place on Sunday.

Children's footprints, tyre marks. Unusable scribbles and a glove compartment with no gloves. Midnight trips to petrol stations. Warm, underage hands.

Now the abyss looked different. No matter where she found herself, she was in the middle of it.

"Please go, O.K.?"

Landen opened the car door. "Call me tomorrow."

She nodded.

"Or I'll call." He got in.

The headlights moved away and left her in the dark.

As she watched the Volvo's red taillights she slipped her hand into the pocket of her anorak. Then she sank backwards.

10

At around half past seven she was in Freiburg. The snow had thawed. A digital display on the side of a building read 6 degrees. With a touch of imagination you could summon the fragrance of spring flowers in the air.

Roman, the community service assistant, was gangly, exhausted, and trying to combat the misery of the hospital with his indefatigable willingness to help. He knew about every patient in intensive care, and on the way from reception he gave her potted biographies of four individuals including their full tales of woe.

Hollerer was his favourite patient. Every day he read him two pages of *The Outsider*, whether Hollerer was asleep or not, and he knew his patient file by heart. "He's over the worst," he said, smoothing the stubble on his head with his palms.

On a chair by the entrance to the ward sat a pale, thin man. He was wearing a dark-blue suit, a tie and a light-brown leather winter jacket. "Evening, Herr Ponzelt," Roman said, and the man nodded.

It took her a moment to place the name: Ponzelt, the mayor of Liebau and the man who'd wanted to lead a crusade. One of those people who sensed danger.

Now he didn't seem to be feeling anything. Without stopping she said, "So, how was the skiing?" Ponzelt stiffened.

They walked into intensive care.

Hollerer was asleep. He only remotely resembled the grim-faced, red-cheeked man she pictured when she thought back to their meetings.

She stayed with him for half an hour, holding his horrifyingly feeble hand. When she imagined the moment that he regained consciousness she felt sick. The first thing he'd have to do was come to terms with the fact that Niksch was dead.

Roman escorted her out. Ponzelt asked who she was, but she didn't reply.

Outside the main entrance Roman lit a cigarette. She stood close to him. "Do you know who Niksch is?"

He exhaled smoke noisily and nodded.

"Tell him when he wakes up. I think you'll find the right words. Would you do that?"

Roman nodded again.

As she got into her car she watched him extinguish the cigarette, put the unsmoked half into his pocket and go back inside the hospital.

The entire Liebau task force seemed to be out and about. Entire corridors of police H.Q. were dark and deserted. Were Bermann and the others following up on a new lead? Had Taro been found? In her office she rang Lederle from her mobile. It took him a while to answer. "I can't speak right now," he muttered. "I'll call you back."

"Just tell me if . . ."

But Lederle had already hung up.

She sat down in his chair. On his desk were two piles of files relating to the Liebau case. With her free hand she stroked the perfectly aligned horizontal edges of one pile. With the other she pressed the last number redial button.

This time Lederle's mobile was switched off. She waited for the beep and said, "Reiner, if you've found Taro I want to know."

She jiggled her mobile in her hand for a moment. If he didn't call back in the next half hour she'd ring Bermann.

And then Landen.

What did Landen mean by "tomorrow"? "Later"? Did he only say "tomorrow" because as a married man and father-to-be, he hadn't dared say "later"? Would he prefer it if she rang "later" rather than "tomorrow"? Did he like women who were four and a half kilos off their normal weight? Was Tommo a sharpened pencil when she wasn't pregnant?

She smirked.

In the past Lederle's chaos had been legendary. But now, since his wife had been ill, he had been devising a number of increasingly perfect systems of organisation. For the Liebau case, besides the evidence file, there was a main dossier and a copy, and subsidiary files marked "Hollerer, Johann Georg (Sergeant)", "Schmidt, Nikolai (Niksch, Senior Officer)", "Taro (Buddhist monk)" and "Index of names", as well as the obligatory reference file.

She held the main dossier for a moment in her hand before putting it aside and opening the evidence file. In addition to photographs of the tyre marks there were transcripts of conversations with Ponzelt, other inhabitants of Liebau, the postman from Badenweiler as well as the farmer and Catholic priest of Unterbirken. The reports by the Freiburg police officers, which she'd already seen, and Wallmer's summary of her visit to the Kanzan-an were also there. She browsed the brief transcripts and learned nothing new.

The report of the monastery visit was more substantial.

Justin Muller had spoken to the roshi – Schneider and Wallmer called him the "dean of the monastery" – but failed to glean any information. The names, ages and nationalities of all the monks and nuns had been meticulously listed – obviously a friendly favour by Muller. He hadn't spoken to the "employees of Asile d'enfants" because the carers and children had spent the day at a nearby pony club. He would go back and do it later.

She skimmed the report a second time. Muller had asked the roshi important questions that she'd forgotten to ask. Where might Taro have been going? The roshi didn't know.

Was there another Zen centre in the direction Taro had been heading? No.

Louise could picture vividly the expression of anger on the roshi's face.

The monastery had not yielded any concrete leads. All the same their French colleagues would undertake a more thorough examination of the Kanzan-an. Bermann and Almenbroich must have applied the pressure. Schneider and Wallmer wrote that they needed detailed information on the origins of the place and its owners, its financial situation, biographies of the current and former inhabitants, floorplans, as well as an inspection of sale contracts and visitor lists, and so on.

They cited three reasons for their demands. First, Taro, "the only suspect so far", lived at the monastery. Second, according to Muller three strangers – "probably of eastern European origin" – had enquired about the Kanzan-an over the past week in Zillisheim. Third, the Federal Criminal Police Office and the Federal Intelligence Service had issued repeated warnings of possible terror attacks by foreign groups.

At the very bottom of the file were the photographs that Niksch had taken. Taro from behind, Taro from the side, Taro as a small dot in the barren expanse of white. Louise and Hollerer in the patrol car. Louise and Hollerer standing by the patrol car. No identifiable faces in any of them.

Quickly she reached for the reference file.

Bullet points by Lederle from the Liebau task force briefings showed that, for want of any alternatives, the investigation was focusing on the Kanzan-an. She wondered whether the monastery was under observation. If so, the French police would have seen her and Landen.

She continued to go through the documents. A note from Bermann: date, time.

Spoke to Asil d'enfants (Jean Berger) in Basel. Promised to get the children out of the monastery discreetly.

Bermann, the child obsessive. Nobody at police H.Q. had ever seen his wife *not* pregnant. She was now carrying their fourth. Bermann had become something of an expert in the delivery room and was now permitted to help out with the births.

As she closed the file her attention was drawn again to the main dossier. There wouldn't be much more in there. The crime scene report. The forensics report.

The photographs of Niksch's dead body.

She looked again at the evidence file. At the top were images of the footprints of Hollerer's and Niksch's pursuers. No remarkable characteristics. The prints came from a narrow track nearby, where a car had been parked. She looked at the details of the tyres; they didn't match the impressions in the Kanzan-an car park.

She then laid out the pictures of the tyre tracks taken by the technicians beside the forest east of Liebau, in the order that Lederle had put them: first the reference photos and pictures of the tracks, then sections, followed by close-ups with accompanying scale.

The tracks in the snow showed that the car had driven alongside the forest, then turned and driven back. She put her abortive sketches beside the images. The measurements were roughly the same. And if her memory served her well, the impressions had similarities.

Then the first potential differences emerged, increasing in number with every passing minute.

She took a glug, then another, but the differences remained.

After ten minutes she gave up. In exasperation she kept one of the detailed photographs and returned the rest to the plastic sleeve. She put the files on top of each other.

Only Lederle would notice that two piles had become one.

On her way home she stopped outside the sushi bar. Through the steamed-up window she could see it was very busy inside. Enni was at the counter, surrounded by customers on three sides. His yellow hair shone in the harsh light. He took orders with a stoical calmness. She saw him nod, speak, then nod again. In his right hand he held a pen. He stuck it behind his ear, reached for it again. Smiled, wrote something down.

She got out of the car, and as she approached the entrance she thought of Schneider and Wallmer's report, and was seized by a vague feeling of anxiety. What went on at the Kanzan-an? Were Annegret Schelling, Pham and the other children in danger?

As she opened the door she was met by the aroma of fish. Although there must have been at least twenty diners in the tiny room there was no noise. Nobody was talking loudly and there wasn't any music. A man gave a muffled laugh.

Two young policemen in civvies were standing at one of the bar tables, leaning on their elbows. Still chewing, they stood up straight and gave her a nod. Louise returned their greeting. Only when she'd passed them did she realise that she hadn't smiled.

"Hey!" said the woman she pushed aside at the counter. Enni said, "Good evening, Inspector."

She gestured to him to give her his pen and pad and jotted down her landline and mobile numbers.

Enni nodded. He seemed to have known she'd come back to him for the journey to the centre of the universe. And unlike her, he seemed to know if this journey went inwards or outwards.

She drove the Mégane into the underground car park. In the lift she considered paying Ronescu a visit with the țuică. To sedate the escalating cravings in her body. But she decided against.

Her apartment was chilly. She turned the heating up to its highest setting and got undressed.

Under the shower she thought of Richard Landen. In front of the mirror she thought of Landen's wife.

At around half past eight Lederle rang and said, "Well, well, it looks like we had a visitor." He sounded tired and disappointed.

She slumped onto the sofa. "As soon as we know who killed Niksch you'll be rid of me, I promise."

Lederle said nothing.

"I *can't* stay out of it, Reiner."

"We don't want to be 'rid' of you, Bonì. We want you to get better and come back to us soon."

"Is that what Rolf thinks too?"

"Rolf is Rolf. It's what I think, it's what Almenbroich thinks and a couple of others as well. You're not at your mother's anymore, then?"

"No, I'm back home."

"For what reason?"

"To think. To support you lot."

"And to talk to the psychologist?"

She grimaced. "Sure, that too. I mean, that's the main reason."

Lederle sighed. "What do you want to know?"

"Have you found Taro?"

"No."

"Has Muller got the monastery under surveillance?"

"Not yet. He's having difficulty convincing the investigating judge. The judge says: Are we talking about north Africans or Arabs? No? Then we need more proof." He laughed.

A brief silence ensued. Lederle's laughter still rang in her ears. Cynicism was a new thing for him. Even he seemed shocked.

She went to her kitchenette and kneeled in front of the sink. Crawling halfway into the cupboard below it, she fished out a bottle of vodka from behind the fabric conditioner. When she stood up again she asked, "How's Antonia, Reiner? I mean . . ."

"Let's stick to business," Lederle said.

He told her that over the course of the day the Liebau task force had conducted a second search of the section of forest where Niksch had been found, with the help of a hundred rapid reaction officers and a pack of dogs. Again they'd found nothing. "*Nothing*, Louise," he said.

She sat back down on the sofa. "What were you expecting?"

"Taro was carrying a bowl and a staff. If there had been a struggle . . ." Lederle didn't finish his sentence.

She nodded but said nothing.

Police officers were always dangerous when they didn't find

anything. They would cling to the little they had, twisting and turning it until it lost its innocence.

And what did they have? A strange Japanese monk who had vanished without trace and who was mixed up in the murder of a policeman. A remote Buddhist monastery where no-one was especially willing to divulge information. People who walked in sandals through the snow and slept in caves, trying to emulate a monk who had lived fifteen hundred years ago.

She grunted. Somehow she could almost understand Bermann. *What about these eastern Europeans?*

A week earlier, three Romanians or Hungarians or Bulgarians had made enquiries in Zillisheim about the Kanzan-an. They had something to drink in a café and left after a few minutes. Half an hour later they returned and asked the barman in broken English where the Kanzan-an was.

Three eastern Europeans, Bonì thought. Three men had been following Taro. "They didn't find it straightaway," she said.

"No."

"Last week?"

"Wednesday or Thursday."

"Taro left the monastery on Thursday morning."

"Yes," Lederle said.

"Did the barman see their car?"

"The second time, yes. A red Audi or a Passat."

"Not a 4×4?"

"No. What makes you think that? Oh yes, I get it." She heard him rustling papers. "I see you helped yourself to a photo. Got it in front of you?" She fetched the print. Lederle paused then said, "Asymmetrical profile with two circumferential grooves, 215 millimetre. Four-wheel drive. Winter tyres. Hmm . . . ContiWinterContact T.S. 790. Or T.S. 790 V? Which of those has lateral grooves?"

"Does Conti mean Continental?"

"Yes. But it doesn't look to me like a tyre for an off-roader, more like an M.P.V. The tyres would be wider otherwise, and anyway . . ." Lederle read out the measurements of the wheel base and axle track. They also tallied more with an M.P.V., he said. They hadn't been able to get the measurements down to the millimetre. "Otherwise you'd probably know by now what make of car it was."

"Any idea at all?"

"The wheel base and axle track are consistent with a Ford Galaxy. The Seat Alhambra and the Sharan are possibilities too. Although I don't know if they're allowed to drive with the T.S. 790 215." He continued leafing through his document and asked cautiously whether they might disregard the tyre tracks. An M.P.V. by the forest – a family outing, maybe?

She took a swig. She didn't want to disregard the tracks. "Yes," she said, changing the subject. "Tell me, what do eastern Europeans look like anyway?"

"No idea. Sort of poor, cheerless and violent?"

They laughed.

Louise asked about the results from ballistics. "Two different automatic pistols," Lederle said. "For Niksch a Walther P5 and Hollerer a Heckler & Koch P2000." Nine-millimetre pistols. One old, one new. Twenty-five thousand police officers in Baden-Württemberg had just been issued with the P2000 V5.

Silence again. For the first time Louise sensed that the task force was making progress. Three men had been seen as well as a red Audi or Passat. The Heckler in particular might bear fruit. The model was just a few years old and not yet in wide distribution.

Not much to go on, but these were the first concrete leads.

She asked what was planned for the next day.

In the morning Bermann, Schneider and Lederle would drive with Justin Muller, Hugo Chervel and a Japanese translator – not Landen – to the Kanzan-an. Wallmer, who spoke fluent French, would work with French police in Mulhouse to dig up information about the monastery and its inhabitants.

145

Lederle yawned. "Sorry."

He was about to leave H.Q. Bermann had sent everybody home apart from a skeleton team of which he was part. He had put down a mattress in his study in case he got tired. His wife had brought him underwear, shirts and a pair of jeans. "The dead young lad isn't allowing him any peace," Lederle said.

"The dead *policeman*."

"Whatever. Your father called again, by the way. He's going to try again tomorrow."

"Tell him I'm on holiday. Tell him I'm at Robinson Club in the Domrep."

"Is that how I should say it? Domrep?"

"Yes, just like that."

"Will he understand?"

"He'll think it's a feminist commune where white women have sex with the natives. Why don't you pop over?"

"I can't. Antonia's got dinner ready."

At ten o'clock she noticed that she was hungry. The fridge was empty apart from butter and jam. She made do with orange juice.

As she drank she thought of Ponzelt, the mayor. Was he spending the night on that chair outside intensive care? And if so, why?

She knew there was something she ought to ask him, but she couldn't think what.

She sat down in the sitting room and, for the first time since her split with Mick, wished she had bought a television set. At the time Lederle had said, "You need a T.V. if you're going to be living on your own." She'd laughed and replied, "The last thing I want is to be tied down again straightaway."

She went to lie on her bed. After a few minutes she went back into the sitting room and picked up the telephone.

Tommo / Landen weren't in, or they weren't answering. She pressed number recall, hung up, then called a third time. The same number on the display three times, but no message. Landen would know that it was urgent.

And maybe *why* it was urgent too.

And that perhaps rather than ringing back later it would be better to wait until tomorrow.

At around midnight a name began to worm its way from her memory into her consciousness. At first the image accompanying it consisted only of two huge earlobes. Then she heard a laid-back voice.

She called directory enquiries and was connected. "Hello?" Anatol said.

"I'd like to return your sunglasses. Why don't you come over?"

"Who . . . oh, you." He yawned. "Now?"

"Yes. Have you eaten?"

He gave a sleepy laugh. "Not so far today."

She suggested breakfast. A midnight breakfast. "But you've got to bring the bread. And, um, *time.*"

Anatol paused, then said he didn't have any bread, only deep-frozen pizza. "Vegetarian. I'm a veggie." He cleared his throat.

"Looks like it's pizza then."

She gave him her address. As she hung up she heard him laugh in disbelief.

But he came. He gave two short rings of the bell, a trusty friend of the early hours. As she buzzed him in she thought of Landen. The slow, confident footsteps on the stairs could have belonged to either man.

She waited by the door wearing fresh pyjamas. She'd taken a very quick shower, washed her hair, brushed her teeth and now felt very young and very old.

Hands appeared on the banisters. The curly hair was uncombed, only the sunglasses on the forehead gave any structure to his face. "Hi!" he said with a smile.

"Hi!"

She found him thinner and even more laid-back than she remembered. And taller.

He kissed her on both cheeks, took off his shoes, slid the pizza onto the work surface in the kitchenette and said, "It's warm in here. Nice, too."

She raised her eyebrows.

"I mean, compared to my apartment."

She followed him in, leaned against a kitchen cupboard and crossed her arms. For a moment neither of them said anything. Then she asked, "Have you got experience with this sort of thing?"

He nodded thoughtfully.

"I don't."

"Hmm. O.K."

His calmness didn't appear put on, but there was something weary and jaded about it. It made him seem older than he probably was and it lingered in his eyes when he smiled.

"Should we eat beforehand?" she said. "Or have something to drink? Maybe a drink first?"

"O.K."

She fetched two glasses, poured vodka in them and pushed one over to him. He shook his head, surprised. Not now. Later. She drank and said, "So what do we do now?"

"Well, we do what we want."

He took a step towards her. They were a couple of metres apart. She noticed that he hadn't introduced an unfamiliar smell into the apartment. No *eau de toilette*, no sweat, no smell of body or outside. In Mick's time everything had smelled of Mick. Even her underwear.

"Sure, but what do we want? I mean, how do we get to what we want? Should we chat a little beforehand? Should we get to know each other before we do what we want to do? I mean, do we first have to do what we don't want to do before we can do what we want? Do we have to *talk* for a couple of hours first?"

"We can talk if you like."

She sighed and said impatiently, "A-na-tol."

He grinned. Another small step.

She put her hands on his chest. "I'm a chief inspector in the serious crimes department and have been a police officer for twenty years. My favourite authors are Clavell, Mankell and Pilcher, I like Wagner, Beethoven, Pink Floyd and Wham! and, ashamed though I am to admit it, I can't do without Barclay James Harvest. I'm forty-two, divorced and I don't have any children, luckily. And . . ."

"And?"

"And I've put on weight."

"Now, now," Anatol said, moving closer.

Anatol kept going till three in the morning, then said, "O.K., that's enough," and fell asleep in a flash. She didn't want to lie next to him; she thought he was too young for that. So she went into the bathroom and took another shower. Her legs were shaking; her breasts and womb were aching. She grinned. There were advantages to having a man who was experienced but still half a child. He was capable of everything and did whatever you asked him to.

In front of the mirror it struck her that in the past two and a half hours she hadn't once thought of Landen, and only once – while she was undressing – of Tommo the pencil. But Anatol had worked with such relish on her problem areas that she had quickly forgotten her.

And yet . . . she wasn't happy with the signs she read from her body. As the psychologist Katrin Rein had said, there was a lot to do.

Well then, she thought, let's get cracking. She wandered into the sitting room, curled up on the sofa and went to sleep.

Four hours later she woke up. As soon as she opened her eyes she knew what she had to ask Ponzelt: had the red Audi or Passat and/or the M.P.V. been spotted in Liebau over the weekend? In most villages there were people who saw, heard and knew everything.

She sat up. This morning she would drive to Liebau and seek out these people. If one of the cars had been seen there this might lead to more information. A face, a voice, a number plate.

Then, in the afternoon, when there was no danger of bumping into Muller or her colleagues, she would go back to the Kanzan-an.

Deep breathing was coming from the bedroom. For a brief moment the apartment felt busy and cramped.

Outside it was beginning to get light. She reached behind her and pulled the curtains to one side. No snow. There was the hint of a life beyond the winter. A life without images of Calambert. Or of Niksch.

A life in the abyss.

What was there apart from fighting and submission? She would ask Landen this question. Or Enni.

The roshi.

Zensu no harm people. Zensu look Buddha-nature. Look own-nature. Look shunyata. Could a person who thought and spoke like that be involved in a murder?

Only if he were lying.

Was the roshi lying? A man striving for a complex form of emptiness? Who stripped things down to their bare essence? Who looked for their true nature, whatever that might be?

These people are different, Landen had said. They're not interested in the things that people lie about. Everything these people need and are looking for they can find within themselves.

No, she thought, the roshi wasn't lying. She wasn't so sure about Georges, the French novice. Georges might be lying. And she didn't know the other monks and nuns.

But even if they, like the roshi and Taro, were not interested in the things people lie about, it could only mean one thing. The willingness to use force to abduct someone and shoot at policemen hadn't originated from the Kanzan-an. It had been introduced into it.

By three men who looked eastern European.

Who else was there? She sat on the sofa. Asile d'enfants.

150

They ate the pizza for breakfast. In the ex-post facto light Anatol was just as laid-back as in the ex-ante facto dark. Without the sunglasses to hold his hair in place, the locks tumbled over his eyes. He drank worrying amounts of coffee and yawned copiously. He gave her the occasional smile, but said nothing.

This suited her to begin with. She thought of Annegret Schelling and Pham, who would have new parents. Of what Georges had said about the orphans in the Buddhist and Christian children's homes in the Far East.

What else did she know about Asile d'enfants? That in Basel they had a man called Jean Berger who had promised Bermann to get the children out of the monastery. That on Monday the carers had taken the children to a nearby pony club and had therefore not been available to talk to Justin Muller.

On Monday. The day *after*.

But what could link Asile d'enfants with three eastern Europeans who were suspected of murdering Niksch and wounding Hollerer? An organisation that worked in conjunction with U.N.I.C.E.F. and Terre des hommes?

She wondered if she would have had the same thoughts had she been with Bermann, Lederle and the others rather than having been invalided. If she had been party to the same information as them and had taken part in the briefings. Talked to them on a regular basis.

She stood up and went to the sink, then kneeled down. Anatol didn't notice a thing.

When she sat down again she said, "Well?"

"Well what?"

"Anything we should talk about? Have you fallen in love with me? Have you got a bad conscience because you identify me with your grandmother? Do you regret it?"

"Yes, there was one thing." He poured himself more coffee. "What's Barclay James Harvest?"

She grinned. "Addictive seventies' kitsch. You do know there was a time we call 'the seventies'?"

"I've heard of them."

"How old are you?"

"Twenty-four."

"That means they're immortalised in your driving licence."

He nodded. "Sometimes I ask myself: What came before? Before the seventies? It's so far back that I wonder whether there was anything at all."

"No, there wasn't anything. Only chaos. Listen, I'll hang on to the sunglasses, O.K.?"

"O.K." He got up.

"Where are you going?"

"To take a shower."

"Later, An-a-tol," she said, slipping off her dressing gown.

11

In Liebau grey remnants of snow lay by the roadside. Few people were out. In front of the town hall a drooping Baden-Württemberg flag hung at half-mast. Beneath it were several police cars and other vehicles. Louise parked in a side street, and as she got out of the car she was met with an unreal hush, as if the entire village had fallen silent in shock.

It was just after ten in the morning. She had telephoned; Ponzelt had been at his desk since eight. As Louise walked along a short corridor it occurred to her that Landen hadn't yet rung. She quashed a faint feeling of disappointment.

A secretary showed her to Ponzelt's office. He recognised her at once and nodded when she introduced herself. She apologised, explaining she'd been in shock at the hospital the day before, because of Hollerer. He said nothing. He was thin and about her age. She got the impression that he didn't particularly like her.

He gestured to the chair by his desk and she sat down. She asked how Hollerer was.

Ponzelt had rung the hospital a short while earlier. Hollerer had been awake for an hour that morning. His condition was stabilising all the time and he'd answered some initial questions. What these questions were Ponzelt didn't appear to have discovered, or he didn't want to tell her. His voice was quiet in a menacing way.

"Who was with him?"

"Your section head."

"Bermann?"

The slightest of nods. Then Ponzelt said, "I thought you were on leave, but clearly that's not the case?"

She leaned back. This promised to be a fascinating conversation. "In theory, yes I am."

"Interesting." Ponzelt glanced out of the window then turned back to her. He looked exhausted, but very determined. "Explain the difference between being on leave and being theoretically on leave."

"One question, then I'll go – O.K.?"

"I'd rather you went now."

She shook her head. "Answer my question, then I'll leave you in peace."

Ponzelt leaned forward on his elbows and gazed at her. The coldness in his eyes was piercing. "I don't know how long I'll be able to remain polite."

"You think you're polite, do you?"

He glared at her in silence, and then said, "There's one thing you don't understand." He stood up and went to the window. Only now did she realise *how* thin he was. Like a hyena, a vulture, with a long and knotted neck. She grinned.

But she sensed that his shock at the course of events was genuine. A sycophant who'd been reeled in by shock on his ruthless way to the top. She couldn't tell how significant it was that he'd been skiing with his sons when Hollerer and Niksch were shot.

"What don't I understand?"

"That you're the only reason any of this happened. If you and the Japanese guy hadn't been here none of this would have happened. Niksch would still be alive and Hollerer would be sitting where you are, as he has done every Wednesday morning for years." No rebuke, no interpretation, no opinion – his feeble voice had left no room for doubt: this was the *truth*.

Bonì caught her breath, but she managed to hold Ponzelt's uncompromising gaze. She wanted to get up, vacate Hollerer's chair, but felt unable to move.

"That's why," Ponzelt said, "our people don't want women like you and strangers like the Japanese monk here. All you bring is destruction. You don't respect our traditions, you import a world we don't want. You don't fit in here . . . You bring *destruction*." He swallowed with a hard, dry sound. "What were you doing here? What were you and the Japanese man doing here?"

Finally she managed to stand up and move a few paces away. A simple, anthracite-coloured office chair with brass arms, narrow, hard and angular. As she looked at Ponzelt she wanted to tell him that Hollerer couldn't have found that chair particularly comfortable. From a distance his voice wafted into her consciousness. He repeated what he'd just said, using different words and raising his voice. Louise approached him and he broke off. She stood right beside him. The long neck and skinny torso shrank, consternation flashed in his eyes. For a moment she thought he was afraid. She imagined grabbing the vulture neck with one hand and squeezing hard until her fist was fully clenched.

But he wasn't afraid. What had happened had thrown him off track and he couldn't find the way back.

Instinctively she placed a hand on his shoulder. Both of them gave a start. Ponzelt narrowed his eyes and looked down. Louise withdrew her hand and gazed out into the street.

A white Mercedes coming from the right, then a blue Fiat from the left.

In a hoarse voice she said, "If the people we're looking for drove through Liebau at the weekend, who might have seen them? Who picks up on things like that?"

"Eastern Europeans in a red Audi or Passat," Ponzelt muttered.

She nodded. "Or maybe an M.P.V."

"No-one said anything about an M.P.V."

"They have now."

"Me," Ponzelt said, looking up. "That's my job – to see and know everything that could be of importance for Liebau. But I didn't see anything. They must have come through here, right past my window, but I didn't see them."

He quietly made his way back to the desk and sat down. They looked at each other.

"It was snowing heavily at the weekend," Louise said.

"Yes." Ponzelt glanced down at his hands. "Yes, perhaps that's why I didn't see them."

She went to the door and turned around. Their eyes met. "Thanks for answering my question."

Ponzelt pursed his lips and nodded.

Five minutes later Landen called. She'd just turned on the ignition; now she switched it off again. "Where are you?" he said.

"In Liebau. You?"

"At home. Do you want to come past?"

She grinned. Was it that simple?

She had arranged to visit at 12.00, which gave her an hour and a half to follow up a question that was nagging her: what connection was there between the three eastern Europeans and the Kanzan-an, assuming that Landen was right in his belief that the roshi, Taro and the other inhabitants of the monastery were innocent?

Given that the eastern Europeans had made enquiries about the Kanzan-an, it was likely that they'd gone there. Why? Who had they met there?

Asile d'enfants?

Justin Muller and his people were dealing with those living at the monastery. Were they also dealing with Asile d'enfants?

She needed to know what questioning of the Asile staff had thrown up. But it was too soon to ring Lederle.

She wound down the window. Spring air. The fields on either side of the road had thawed. Now they looked muddy and weary, radiating meekness and contentment. January was almost over, February only on its way. Winter was forecast to return at the weekend.

Let it snow. She would sleep during the day at the weekend; Anatol was coming over on Friday and Saturday night. No more snowmen, just midnight men.

There were U.N.I.C.E.F. and Terre des hommes offices in Freiburg. The U.N.I.C.E.F. number was engaged, Terre des hommes had a recorded message. A child's voice squawked, "We're on holiday, but you can call Baba at the following number!"

Baba's full name was Barbara Franke, and she had a call divert on her mobile, but no time.

"Ten minutes," Bonì said. "It's important."

"Not today, I've got to go to court."

"It's *very* important."

"Shit!" Barbara Franke said. She suggested they meet at 11.00, at the fountain by the Adelhauser Neukloster. "Light-brown coat, blonde hair, laptop," she said and hung up.

Blue anorak, dark hair, bottle, Bonì thought as she opened the glove box.

Barbara Franke was in her early thirties and at first glance appeared to be a classic Mick type – light-brown suit, very feminine figure, very long blonde hair, very beautiful. At second glance this assessment was shattered by the "Baba", her commitment to Terre des hommes and her confidence.

And of course by the fact that she was a lawyer. Lawyers hadn't come up on the chairlift at Scuol. Only secretaries, cashiers, cleaning ladies, saleswomen, waitresses. A writer too. But no lawyers.

So she wasn't a Mick type. But the ideal wife for Landen.

They greeted each other. "Interesting perfume," Barbara said.

It took a few seconds for Louise to understand. She felt herself blushing. She snuck a chewing gum from the pocket of her anorak. Then another.

Barbara touched her arm.

"Are you on duty?"

She shook her head.

"Good," Barbara said smiling. "Ditch the car, will you? You've got nine minutes." She set off towards Fischerau, Bonì walking beside her in silence. Barbara apologised for the hurry; this was the most important court hearing she'd had for ages. She was prosecuting a business for grossly negligent environmental pollution. "I'm going to make mincemeat of them today."

"Eight minutes," Louise said.

"I'd have more time at the weekend."

They crossed the Gewerbekanal. Bonì said the court was in the other direction. Barbara said she had to pick someone up. She stopped by a café in Gerberau and looked at her watch. "Shit."

Questions about Asile d'enfants floated through Louise's mind and remained unasked. Her gaze fell on the green canal railings. Metal triangles, squares, a circle – Mick shapes. Briefly she thought of the puzzling lines of the calligraphy in Landen's hallway. But thinking of Landen now was not helpful.

"Sorry about earlier. It just slipped out."

She looked up. Barbara was leaning against the railings, her hands clasped. She wore three gold rings on the ring finger of her left hand. What did that mean? Three husbands? I have sufficient love for three lives? The black laptop was wedged between her tummy and her arms. Louise nodded. She didn't know whether to hate Barbara Franke or admire her. She had two contradictory urges: to give the woman a shove and watch her flap about in the canal in her beautiful light-brown suit, or get down on her knees and beg for help.

Resisting both, she said, "Asile d'enfants."

Barbara twitched her nose and said, "I've heard of them."

"What impression do you have of them?"

"Hmm. Secretive."

"Do they work with Terre des hommes?"

"Not that I know of."

"Not at all, or just not in Germany?"

"Not in Germany."

"In the Far East?"

"It's possible. I don't know." Barbara's mobile rang. She turned her back and muttered a few words. Then she put the mobile away and said, "To the court, we're meeting there."

They hurried over the bridge again, back in the direction they had come.

"What do you know about them?" Louise said.

"Not a lot." Founded and run by Jean Berger, H.Q. in Basel, clandestine operation. What Asile did was to place orphans from the Far East with adoptive parents in Europe, i.e. overseas adoption. "Just for your information, Terre des hommes no longer arranges overseas adoptions. We're not against it in principle, but we think it makes more sense to find adoptive or foster parents in the country concerned, or to reintegrate the child into its original family if that's possible." Now Barbara was speaking as fast as she was walking.

"But they're not prohibited."

"Not if the parties involved stick to the prescribed channels."

"Which are?"

"Placement via youth welfare offices and other recognised authorities, rather than private individuals or semi-public agencies."

"Why is it administered so strictly?"

"Because that's the only way of guaranteeing that the child's welfare is given the highest priority. Ensuring that children aren't sold, reduced to commodities. You can earn good money with children, you see? Are you free at all on Saturday morning?"

"No."

"Shit."

"Does Asile stick to the prescribed channels?"

"I don't know. What about later this evening?"

"Possibly, but unlikely."

"Can I call you?" Boni handed her a business card. Barbara glanced at it without stopping. "Section 11, yes?" She knew Bermann. A colleague from her law firm was representing one of the suspects in a serious arson case. Bermann had arrested him and Louise remembered the case. Barbara laughed jovially and said she couldn't understand how a man like Bermann could stick it out in Freiburg. Somewhere there must be a secret hideout for displaced machos, where he could spend the odd hour or two with kindred spirits. A chauvinist hole in a damp cellar where five body-builders with handlebar moustaches sat around a camp fire, exchanging jokes about blondes.

"Police H.Q.?"

Barbara gave a crooked grin.

They stopped outside the courthouse. Only now did Lousie realise that she was sweating profusely and out of breath. Panting, she asked, "Do you know Annegret Schelling? She works for Asile."

Barbara shook her head and made a note of the name. She promised to find out more and ring Bonì that evening. "Once again, sorry about earlier." They shook hands. "Wish me luck for my battle." With an excited smile she vanished into the courthouse.

Louise watched her go. She briefly considered taking Barbara's advice and leaving the car where it was, but then dismissed the idea.

On the way back to the Adelhauser Neukloster she imagined Barbara in the cold little house in Provence. She saw her sitting at the kitchen table with her mother. The two of them fired up, delivering impassioned speeches, warriors together.

She parked outside the sushi bar. Enni was standing in the open doorway holding a newspaper. When she got out he looked up. He folded the paper and said, "Sorry, Inspector, I forgot."

She waved a hand dismissively. "I've got a quarter of an hour. Will that do?"

"For what?"

"To explain to me why the centre of the universe is in my tummy."

Enni laughed. "That depends, Inspector."

"Has it got anything to do with Buddhism, with Zen?"

He nodded.

"And? So?"

"Zen is doing, Inspector, not talking or knowing, not explaining or thinking. Doing." With a smile he opened out his arms.

"Smart arse. So *what* do I have to do."

"Start by breathing."

"Breathing?"

A broad grin. Enni looked over his shoulder and called out something in Japanese. A man's voice replied from the kitchen. He took a turquoise autumn coat from one of the hooks. "Let's go to the Seepark. Have you ever been to the Japanese Garden, Inspector?"

"No." She didn't move.

"Did you know that Freiburg is twinned with a city in Japan?"

"No. Look, Enni, we're staying here. I don't have time for the Seepark."

"Matsuyama. It's on Shikoku Island, seventy kilometres south of Hiroshima."

They sat at the tram stop. The sun was shining and it was milder than the day before. She was still freezing though. Her sweat had dried and turned cold, and it stank. "What's that got to do with my belly?"

"I was born there," Enni said. "In Matsuyama. How about that? I live in cities that are twinned." Born in one, grown up in the other. One his mother, the other his father. Matsuyama and Freiburg. Enni nodded with satisfaction. Two cities that were more than two cities; they were *one* city. *One* organism. One was the other and vice-versa. Through him Matsuyama was Freiburg and Freiburg Matsuyama. "So to speak."

Louise nodded automatically. She needed to change her clothes. There was a fresh T-shirt in her rucksack in the car. There was no way she was going to Landen's house reeking of sweat. "Enni, I've got to go now."

"O.K., Inspector." Enni told her that in Japanese the centre of the body was called *hara* and it was the seat of energy. Given proper training you could "push" energy – *ki* – from there to other areas.

She yawned. "What's the point of doing that?"

"It keeps you healthy. Physically and mentally."

"Now it's getting interesting. How do you learn it?"

"Through meditation."

"I might have guessed. That's all you orientals ever think of."

Enni laughed. All of a sudden his head was very close to hers. He had snow-white, strikingly straight teeth. His breath smelled of fish and cigarette smoke. Putting his left hand on her shoulder he said, "Focus on the breathing, Inspector. Breathe in through your nose, out through your mouth. But first you have to sit properly or you'll slide off the bench. Straight back, the spine mustn't be curved."

She did as she was told. His hand was on her back. She thought of Anatol and his hands, and how they'd fought heroic battles the night before.

"Keep the spine straight, Inspector. Close your eyes. Breathe in through your nose, out through your mouth. Do you know how to breathe correctly?"

She nodded.

"Then do it."

She shook her head. Four and a half kilos heavier than her normal weight, she was not going to breathe into her stomach in public. Japanese tourists would stop and gape, cyclists would come racing towards the balloon of feathers and fat.

Enni giggled. "Follow the path of your breathing through your body, inspector. Think of nothing apart from your breathing."

She nodded and concentrated. She fleetingly felt that one day she might attain some sort of peace if she sat here for many years and kept going like this. That she was beginning to sink into a dark, whooshing, *redemptive* abyss.

Then she thought of vegetable sushi, Bermann, her mother and Niksch. She heard Landen's voice and felt the tingling of happy expectation in the back of her neck.

She fell asleep.

When she awoke her head was on Enni's shoulder. The world was turquoise. She sat up. Enni looked at her.

She had dreamed of Pham, the boy from Vietnam. Calambert had tied him up and stuffed him into the boot of his car. Then he'd turned around and told her that he was Pham's new father. She'd been standing in the snow but it was very warm. Calambert had put his hands up and she'd shot him.

She'd woken up because it was getting warmer and warmer. Now she realised that the warmth was coming from Enni. She glanced at her watch. 11.50. "I've got to go. Can I use your loo?"

Enni nodded. She stroked his short, firm hair and got up.

Much sooner than Louise felt comfortable with, she found herself standing back in front of the little house with the wooden fence. Nothing had changed. The willow's fingers above the roof, the stepping stones, the shed that might be a teahouse. Only the snow was gone.

And Niksch.

She looked at the letterbox. TOMMO / LANDEN. Funny names, Niksch said in her head. He'd been nervous and suspicious, as if already sensing that his life was in danger.

But not here, at this place, not from these people.

She didn't know how long she stood motionless at the garden gate before ringing the bell.

Tommo opened the door.

No sign yet of Landen's child: a firm tummy, narrow hips, a small white face. Tommo gave her an enchantingly weary smile. "I'm Shizu Tommo. How nice that you've come to visit us." She spoke slowly and with a strong accent.

Us.

For a second or two Bonì wondered whether she ought to drive off again. Then she pushed open the garden gate.

Tommo's handshake was soft and timid. She was finally meeting "the inspector", she said. She wore her neat black hair short. Dark rings around her eyes shimmered beneath a layer of powder. Her fluffy yellow jumper smelled of spring-fresh fabric conditioner. She was a head shorter than Louise and half as large, a gorgeous splash of colour in the winter grey.

Then Louise was standing by the calligraphy again. Happiness and friendship – Niksch had thought of death. She stared at Tommo, who returned her gaze and was perhaps able to guess what was going through her head, or perhaps not.

"Should I take off my shoes?"

Tommo nodded gratefully.

Bonì breathed a sigh of relief when Tommo took her into the living room rather than the kitchen. The kitchen was where the china cat and Niksch sat.

"Would you like some tea?"

She said no, and shuddered.

The living room was decked out in German–Japanese style. A dining table in light wood and soft beige cushions rather than chairs or a sofa in the sitting area. Where was Landen? On the floor of a windowless alcove stood a vase with three flower stems; above it hung a calligraphy. Tommo noticed her gazing at it. "It's just for decoration. I'm not a . . ." She thought about it. "Prac-ti-sing Buddhist."

"Already onto religion?" Landen said as he entered the room. "Hello."

"Hello." They shook hands. His eyebrows were slightly raised and he was smiling. He looked a picture of innocence, apparently unaware of the effect of his telephone call. Landen was wearing jeans and a dark-blue corduroy shirt that came down to his thighs. Not for the first time she thought he could pass as a model for clothes for men in their forties.

And yet he remained inscrutable. Why had he invited her if his wife was at home?

"Tokonoma, the picture recess," he said, gesturing to the alcove with his chin. "Like some tea?"

Tommo and she shook their heads in unison.

They sat on the cushions. Louise could detect a faint and pleasant smell of sandalwood. She was glad she'd changed her T-shirt. When Landen asked about Taro she told him there was no news. He sat opposite Tommo, and closer to her. Both of them looked at Bonì rather than each other.

They spoke about Taro, the monastery, the roshi. Tommo knew all the names, knew about everything. She nodded a lot, said little and didn't move. She looked elegant, educated and compassionate. Louise thought that she would have gone well in the picture recess, in place of the vase with the flowers, just for decoration. She wondered what might stir her passion. What did Tommo laugh about? What did she cry about? What was it like sleeping with her? Where did those rings around her eyes come from?

In the presence of his wife Landen was even more reserved than normal. He seemed to be gauging his words before opening his mouth, moderating the intensity with which he spoke. Everything about him spelled caution and aloofness. Sieved through a fine-mesh net of deliberation.

Now she knew three Richard Landens. The didactic one, the engaged one and the secretive one. The first was boring, the second erotic and the third depressing. After twenty minutes she said she had to go.

"Stay a while longer," Landen said.

"Yes, please do," Tommo said. "Stay for lunch. I've made pasta parcels."

So she stayed. And had her time alone with Landen, as Tommo got up shortly afterwards to prepare lunch. Some traditions had their good sides. Tommo vanished without a sound. Rings around the eyes, Louise thought, were either down to a lack of sleep or tears. Although she couldn't imagine Tommo crying, she began to relax.

Landen said nothing. The precious seconds were passing idly and in silence.

"What does your wife do for a living?" she said eventually.

"She's a software expert for a Japanese firm."

"In Freiburg?"

"Yes."

"Did you meet in Japan?"

He nodded. During his time "over there". Three years ago, when he returned to Germany, Tommo came with him.

Little by little Landen became animated. He talked of Japan, of researching for a book about the Japanese forms of Buddhism, of a six-month stay at the Zen monastery Nanzen-ji in Kyoto. About Tommo and her family, who for a long time were sceptical and cool towards him. But then they relented and began to treat him like a son.

"But you did come back to Germany. Why?"

"I . . . you know, I was homesick." He smiled. "The longer I spent in Japan, the more foreign I felt there. By the end I was so well integrated – as well integrated as you can be as a westerner – and yet I felt like the loneliest person in the world."

"In spite of Shizu?"

"Yes, in spite of Shizu. Do you understand what I mean?"

"No."

They laughed. Landen said, "It's only when you know something well that you realise just how *little* you know it. It doesn't matter whether it's a country or a person. That's my experience at least."

"Do you find that's the case with everyone, or just with . . . er, other nationalities?"

"With everyone, ultimately. The longer you know a person, the more of a riddle they become, irrespective of where they're from. You accept that you'll never be able to really know or understand them, because they're not you."

"Aha."

"Don't you find that too?"

"I've never really thought about it."

"Can I ask you something?"

She sighed. "Depends."

"Do you always work alone?"

"No."

"So why now?"

"Because I'm on holiday."

"You could terminate your holiday."

"I like being on holiday." Landen laughed. Louise said, "When's the baby due?"

"The . . . oh, end of July, beginning of August."

She nodded. Tommo was in her third month. But something wasn't right. She felt that Landen didn't like talking about the baby. Didn't he want children? Was it just with Tommo that he didn't want children? Was Tommo, as a software expert, unsuited to marriage and having a family?

"What did you and the roshi talk about in the monastery?"

Landen raised his two-tone eyebrow and smiled. His gaze wandered to where Tommo had been sitting. The three Landens seemed to be wrestling with each other. The second Landen – the dangerous one – was the victor. "I told him you have a special gift – an emotional sincerity. Anyway, um, this sincerity sometimes *sprays* out of you like . . . like . . . like water from a burst hose."

She pursed her lips. *A special gift.* Bermann had called this special gift "an irritating lack of self-control". On the other hand, Bermann would never invite a woman over if he were not alone. She felt herself starting to sweat again. "Why did you call me today?"

Landen gave a somewhat strained smile. "Because yesterday evening you . . ." Once more he lowered his eyes to the empty Tommo cushion. "You didn't look as if you were in a very good way."

Anger stirred deep within her. Was this just *pity*? But she sensed that he had too much respect for her to feel only pity. "Let's just say, not all my colleagues share my opinions as far as the Kanzan-an is concerned. Well, in fact, *nobody* does." She waited for him to look at her again. He didn't seem to notice her blushing. "Apart from you."

The eyebrows moved upwards. "So you believe the roshi."

To hell with the roshi. She nodded.

"And Taro."

To hell with Taro too. "Yes, if you ignore the fact that Taro didn't say much that I could believe. I mean, apart from 'No'."

Landen didn't laugh. "I can't stop thinking about him," he said. "Taro. No matter what I'm doing, I see him in my mind and then I ask myself what was he afraid of, why didn't he want to talk to me and how could I have helped him. I wonder where he is. To think that he . . ." He broke off. Neither of them spoke for a few seconds.

Then Landen cleared his throat and asked why she'd measured the tyre tracks. As she talked of the tyre marks east of Liebau it struck her that she wasn't being particularly professional. But Landen's interest and attentiveness were far too beneficial to make her want to behave professionally.

Only when he asked what she concluded from all of this was her answer evasive. Although she didn't mention Asile d'enfants and Pham, he said he wondered how Pham would get on with his new family. Whether he'd be able to forget what he'd gone through. He gave a sad smile. "This morning I started learning Vietnamese."

At that moment Tommo entered the room to say that lunch was ready.

"Come," Landen said.

They stood up. As they went out into the hallway Bonì realised they'd be eating in the kitchen. She placed a hand on Landen's fore-arm. "I can't," she said. "I can't eat with you." She put on her shoes, staring at friendship, happiness and death as she did so. Without look-ing back she left the house and closed the door.

On the way to the garden gate it felt as if the willow were bending down and grabbing at her with its hard, twiggy boughs. She had to resist breaking into a run.

She got to Mulhouse at 2.00 p.m. She parked and called Lederle. "Oh, Bonì . . ." He groaned.

"Are you still at the monastery?"

"We just left." Lederle was distracted, he had to concentrate on the dirt track. Muller, he told her, had chatted briefly to Annegret Schelling. The other Asile people were looking for somewhere else for the children to stay. This evening Annegret would be leaving too. She'd given them the address of two nearby farms where the carers and children could spend the night.

Louise asked what Lederle thought of her. "A good 'un," he replied. She'd been cooperative and understanding. Concerned about the children. Shocked by what had happened. She knew Taro by sight. She couldn't imagine the roshi having anything to do with it all.

Louise felt uneasy. "What made her mention the roshi? Did she see anything?"

Lederle cleared his throat. "The eastern Europeans."

"With the roshi?"

Lederle was silent for a moment. Then he said, "She can't swear by it, she said. It was rather dark. They were standing near the office on the ground floor."

"And what if *she's* involved, Reiner, rather than the roshi?"

"Annegret Schelling? Asile d'enfants?" Lederle sounded very patient. "Everything's possible. But it's hardly probable."

She bit her lip. Had she become further entangled in the web than she'd realised? Possible but not probable? Why was she the only one who thought it possible *and* probable?

But *did* she think it probable?

"What's the next move?"

"Tomorrow Chervel's going to get a search warrant for the monastery. Rolf and I are allowed to be present." Lederle paused. She could hear his short breaths. With sudden anger he said, "What about you, Bonì? What's your next move? How much longer are you going to hide away? The psychologist came to see me today. Call her, make an appointment. Do you really think Almenbroich and Bermann are going to forget the whole thing just because you're out of their sight for a few days?"

"Yes," she said, then hung up.

She wondered if Lederle knew she'd been to the Kanzan-an with Landen. Had Georges talked? Annegret Schelling?

Then she thought of Katrin Rein. The Bermann woman who was worried about her. Who'd stood in her stairwell, who'd now gone to see Lederle and was waiting for a call that might never come. It was a while before she could banish the thought of the psychologist.

Had Annegret's statement that she'd seen the roshi with the eastern Europeans changed her attitude towards him? The answer was clear: not at all.

Or completely?

Furious, she slapped both hands on the steering wheel.

Another question was beginning to elicit new doubts in her too. Asile d'enfants placed children from Far-Eastern countries with European adoptive parents. Barbara Franke had said that there was money to be earned with children. But was the trade in adoption so lucrative that the proceeds justified kidnapping and the murder of a police officer? How much did you earn by selling Asian children to adoptive parents in Europe bypassing the recognised authorities?

How much was a child worth? She shuddered.

This was the worst thing about her profession. You were forced to adopt the same mindset as those you were up against. However much you strove to set yourself apart from criminals, there was always an overlap, even if you approached it from a different angle. There were common paths, common categories and common thought processes. What would you say in your statement if you were the guilty party? How would you kill the rich wife or the rich husband without drawing suspicion to yourself? Where would you hide? How much money would you demand for a child?

Where would you go if you were Calambert?

The criminal and law enforcer both considered the same solutions to potential problems. Opting to go down the criminal route was weighed up twice: by both perpetrator and their pursuer.

How much was a child worth? Was an infant worth more than a three-year-old? A boy more than a girl? A light-skinned child more than a dark one?

She didn't want to know.

But the question remained: was the illegal placement of Asian orphans with European adoptive parents so lucrative that you would kill for it, or have someone killed?

Or was there more behind it?

III

ASILE D'ENFANTS

12

Rather than take the road to Zillisheim, she drove south towards Steinbrunn-le-Bas to avoid the possibility of meeting anyone she knew. On the way she had lunch: a salami sandwich, pretzel sticks and a king-size Twix. She washed it all down with Evian, which was fresh and yet tasted mercilessly dreary.

In Steinbrunn-le-Bas children were waving as they got off a bus. In Steinbrunn-le-Haut a tiny road branched off to the north towards Flaxlanden, a few kilometres from Mulhouse. She took it on the off chance, to see whether you could access the Kanzan-an from the east as well as from Illfurth in the west. After all, the road from which the track ran to the monastery must lead somewhere. But the few bumpy lanes heading to the west all ended in fields and quiet farmsteads.

So she turned around, drove back through Steinbrunn-le-Haut and then further on to the south. Just before Obermorschwiller she took the turning for Illfurth. About halfway to the village of Suedwiller she came across an asphalt road leading north that vanished into the hilly landscape. She chanced it. A few minutes later the dirt track and wooden sign came into view.

The bumpy ground felt familiar. The car park was empty. As she walked through the wood to the monastery she felt alone. It made her angry to realise that she was missing Landen.

There was nobody to be seen in the clearing. Yesterday at around this time monks and nuns had been at meditation. She entered the silent building, knocked in turn on the doors to the visitors' room, kitchen and office and peered into empty rooms. When she returned to the entrance the soft clangs of the gong sounded. She waited on the outside steps.

First came the light-grey cat, which loped across the clearing and disappeared behind the house. Then the roshi and the rest of the monks and nuns appeared on one of the stepping-stone paths between the damp hillocks.

Once again she expected the roshi to send her packing; once again he didn't. As they shook hands his expression was unchanging. His wrinkles seemed more furrowed than the day before. He said, "You find Taro?"

"No, I'm sorry."

The roshi nodded thoughtfully. They went inside.

"You come alone."

She suspected he was referring to her colleagues rather than Landen. In the morning half a dozen French and German police officers, in the afternoon just her. A shiver ran down her spine. There's a lot to do; let's get cracking. For the first time she wondered how much longer she would be able to keep going. A few hours? A few days? "I need your help."

"We drink tea, we talk."

She had to smile. An enticing prospect despite the tea bowls, which weren't made for her hands. To sit beside the roshi, feel his warmth and energy, talk to him. Maybe close her eyes again as with Enni, focus on her breathing, capture the feeling that inside her lurked not only a dark abyss of terror, but maybe a redemption from it too. *Buddha-nature own-nature. Understand? Own-nature.*

But there was no time for that now. She thanked the roshi and told him what was on her mind. Who at the Kanzan-an had contact with the visitors at the monastery? Who could answer her questions about Asile d'enfants? He raised his eyebrows. She pointed towards the ceiling. "The children."

He nodded. "You talk Chiyono. Chiyono care guests."

176

Chiyono was German, around seventy, and a head shorter than Bonì. Her white hair was cut very short. She wore rimless spectacles, one arm of which was stuck with a plaster. Her eyes radiated concentration and alertness.

They sat in the small office, Louise on the visitor's chair, Chiyono behind the desk. In front of her lay one of the white folders from the shelves. Louise's eyes followed the slow, deliberate movements of the woman's hands and arms as she opened it. *You come alone.* The roshi perceived more than she felt comfortable with.

She cleared her throat. "Can I ask you something?"

Chiyono looked up. "Of course."

"What's your real name?"

"Chiyono."

"I mean the name on your I.D."

Chiyono smiled. "Oh, that. I don't remember." She bent forward slightly as if about to tell Bonì a secret. "It was associated with a person who had an ego. This person and this ego ceased to exist years ago."

"I see. So now Chiyono exists."

"Yes."

"Was Chiyono a Zen nun?"

"Yes."

"And for you her name is a sort of . . . manifesto? A mindset?"

Chiyono smiled again. "Yes, sort of."

"For what?"

"For the moon and the water, for sitting, for breathing, for the Zen spirit. For a pail that breaks."

Bonì scowled.

Chiyono laughed. "I'm sorry. I'd love to tell you more, but you're in a hurry."

"What more would you tell me if I weren't?"

"What would you like to hear?"

"How, for example, I could exchange my old ego for a new one."

"You don't exchange it. You overcome it."

"Oh. But how?"

"You leave the ego, the self, behind you."

"You mean you live *without* an ego?"

"Yes. The ego is the spiritual enemy."

"But if you don't have an ego, what's sitting in front of me?"

Chiyono laughed again. She seemed to like the way the conversation was going. "The Buddha said, 'This six-foot-tall body, equipped with perception and consciousness, contains the world, the beginning of the world *and* the path leading to the world's end.' He never spoke of an ego. In my case it's probably only five feet, but that changes nothing of the contents."

"So you don't have an ego?"

"No, I don't. What you would describe as an ego we call the five skandhas. These are the parts of the body, emotions, perception, mental powers such as will, concentration, drive etc., and consciousness. All this is continually changing. It's not fixed or consistent. So how can you give it a concrete definition? How can you call it an ego?"

"No ego?" Louise mumbled.

"In the Buddhist sense, not the psychological one."

"Very reassuring. So, Chiyono-without-an-ego, what do you know about Asile d'enfants?"

Asile d'enfants had been coming to the Kanzan-an since 1997, and twice a year since 1999 – summer and winter. The size of the group varied, from two to four carers and three to eight children. The length of their stay always varied: at least one week, and two at the most. The organisation was based in Basel and Chiyono's contact was Annegret Schelling. She knew the other Asile carers only by sight, if at all.

Chiyono put the lists of names of carers and children on an ancient mini photocopier, which spluttered out poor facsimiles. Louise skimmed them. The names of two carers appeared on every list: Annegret

Schelling and Harald Mahler. Other names were Klaus Fröbick, Paul Lebonne and Natchaya Mahler. Jean Berger didn't crop up once.

The children's first names were listed along with their age and country of origin. Most were between one and three, or six and nine. Many came from Cambodia, Thailand and South Korea, a few from Vietnam and Laos. On the final list Louise found Pham: *Pham 3½, Vietnam.*

Chiyono had never seen the eastern Europeans. Neither with the Asile people nor with the roshi.

As far as she knew there had never been any problems with Asile. The group paid generously and in advance, provided their own food and ate in a common room on the first floor. During the day they visited farms, lakes and animal parks. At night the thick walls swallowed up any sounds.

Bonì could not help shuddering. Chiyono, who was about to explain what she meant by that comment, paused. Only now did she seem to realise why Louise was interested in Asile. The two of them gazed at each other in silence.

"It's just a possibility," Bonì said. "No more, no less."

"A possibility?" Chiyono said.

"A horrendous possibility."

Chiyono accompanied her back to the car. In the clearing she stopped and turned. Her eyes were on the building. "I hope you're wrong," she said.

They didn't speak as they walked through the wood. When they reached the Mégane, Louise said, "Some time you'll have to tell me why you live here. I mean, why you live in this way."

"Yes. When you have the time," Chiyono said. She put her hands together and bowed.

Louise raised the hand that was holding her bunch of keys. They jangled hectically. She smiled and got in.

In her wing mirror she could see that Chiyono was watching her leave. It was as if she were trying to put off Louise's return visit for as long as possible.

Lederle was sitting in Justin Muller's office, drinking *café au lait* and waiting for Anne Wallmer. Bermann had gone back to Freiburg. "We're having a chat, Justin and me," Lederle said with a weary satisfaction in his voice. His anger at Bonì seemed to have dissipated. Or perhaps he'd simply given up on her. "Two elderly gentlemen," he said, "who've seen too much and are allowing themselves a little break to talk about pleasant things."

Louise avoided a pothole. Stones knocked against the bottom of the Mégane. "Let's get back to the unpleasant ones then. Could you check a few names for me?"

"Later, love, or my coffee's going to get cold."

"Get a pen, would you, love?"

Sighing, Lederle said, "Go on."

"Annegret Schelling, Klaus Fröbick – that's 'c-k' at the end – Paul Lebonne – '-bonne' rather than '-bon' – Harald and Natchaya Mahler – N-a-t-c-h-a-y-a and Mahler with an 'h'."

"Hmm," Lederle said. She sensed that he'd stopped writing. All the same she said. "I need everything you can find, including addresses."

Lederle cleared his throat.

Perhaps, she thought, it would have been better to call someone at the station and ask them to run the check. A young detective sergeant, a secretary, a colleague from a different section. But nobody stuck with Bonì like Lederle did. Nobody except him would have been prepared to stay in contact with her, disobeying both Bermann and Almenbroich.

You come alone.

Louise took her foot off the accelerator and let the car coast. The Mégane came to a stop twenty metres from the road. Her eyes were on the weather-beaten wooden sign. Two years ago, on the day she'd shot Calambert, she had been on her own at the end too. But at least then she'd set off with Bermann, Lederle and the others. She had been part of a team. Now she was no longer part of the team.

A movement made her glance to the right. The light-grey cat loped slowly down the hill and sat by the edge of the track.

"Reiner."

"It can't go on like this."

"I need your help."

"You need a different sort of help. Please understand that."

"One last time, O.K.? Do I really have to *beg* you for this one last favour?"

Lederle did not respond. The longer the pause lasted, the more pathetic these words sounded in her head. She grinned in spite of herself.

Now the cat turned and looked at her. She preferred its expression to that of Landen's china cat – not stubborn, but interested. Friendly.

She wondered what was going through Lederle's head. Did he feel sympathy for her? Probably. Did he have a bad conscience? Even though they'd been working together for years, he hadn't identified the reason behind her mood swings, tiredness and moments of madness. He hadn't realised what the Calambert case had meant to her. He partly blamed himself for her problems. *Of course* he had a bad conscience.

But Lederle was a good policeman too. Even if he considered her suspicions to be far-fetched, he knew that nothing was yet proven. There was a tiny possibility that she was right. Good police officers kept tiny possibilities in mind.

The cat crossed the track and vanished into the wood. "Fine," Lederle said. "But it might take a while."

She turned left towards Suedwiller. A hundred metres further on, a path she had noticed on the way led into the forest. She reversed onto it and parked her Mégane on the soft earth. Here the trees were quite dense. Unless you turned your head at precisely this point on the road you'd never notice the car.

She put on a pair of trainers and took from the boot the rucksack she had packed. When she opened the glove box she thought of Barbara Franke. But Barbara was far away.

On the way back to the road she felt the urge to call Anatol. To mumble raunchy, tender, secret things to him, whisper pet names. Fuel her anticipation for the weekend.

The ringing was replaced by the distant sound of an engine. "Hi!" Anatol said.

"Hi!"

She looked up. On the road in front of her a silver car was heading for the monastery track.

Her brain shifted only slowly into gear. A box-like car rather than a saloon. Large, light-coloured.

A silver M.P.V.

"Shit!" she said, switching off her mobile.

Fifteen minutes later she reached the car park. The M.P.V. was there, but she couldn't see anybody, either in the vehicle itself, or on the path to the wood.

She crept up to the car, one hand on her pistol. A Cologne number plate. She committed it to memory. After a quick glance inside she ran her finger over the letters on the back: SHARAN.

Bonì knelt to examine the tyre impressions in the dried earth. An asymmetrical profile with two circumferential grooves. The same tracks as on the photograph she'd swiped from Lederle's dossier. She crawled in front of the left rear tyre. ContiWinterContact T.S. 790, 215/55 R16. As Lederle had suspected.

The car that had been east of Liebau on Sunday and here yesterday evening. The car that Ponzelt hadn't seen.

She stood up. She had to call Lederle or Bermann. Then it struck her that Lederle and Bermann weren't interested in the M.P.V. Only she was.

*

She walked through the wood but didn't venture into the clearing. Although dusk was settling in, she would have been spotted immediately from the windows on the first floor. Kneeling, she leaned with the rucksack against a tree trunk at the edge of the wood. From here she had a view of both the monastery and the path. If nothing had happened by midnight she would steal her way into the Kanzan-an. If someone came out to the M.P.V. before that, she'd try to follow the vehicle.

It turned dark rapidly. About halfway between her and the main monastery building there was a soft, yellow glow above the clearing. The dharma hall. What happened in a *teisho*? What did the roshi say to the monks and nuns? From his face she'd seen that the recent events had left their mark. That he was worried about Taro. Did he talk about him?

The thought of Taro made her freeze. The cold had to be fought off with warmth. As she unscrewed the small bottle the soft, reassuring gong resounded. She closed her eyes.

We drink tea, we talk.

At some point, when she had the time, she would tell the roshi everything. Ask Chiyono why and how she'd become who she was. Take part in a *teisho*.

Confront her spiritual foe.

What, she wondered, might you find within yourself if there was no longer any ego? What was *own-nature* if not your own self? All those different questions and all the different answers depending on your conviction. Some were looking for their ego, others trying to liberate themselves from it. Christians went to church and prayed, Buddhists to dharma halls to meditate. Not to mention what Jews, Muslims and Hindus did.

What *did* Jews, Muslims and Hindus do?

When she had the time she would ask Landen these questions. Perhaps he also knew what newborn babies were before they were baptised. Were they already Christians, or were they nothing?

She grinned. Were they perhaps *heathens*?

A question she wouldn't mind putting to her father – when she had the time. He would go silent and turn pale. Over the decades he'd become increasingly faithful to the Church. Increasingly German and increasingly religious.

A barely audible crack made her spin around. She held her breath and listened. A small, light-grey creature moving away from her and bounding into the clearing. The cat.

She sank back down. Her pulse was racing. She hadn't been paying attention.

Then it was pitch black. Tiny lights flickered at certain points on the ground floor of the Kanzan-an. On the first floor a few candles were alight in the long corridor. The top floor was not visible.

If the Asile people didn't use torches she wouldn't notice them immediately. Too late, perhaps, to creep back to the car park and her Mégane, which meant that she wouldn't be able to follow them. Why hadn't she thought of that before?

She stood up. She'd wait near the Sharan.

At that moment a small, circular light flashed close to the entrance to the monastery, followed by two more. They were stationary for a few seconds before moving slowly in her direction.

Adrenalin shot through her veins. They were coming.

As quietly and yet as quickly as she could, Bonì ran to the car park. When she reached the Sharan she stopped and caught her breath. What now? Wait here to see who got in? Run to the Mégane and try to follow the M.P.V.? She cursed under her breath. There were so many reasons why officers worked in teams.

It then dawned on her that she hadn't thought to memorise her surroundings. She'd forgotten to get her bearings at the critical moment, scout for paths and make a plan.

Her Jägermeister thoughts were being joined increasingly by Jäger-meister lapses.

No lights were visible in the wood, so she still had time. To the right of the track there was a shallow hill. She would have a good view from the top. But the Mégane was in the forest to the left of the road. What was between the road and the edge of the forest on her left? A ditch? A stream? A narrow meadow? A meadow with a fence? Without a fence? She had no idea.

She ran along the soft verge to the left of the track towards the road. She could scarcely see a metre in front of her. She'd thought to bring a torch. She hadn't thought she might not be able to use it.

A shimmer of light appeared on the horizon beyond the road.

After half a minute she got a stitch and had to stop. She turned around. No lights. She pressed her hand against her side and stumbled on, but the pain quickly grew acute. Her breathing was hasty and irregular, however much she tried to calm it. And the horizon wasn't getting any closer. She stopped and clasped her knees with both hands and looked behind her, panting.

Still nothing.

She dropped to her knees and stared into the darkness. No dots of light. The Sharan must still be in her field of vision, even if she couldn't see it. Had they switched off their torches? Were they walking that slowly? Were they not going to the car park after all? Was it possible that the light had come from inhabitants of the monastery rather than the Asile people?

No. *No batteries China of Kanzan, no batteries here.*

She continued at a steady pace. Only when she was about fifty metres from the road did she see lights dancing away in the distance behind her. Relieved, she wiped sweat from her face and ran the last bit to the junction.

At the wooden sign she turned one final time. In the darkness the Sharan's headlights flared on.

13

The Sharan went in the same direction it had come from. Once it had passed the forest track, heading towards Suedwiller, Louise set off, keeping her headlights off until she reached the road. The Sharan was nowhere to be seen. She accelerated. Two bends later, tail-lights and silver silhouettes appeared ahead of her. On one or two occasions the beam of her headlights lit up the driver's side. There were several people in the Sharan, but she couldn't say how many.

They took the Obermorschwiller turning, then drove westwards through the village towards the French–German border. The M.P.V. stuck rigidly to the speed limit, staying on narrow country roads and crossing through tiny villages.

As they were leaving Magstatt-le-Haut, Bonì braked spontaneously and coasted into a dark farmyard. For a few seconds she waited next to a crazed, chained-up bulldog. Then she drove for a kilometre without lights on, slowing whenever she got to a bend.

After a while she switched on her dipped headlights and put her foot down.

Beyond Uffheim she turned on her mobile and placed it in the hands-free cradle. There were two messages on her voicemail. The first was Anatol asking nicely *what* was "shit", following by engine noise and a screeching as if a tram were braking. A cool, barely comprehensible voice said, "Louise? Barbara Franke here. Give me a call at the office."

But first she rang Lederle's number. Before she could speak he said, "I'm still on it, I'll let you know." She could hardly understand him either – he seemed to be eating.

"Wait, Reiner." She told him about the Sharan with the Cologne number plate and the ContiWinterContact T.S. 790. Explained how she'd waited at the Kanzan-an, followed the Asile staff, how they had given Mulhouse a wide berth, eventually crossing the border at Ottmarsheim or Chalampé.

She heard Lederle chew, swallow and drink. Then he fell silent. "Say something, Reiner."

"No."

Anger rose inside her. "Shit!" she cried. "I can't understand why you won't at least *consider* the possibility that it might be Asile rather than the Buddhists!"

"It's for your sake," Lederle said wearily. "I don't know who you are anymore, what you're doing, why you're doing it, how you're doing it, what's going on inside your head – I don't know *anything* anymore. Apart from the fact that you're refusing to talk to the psychologist."

"What do you mean, *how* I'm doing it?"

"What you're doing right now, are you doing it sober? Are you doing it drunk?"

"I see." She gave an irate laugh. "O.K., let's assume I'm drunk."

"You see?"

"And let's assume it's Asile that's involved."

Lederle drank and sighed. "Alright, fine."

"Would my state have any bearing on the fact that Asile's involved?"

"Oh dear." Lederle laughed sadly.

"Exactly."

The taillights of the Sharan were getting closer. She cut her speed. About fifty metres apart, the two cars crossed some kind of highway. The red lights moved away again.

"Apropos," she said, "what are *you* drinking at the moment, Reiner?"

Lederle didn't reply, nor did he need to. Despite his wife's diagnosis some of his habits hadn't changed. There was scarcely a day he worked that didn't include an early evening beer.

She felt shabby. On the other hand, what was the point in standards if they didn't apply to everyone?

She said, "I need both the addresses Annegret Schelling gave you."

"You're in *France*, Louise."

"Oh really? Tell that to Niksch, Hollerer and Taro."

Seconds passed without either of them speaking, then she heard Lederle leafing through some paper. His voice sounded reedy and unfamiliar. Two farms in the southern Vosges. One near Thann, the other in Ferrette. She opened her map. Thann was to the west of Mulhouse, Ferrette to the south. The Sharan had been heading eastwards, then north-eastwards.

She flinched when she was overtaken. A yellow V.W. Beetle stuck itself between her and the M.P.V. Below them ran the Basel–Mulhouse motorway. Ahead lay Kembs.

"Thanks, Reiner."

"We need to talk," Lederle said hoarsely. "There's something you ought to know. Let's talk next week, Louise." He hung up.

Before she could consider what he meant, her mobile rang. "I've got something for you," Barbara Franke said, this time with no noise in the background.

"Have you won the war?"

"Almost. The enemy's on the point of surrender. But I'll cut to the point – I've only got a minute. I've found out nothing about Annegret Schelling, but I do have information on Asile d'enfants."

Barbara had quizzed other members of Terre des hommes about Asile. Hardly anybody knew more about the organisation than she did – name, founder, activity. One TdH friend, however, by the name of Franco, seemed to recall that several years ago an adoption in Germany arranged by Asile had been revoked. The child, a seven- or eight-year-old Thai girl, had been put in a Bangkok orphanage by her mother. Franco couldn't remember exactly why, but it was generally done for financial reasons. At any rate the girl, Areewan, was *not* given up for adoption. And yet for some unfathomable reason, Areewan was placed with adoptive parents in Germany. Months later her biological mother learned of this and through the courts in Bangkok and Germany managed to have the adoption annulled.

"It shouldn't happen, but sometimes it does," Barbara said.

Areewan, Boní thought uneasily. The name seemed vaguely familiar. She reached for the photocopies Chiyono had given her. Without reducing her speed she skimmed through them at the wheel. On the list dated autumn 2000 it said: *Areewan, 10, Thailand.*

Carefully she placed the sheets of paper on the passenger seat.

When she looked up she noticed that the distance between her and the M.P.V. had substantially decreased, so she took her foot off the accelerator and fell back. They had passed through Kembs and headed north for a while on the D52, then turned off onto a smaller road.

"Louise?" Barbara said impatiently.

"When was this?"

"Mid or late nineties, Franco says."

"Is Areewan a common name in Thailand?"

"I don't know. It's certainly not uncommon. Why?"

"On the Asile list from autumn 2000 there's an Areewan from Thailand. She was ten at the time."

"A coincidence."

"How can we be sure?"

"Fly over there." Barbara groaned. "Alright, I'll sort it out. *Shit.*"

"But do it discreetly."

"Yes, yes. See you later."

"Wait. How much could you get for an orphan illegally placed with adoptive parents?"

Barbara paused, then mentioned some figures before hanging up. Deep in thought, Louise pressed the button on her mobile to end the call.

A child cost between five and twenty thousand dollars, depending on their background, age, sex and demand. Even in this business, however, special offers were available, Barbara had said. In India several years back, an employee of a charitable organisation had been offered children for adoption at around 450 marks. The laws of the market. When there was a surplus of goods, the price sank. As so often, the poverty of the Third World and the desires of the First had entered a fatal pact.

Soon afterwards the Sharan stopped by the side of the road. She maintained her speed. About 150 metres now separated her from the M.P.V. Three figures got out of the passenger side and walked away from the road. One was blonde. Annegret Schelling?

Eighty metres.

Between her and the Sharan a small road forked off. Should she take it? Unsure, she eased her foot off the pedal. At that moment the Sharan started moving again, but instead of driving on, it steered towards the other side of the road, as if to turn around. But it stopped in the middle and blocked the road.

She had been discovered.

Cursing, she slammed on the brakes. With an ugly screeching of the tyres, the Mégane skidded along the tarmac past the fork, coming to a stop fifteen metres from the Sharan. Instinctively she jammed her foot on the clutch to avoid stalling. Then she pulled out her pistol.

She could only make out the silhouette of the driver – the Mégane's headlights illuminated the field to the left of him. From the position of his head she could see that he was looking at her. Her eyes darted to the right. The three figures were now around twenty metres from the road, moving slowly. Where they were going she couldn't tell. There was no house or farm in sight, just a fenced-in pasture and the odd solitary tree in the distance.

She turned back to the M.P.V. Seconds passed without anything happening. What was he planning to do? She decided to wait for half a minute. Then she'd go and haul him out of his car, even though they were in France.

Assuming the traffic allowed.

But there didn't seem to be any traffic on this road. All she could see in front of her was the Sharan. She glanced in her rear-view mirror – and flinched. A few metres behind her was a red car without its lights on. Four rings in its radiator grille. An Audi. It was a moment before she realised why it was empty.

She put her foot down and the Mégane shot across a small embankment. She heard the rear window shatter and her head was thrown to the side. A burning pain spread from her right temple. She ducked. A muzzle flash was reflected in the wing mirror and she felt several hard clunks in the metal. Then the window next to her exploded and shards of glass shot into her hair.

She glanced over the steering wheel. The field was dancing before her. There was water in the furrows and the Mégane made slow progress. The wheels kept spinning and the rear of the car swung out to the side. More bullets burrowed into the metal without her hearing the shots. Silencers, she thought. They're using silencers.

Asile d'enfants hired professional killers.

From far away furious cries reached her ears. She realised to her amazement that they were coming from her belly and throat. Louise shut her mouth and the cries stopped. A strangely unreal calm filled her head. The engine noise, the blows against the undercarriage, and the groaning of the bodywork all became quieter. Faces popped into her head. Niksch, Taro and Hollerer staring at her, then Niksch again, then the images froze on a child's face.

Pham.

She heard a shrill humming and ducked in terror as a projectile thudded into the dashboard, shattering the speedometer. She pressed her foot down, but the accelerator was already on the floor.

Pham, 3½, Vietnam.

Pham, who couldn't wait to meet his new parents. Who had become a commodity and had cost five or ten, or maybe fifteen thousand dollars. Pham, who had vanished without trace.

She manoeuvred the Mégane slightly to the right and turned her head towards the road. The Sharan was facing the right way again and the passengers were coming back out of the darkness. Two of the three men who'd fired shots were running into the field after her. The third was hurrying back to the Audi.

More bullets hit the passenger side, but they had no penetration and ricocheted off. She was too far away.

Fifty metres further on she hit more solid ground – a meadow. Taking her foot off the pedal, she allowed the car to freewheel. Without letting the two men out of her sight she opened the last miniature of Jägermeister, tipped the contents onto a tissue and held it against the bleeding side of her head. The pain returned with a fury.

Glass crunched as she sank back into the seat. A grazing shot. Painful, but by no means fatal. Worse was that her mobile had been destroyed by a richochet.

The Sharan blocked her view of the three passengers. Now she was almost sure that Annegret Schelling was among them, but who were the others? And where had Asile taken the children? To the farms Lederle had mentioned? Still so many questions and so few answers. Who was in the car? Where was Pham? Why were people being murdered and others abducted if this was "just" about illegal adoption? It would earn two to three hundred thousand dollars per year at most, and involve several people, all keen for a share of the profit?

But was it just about arranging adoptions? What sort of parents did children like ten-year-old Areewan from Thailand get?

The third man had reached the Audi. With his lights off he drove down the small embankment into the field. The two other men had closed to within a hundred metres of Louise, but had slowed and weren't shooting anymore. All she could hear were the drone of the Mégane's engine and her breathing. Otherwise, silence.

Here they were again: Niksch, Taro and the blurred face of a Thai girl with long black hair. And Pham.

The silence grew oppressive. The silence of the abyss. The emptiness into which Taro and Pham had vanished. A silence where no answers existed, only questions. Her eye caught the stereo. She turned it on and switched to cassette.

Beethoven, "*Für Elise*".

The Audi had driven some way across the field, but its progress was sluggish, the driver encountering the same problems. The two other men were now attempting a pincer movement: one coming diagonally from up ahead, the other from behind.

She changed into first gear and put her foot down. The men in the field shot at once, but only the one in front was close, and therefore dangerous. She raised her weapon and fired. The passenger window shattered. The man immediately disappeared from view.

On the hard ground the Mégane accelerated quickly. She looked straight ahead at the Sharan. In the beam of her headlights she could see the driver staring back at her. On the other side there was movement. The doors opened and the three figures jumped in.

She turned her lights on full beam. The driver seemed to be shouting something. He kept turning around, then faced the front again. His right arm was gesticulating and the Sharan kangarooed along. Boní was about twenty metres from the road. She took her foot off the acclerator but did not brake.

Then came the second theme of "*Für Elise*". She wondered whether Pham would like the music. Bermann played Mozart to his unborn children. What did prospective parents in the Far East play to their unborn children? What did Tommo and Landen play to their unborn child? Mozart? Beethoven? Bach? Most likely Bach. What would she do? Would she alternate between Beethoven and Barclay James Harvest?

The first theme repeated as she reached the embankment. She glanced at the approaching Sharan. Good timing, she thought.

The impact was not as violent as she had expected. The Sharan's door was surprisingly robust. She saw the driver yell a metre in front of her and fancied she could hear his voice.

The metre became half a metre.

The bonnet of the Mégane flew open, obstructing her view. Steam shot up in a fountain. The music played on.

She took off her belt and leaped out of the car. The collision had given the Sharan a shunt; its front wheels jolted onto the pasture and the back of the car swerved across the road. As she ran around the back of the Mégane she fired a random shot into the field. In the darkness muzzle fire flared.

Screams were coming from the Sharan. One male and several female voices. She wrenched open the back door. The courtesy light came on and she found herself staring into the terrified face of an oriental woman. "No!" the woman screamed in English. "No! Please! No!" Bonì's gaze fell on her swollen belly. The woman was highly pregnant.

"Police," she said in English.

The woman said nothing.

Beside her sat Annegret Schelling, holding the back of her head and groaning. Her blonde hair was covered in blood. The driver, too, was moaning softly. He had slumped over the gearstick but Louise couldn't see any blood.

Only the woman in the passenger seat was silent. She had turned and was coolly staring at Louise. A delicate Thai woman, twenty years old at most and very beautiful. Well-proportioned, narrow cheeks, eyes as deep as oceans, an exotic dream, a lifelong dream. Every man's dream.

"Natchaya," Louise muttered.

The woman sunk back into her seat and stared into the darkness.

Bonì glanced across the roof of the car. The Audi was still in the field, its engine running but both doors on the driver's side open. A shadow was kneeling in the place where one of the men had disappeared from view. Frenzied voices drifted over. It took her a moment to identify the language. Not Romanian or Bulgarian or Polish, but French. With no accent.

They were French, not eastern Europeans.

Shit, you've got to get me to Steiner!

Can you get up?

Ow! Careful!

Can you stand?

I don't know! Shit, you've really got to get me to Steiner! Fucking hell!

Two voices. Where was the third man? He'd been further from the road, but must have reached the Audi by now. Why couldn't she see him?

Quickly she turned back to the Sharan. What should she do now? She couldn't arrest anybody as she was in France. Not to mention her sick leave.

And she was alone. Without a phone.

And she didn't know where the third man was.

But she couldn't just run. She needed information; she had to know where the children were, how they came to Asile d'enfants and where Jean Berger was.

She slammed the door and ran to the other side of the car.

Annegret Schelling fell towards her when she yanked open the door. Pushing her back in, Bonì hissed, "Where are the children?"

Schelling just moaned.

Right, you're coming with me then, Louise thought, heaving her out of the car. But Schelling could not even stand, let alone walk. Her legs buckled, she fell to her knees with a whimper and vomited.

Louise cursed and opened the passenger door. Natchaya did not look at her, the woman's eyes were half closed. With a soft but surprisingly deep voice she was humming a tune to herself. It took Bonì a moment to recognise "*Für Elise*".

"You're coming with me," she said, grabbing Natchaya's arm.

They ran across the pasture towards the trees, Natchaya in front, Bonì close behind. Although she was delicate, Natchaya moved energetically. She didn't make a sound, whereas Louise was soon panting. After a few minutes Louise told her to stop and she turned around.

There was still no trace of the third man. He couldn't be injured as she hadn't shot at him. Had she failed to spot him by the Audi? Was he already on his way to "Steiner" with the other two?

It was possible. But it was more likely that he was following her.

She tried to remember how many shots she had fired. Four? Five? Which left her with three bullets, four at most.

Natchaya eyed her indifferently and didn't offer any resistance. What was going through the woman's mind? Was she waiting for an opportunity to escape? Sink a knife into her back?

Louise realised that she hadn't searched for weapons. She felt the pistol with both hands. A warm, smooth body that didn't flinch, didn't yield and curiously entrusted itself to her hands.

Natchaya was still looking at her, her expression unchanged. Bonì kneeled and made a swift check of the insides of the woman's legs and ankles. No weapons. She stood up. It was too dark to make out anything in Natchaya's eyes. She radiated a peculiar lack of determination. The un- ending, passive patience of an old dog. Or of a humiliated younger one.

A poor analogy, she thought, and got moving again.

When they reached the trees Louise realised they wouldn't offer any protection. They weren't close enough together and the trunks were too slim. The women would have to go on.

But she couldn't. Gasping, she leaned against a tree and pulled Natchaya towards her. For a few moments she stared into the darkness from which they had come.

No movement, no sounds, no shadows. She couldn't see what was happening on the road as the pasture sloped down to the Rhine, obstructing the view.

"Have you got a mobile?" Bonì whispered.

Natchaya shrugged almost imperceptibly.

"Do you understand what I'm saying?"

Another slight twitch of the shoulders. Louise thought of Harald

Mahler. Was he Natchaya's husband? Her brother, her father? Had he driven the M.P.V.? His name sounded German at any rate. She pursed her lips? "No? English? Français?"

Natchaya shook her head.

"Rubbish," Louise said.

Soon afterwards they came to a broad path that ran alongside a water course, probably the Rhône–Rhine Canal. North must be to the left and south to the right. To the north was Ottmarsheim, the nearest border crossing. It couldn't be far, a few kilometres. She pointed left.

After a few metres she realised they couldn't walk along the path; their footsteps were too noisy on the sandy ground. She pushed Natchaya onto the strip of grass between the path and the canal. The girl's body gave way immediately. A creature without a will, without resistance. Or was Louise not an enemy in her eyes?

Ten minutes later Louise was spent. "Stop," she grunted, sinking to her knees. Natchaya came to her. Her breathing was heavier now too.

Bonì let her gaze wander across the dark pasture. No movement, no sounds, no shadows. Where was the third man? Was he not following them after all?

She felt her temple. The wound had stopped bleeding and the pain had subsided. She needed something to eat and drink, a telephone, Justin Muller, Bermann and Lederle. A new car. Richard Landen. And a pee.

Come on, she thought. Keep going. But she stayed on the ground.

Only gradually did she become aware that something had changed. It was even quieter than a few seconds ago. She could no longer hear Natchaya breathing. Louise looked up. The woman was standing in profile, staring into the darkness to the west of the path. Bonì followed her gaze with her eyes.

Nothing.

Just a sudden bright light and at that same moment an ice-cold pain in her left shoulder.

Then she was lying on her back staring up at the sky. Into large eyes, a dark face looking down at her coldly. Something strange had happened. The eyes and face were blurring. She blinked, but it didn't help. A cool liquid ran down her temples. She could feel her pistol being wrenched away.

A second face appeared, a man's face. "The bitch is alive," it said in French.

Not eastern Europeans. She felt the urge to laugh. Frenchmen who looked like eastern Europeans. Who sometimes spoke like eastern Europeans and sometimes like Frenchmen.

"Goodbye," said the second man in a friendly tone. There was movement, she heard a metallic click.

The face with the large eyes vanished for a moment. Then it was back. In French it said, "No, I'll do it."

"What?"

"Give me your gun."

What are you doing? Louise thought.

Waves of pain seared down her left side. Now the pain was hot and wet, and she grasped what had happened. What the *something strange* was that had happened. For the first time in her life she had a bullet inside her. She felt the urge to laugh again. Then she wanted to cry.

She tried to focus. The entry wound must be below her collar bone. She thought she could feel the bullet. Hello, she thought. Welcome, my little, wicked friend.

Above her an automatic pistol fitted with a silencer was passed from one hand to the other.

What are you doing? Bonì thought.

"Is someone going to pick us up?" the face with the large eyes said.

"No idea."

"Have you got a mobile?"

"Sure."

"Call my husband."

The man's face disappeared. In a swift movement a small hand covered Louise's mouth while the other pressed the muzzle of the silencer against her head. The face with the large eyes came closer to her cheek. She took in its odour; it smelled soft, foreign, young. What are you doing? she thought. The face whispered in German, "You . . . can . . . not . . . save . . . world. Save your*self*."

The muzzle slid along her skull. The sky went "plop" twice, then came the night.

When she awoke she was lying in a bush, branches blocking her view. It was cold. She could hear water flowing somewhere nearby. For a moment Bonì tried to work out where she was and what she was doing in this place, but she could find no answer. She was seized by panic. She wanted to get up but her body refused to move. Instead there was a biting pain in her limbs. She decided to stay lying there.

To stay lying there as long as possible.

She was woken by Calambert. No, he said in her head. No.

Beyond the branches it was now lighter. She was terribly cold. The pain seemed to have subsided, so long as she made no attempt to move at least. She still didn't know where she was and what she was doing there. She pictured herself sitting in Landen's living room. They both stood up and she left because she didn't want to go into the kitchen where Niksch and the china cat were. But she knew that in Landen's eyes she had a special gift.

Then she drove to the Kanzan-an.

All of a sudden her memory returned. The Sharan, Natchaya, her little, wicked friend from the darkness. The false eastern Europeans and Natchaya's bizarre words.

Pham and Areewan and the other children, at risk of disappearing for ever.

She tried to sit up, but her left side was heavy and immobile, like a chunk of metal. Only a resurgence of the pain proved to her that she was in fact flesh and blood. Moaning, she sank back down.

Natchaya and the man had dragged her into a bush between the pasture and the canal. Why hadn't Natchaya killed her? Clearly she wasn't so passive after all, she had shown the determination to go her own way. She had deceived her accomplices and prevented the murder of another police officer. Even though this officer had seen and understood too much.

What did that mean? Was Natchaya only *a little bit* evil? If so, how could she work for an organisation that trafficked children? Children from the same continent, the same country as hers?

A thought crept along the edge of her consciousness, but she no longer had the strength to focus on it.

It was simpler to think of Calambert again. Calambert was more palpable than ever before. Since the bullet had entered Louise's body there were similarities between the two of them. She had seen the sky from the same perspective as he had. She had felt exactly the same as him, been in shock like him. He was now in every fibre of her body. He was a part of her. And she of him.

She took him with her into unconsciousness.

Bonì was found by a dog.

When she came to, the dog was lying on her legs, whining. Girls' voices were calling him. The dog began to bark and leaped up. Shit, stay here, she thought. The dog ran off. Shortly afterwards he came back with the girl.

The girl started to scream.

"The bitch is alive," Bonì said.

14

Lederle shook his head in disbelief, Bermann cursed her, Almen-broich praised and reprimanded her, Barbara Franke kept saying "shit" over and over again. The faces and voices and flowers changed in rapid succession. Only the hospital smell stayed the same. She had no urgent desire to drink, but she was looking forward to her first sip like a child looks forward to Christmas. She waited for Hollerer and Landen, but neither came.

Someone put a newspaper with her photograph on the bed.

Years passed.

After three days Bermann brought some blurred visitors from France: Justin Muller and Hugo Chervel. They held flowers and a basket of fruit, but their faces were serious. "Ten minutes," Bermann said in German. "She won't manage more. And not one word that I can't understand." He sat to her right, Muller and Chervel to her left.

"Feeling any better?" Muller asked, putting a hand on hers, and taking it away again immediately.

She nodded. She dimly recalled that he'd already been there at some point over the past few days. But she couldn't remember if they had spoken. "Almost back to my old self," she muttered in French. The men said nothing, they seemed uncomfortable at the prospect.

Chervel bent forward and rested his elbows on his knees. His face was close to hers. He smelled of cigarettes and aftershave. His eyes were red, the pupils small and light blue, like a husky's. He wore a grey suit and a blue shirt with a starched collar. A gentle, lurking, lone wolf. She liked him. Like Justin Muller, he tried as far as possible to structure the cooperation with their German colleagues according to the needs of the case.

"Your car," he said in French.

She nodded and with her right hand pulled the blanket up to her neck. She couldn't remember the last time she'd been washed.

"I took it in to Altkirch today, to my brother-in-law. He's got a workshop, you see. He's looking after it."

Louise nodded again.

"You were lucky. A Renault radiator against the reinforced side of a V.W. Could have been a different outcome." He grinned and glanced at Bermann.

Bermann said, "Cut to the point, Chervel."

"Tell us what happened, Louise," Chervel said.

"There's a report," she said in French. Chervel smiled meekly and said nothing.

So she explained again what happened after her second visit to the Kanzan-an.

Muller was silent, but Chervel had plenty of questions. What had happened with Taro exactly a week ago? Why had she spent the whole night with him? Since when had she harboured suspicions about Asile d'enfants? And, most important, why? Why had she taken Natchaya with her? Why had she been working alone?

"None of your business," Bermann said in German.

Why hadn't she notified anyone prior to the shootout?

"Ditto," Bermann said in Latin.

Later Chervel listed in a soft voice all the international agreements and national laws she had violated. The fact that she had been "involved in ashootout with French citizens" didn't make things any better.

She rolled her eyes.

"Utter nonsense," Bermann said in German.

"Yes," Chervel said. "But we have a problem."

She sensed that Bermann was leaning on the right-hand side of the bed. Gravity began to pull her towards him. She wondered how he'd react if her bottom suddenly rolled on top of his hands. "If we'd sent a request for mutual assistance," Bermann said, "we'd still have been waiting for an answer at Christmas, for God's sake."

"We?" Bonì said, but none of the three men took notice of her. She glanced at the alarm clock. Ten minutes had become half an hour. The men gave the impression they wanted to spend the whole day in her room.

Through the blanket she could feel one of Bermann's fingers touch her bum. The mattress returned to the horizontal.

Chervel leaned back. "Right," he said with a sigh. "Let's look at what we've got. We've got a monastery in France where French people, Germans and Asians live. But the monastery belongs to us because it's in France. Then we've got a V.W. Sharan with a Cologne number plate. In theory that belongs to you, unless it's in France. The same is true for the owner. We have a Swiss organisation with its H.Q. in Basel, that belongs to Switzerland . . ."

"Switzerland isn't a problem," Bermann butted in. "If we have to go into Switzerland we jump into the car, call operations in Basel, get the public prosecutor on the line, the prosecutor says, 'Are you armed?', we say, 'Yes we are,' and he says, 'Good luck, then, you won't come to any harm.' The Italians aren't a problem either. Even the Russians aren't a problem." He gave a satisfied grin.

"France *is* a problem," Chervel said, now grinning himself. "So, what else do we have? We've got three French pros. They're ours, even if it's likely they've killed a German policeman and drive a German car. We've got German and French employees of Asile; we can share them depending on where they are. Have I forgotten anything?"

"The children," Bonì said.

"Aha," Chervel said.

"Why don't you clear out of here and find them?"

*

A little later a chubby, young senior doctor came in and supplied her with medical details from the foot of the bed. No broken bones, no damaged organs, just muscles and fat tissue as well as an inflammation from the dirt that had entered the wound. She nodded, exhausted. The doctor spoke in a southern Baden dialect, quietly, but enthusiastically. His hands were in the side pockets of his doctor's coat. He kept moving his arms out sideways, as far as the material would allow, resembling an exuberant white putto. She suspected this was the first bullet wound he had treated. His first encounter with a serious crime. With *evil*.

"We were lucky," he said. "With an injury to the arteria brachialis, that's to say the artery in your upper arm – we'd have had circulatory shock after thirty minutes to two hours, so . . . loss of blood, tachyarrhythmia, which means rapid heartbeat, a drop in blood pressure, impaired consciousness, which means we wouldn't have been sufficiently responsive etc. and we'd have needed emergency surgery, but that wouldn't have been possible because we . . . I mean *you* . . . wouldn't have been here."

He smiled sheepishly.

"What else?"

"What do you mean, 'What else?'"

"What else have you established? In general?"

"In general?"

"Is my blood O.K.?"

"Yes, and you're not pregnant, if that's what you mean."

"That's what I meant. Can I keep the bullet?"

"The bullet? Ah, the *bullet*. No, it's with your colleagues in forensics."

The following day, when she was able to sit up again, she called Anatol. He couldn't talk because he had customers. Although he said little more than "Hi" and "Yes" and "Wow!" she sensed he was relieved and pleased. "We've got something to celebrate," she said. "Come whenever you want, but bring a bottle of prosecco."

"O.K. Tonight at nine?"

"I need a jumper. And don't forget the prosecco."

Anatol's laughter sounded devious, as if he knew the real purpose of the prosecco and was deliberating whether he should do her the favour or not.

Later that day Katrin Rein appeared at her bedside. The pretty doll's face was pale, her hand cold, her eyes frightened.

"You're not going to start with your lecture now, are you?" Bonì said.

Katrin shook her head.

"Have you been worrying again?"

Katrin nodded.

She sat on the chair by the bed and emptied Louise's water glass in one gulp. "Sorry. I'm not good at hospitals. Does it still hurt?"

"Sometimes."

"And you were really *shot*?"

Louise nodded wearily. For a ridiculous moment she felt almost proud. Then she remembered how she knew Katrin and the pride gave way to resignation. Katrin Rein, the abyss woman. Whose job it was to have a good poke around in the wound, to make it heal better.

"W...w...where...?"

She pointed cursorily to her right temple, her left shoulder.

Katrin's eyes widened, she poured herself more water and drained the glass. Then she wiped a few drops from the light fuzz on her upper lip. "I did my Ph.D. on the psychological effects of gunshot wounds."

"On the victim or their therapist?"

Katrin stared at her for a moment, and then started to laugh.

Bonì forced a smile. The therapist and patient were joking with each other. Was that a good sign?

In the afternoon Lederle took Louise for a stroll in a quiet, empty corridor. He linked arms with her, clearing his throat in embarrassment as he did so. It dawned on Louise that in all the time they had worked together he'd never touched her, apart from a shake of the hand. It was a nice feeling. It felt like starting again.

He told her he had visited Hollerer the day before. His recovery was slow and he couldn't remember a thing. He now knew that Niksch was dead. Bonì said nothing. The thought of Hollerer and Niksch had destroyed the feeling of starting again. She didn't want to start again, she thought. She wanted to go on living with everything that had happened. In some way she felt that starting again would be a betrayal of Niksch.

Hollerer wouldn't be starting again either.

She decided to visit him as soon as she was able.

"How's Antonia?"

"Antonia's fine, thank you. She sends her regards."

"You said there's something I ought to know. What did you mean?"

"Not here," Lederle said.

"Where?"

"When this is all over, we'll go out for dinner and I'll tell you then."

"You're being transferred."

Lederle smiled fleetingly. "Patience, my dear."

She grinned and laid her hand on his.

Lederle told her that the manhunt hadn't yet thrown up any results. Jean Berger, Annegret Schelling, Natchaya, the Frenchmen, the pregnant woman, the children – all of them had vanished from the face of the earth. The Sharan, on the other hand, had been found. They'd blown it up in a quarry to the west of Mulhouse. The French forensics team were putting together puzzles from charred pieces while the German request for mutual assistance was being processed.

One promising lead was the name "Steiner". A Steiner who might be a doctor. The French were looking; the Germans were looking. "If you're right, they could do with a doctor."

She thought Lederle's voice sounded too sober. But then he said with the same detachment, "I'd hoped to be spared something like this. Years ago we had a case where a ten-year-old girl had been passed around her relatives. I was supposed to head up the task force, but I chickened out. I didn't want to . . . to see any photos or videos – do you understand? I mean, I don't like children, but I didn't want to see that. I didn't want to *believe* it."

"And now?"

"And now?" Lederle repeated. He shrugged. "Now it's not so important what I see and what I don't see."

"Why not?"

"Why not?" Lederle frowned. They were approaching the end of the corridor. Behind them came the sound of soft footsteps, which went away again. The back of Lederle's hand brushed her breast. His hand recoiled, then he said, "By the way, have I given you an apology yet?"

"No-one's given me an apology."

"Then I'll do it now. Please forgive me. You were right. We were . . . oh, I don't know. All those strange Japanese people – it makes you think things you shouldn't." He laughed. "You think before you think."

She nodded. Yes, she had been right, but had she acted correctly? She couldn't answer that. As ever, there was a lot she could have done differently, perhaps *ought* to have done differently. Think things through more thoroughly, be better prepared before acting.

That morning Bermann had asked again and again why the fuck she hadn't called. Why the fuck hadn't she had the courage to come to him and Almenbroich with her theory – *at the right time*? She replied that she hadn't had a theory, just a feeling. So why the fuck didn't you trust your feeling? Bermann had said. I did, you fool, she protested, otherwise I wouldn't be lying here.

"We've just got to get them now," Lederle said.

"Yes."

They had stopped by the window at the end of the corridor. "It's snowing," Bonì said.

"That's what happens in winter."

They turned around and resumed their walking.

"What about the names? Are they genuine?"

Lederle nodded. "They seem to be."

Some things they had managed to find out, others not. They knew nothing about Jean Berger. The report from their Swiss colleagues should arrive today or tomorrow. Harald Mahler, Klaus Fröbick, Annegret Schelling led discreet lives and had no previous convictions. Mahler was an expert witness in compensation cases resulting from car accidents. Fröbick was a secondary school teacher, while Schelling had worked for a bank until a few months ago, since when she'd been unemployed. Fröbick had a family; Schelling was divorced. All three had been regular visitors to Thailand since the early 1990s and Schelling had travelled to other Far Eastern countries too. She lived in a one-bedroom apartment in Freiburg. Fröbick was a member of Freiburg F.C. and went to pretty much every home and away game with his two sons. At the school he was neither popular nor unpopular. He taught German and English, and at home took further education courses online. Besides exercises and learning material his computer contained several hundred video files – all child pornography, including rape. They had found no videos or images on Schelling's or Mahler's computers.

A few days earlier Lederle and Anne Wallmer had been sitting on a flowery sofa in a terraced house in Villingen-Schwenningen, drinking coffee with evaporated milk and questioning a mistrustful Margaret Schelling about her daughter. On the windowsill stood photographs of little Annegret. Annegret ballet dancing. Riding. Holding her father's hand. With her mother by her father's grave. I really don't understand what you want from us, the mother had said. *What* is Annegret supposed to have done?

They'd run a thorough check on the family – after all, many abusers were victims of abuse themselves – but found nothing. No charges, no rumours, no suspicious visits to the doctor, no unusual occurrences according to what they knew. As far as the Schelling parents were concerned, at least, everything seemed to be in order. Lederle hesitated, then said, "But we don't want to rule anything out anymore."

They'd stopped outside her room. "I was waiting at a traffic light today," Lederle said, "and there was a family crossing the road: father, mother, ten- or eleven-year-old daughter. I couldn't help wondering whether . . ." He shook his head.

Louise looked at him. "It's only natural."

"No, it's not. I mean, I don't wonder whether the man coming this way is a bank robber, or if the woman over there is a murderer."

"The hidden figures relating to bank robbery and murder aren't as high as with child abuse."

"You're right. By the way, the man coming this way is your father."

Louise's father sat at the little table in her room, looking alternately at the plaster on her temple and the bandage around her shoulder. She had never seen him so distraught. A small, wizened, empty, grey cocoon that threatened to turn to dust if you touched it. "Come on, Papa," she said. "It was virtually nothing."

Her father didn't seem to have heard. His eyes wandered from her shoulder to her temple. It was as if he couldn't understand why the plaster and bandage were there. What they meant, which was that she was still alive. That he hadn't lost his second child as well.

She sighed. What now? What could she talk to him about now, without risking that the cocoon might shatter? Not about what had happened in France, certainly not about Germain or her mother. Should she tell him about Anatol? About her feelings for Landen, whose wife would soon be having a baby? About Enni, who'd found the centre of the universe in her belly.

Should she confess that she couldn't wait for the prosecco Anatol was going to bring?

Louise grunted wearily. "I'm going to have another lie-down, Papa."

Her father got up and took her hand. She let him lead her to the bed and tuck her in. Then he sat down and clasped her hand.

She remembered how he had often taken her and Germain to bed when they were children. My little butterfly, he used to say, holding her hands tight.

She stared at his grey hands and began to cry.

When Louise stopped weeping it was dark. Snowflakes flew against the window. Her father's grasp was still as firm. At some point, when she had the time, she would tell him about Anatol and Landen, about Enni and the roshi. Let him turn his nose up all he liked, she was going to get him back into her life. She would confront him with herself, her liquid friends and her professional problems, so he knew who she was. Being alive, she thought, was more than just picking up the telephone when it rang.

And at some point, when she had the time, she would help him remember what really had happened with her family in the 1970s. What he had done on a student demonstration.

But not now. Now she wanted to sleep. "Go home, Papa," she said quietly.

She felt the mattress move, and then she fell asleep.

At 8.30 p.m. the telephone rang. Half asleep, Bonì sat up and reached for it. She caught sight of a note on the bedside table. *I'll come back in the morning, darling. I hope you don't mind me staying in your apartment while you're in here. Love, Papa.*

In her apartment?

She sank into the pillows. When had she given him the key to her apartment? She couldn't remember. Louise was gripped by panic as she thought of the cupboard below the sink. The mirrored cabinet above the washbasin in the bathroom. Underwear all over the bedroom, sitting room and bathroom. Barclay James Harvest in the C.D. player. The point at which she was going to get her father back into her life had come quicker than was strictly comfortable.

With a groan she put the receiver to her ear. "Yes?"

"How are you?" It was Barbara Franke.

"Better."

"Great. I'll come and visit you again tomorrow. You were right, by the way."

"About what?"

"Areewan. Her mother gave her up for adoption in early 2000 and she was adopted shortly afterwards. By the same couple that had already adopted her."

"Have you got a name?"

"Two. You know them: Harald and Natchaya Mahler."

Bonì wondered why she wasn't surprised. Then she realised that she was thinking just like Lederle: not ruling anything out. She couldn't be surprised anymore.

Natchaya and Areewan. Two more loose ends tied up.

"They're sisters," Barbara said. "It's a big family. Natchaya is the eldest, Areewan the youngest. Natchaya and two other sisters disappeared years ago, after the father died. To go and find work. The mother testified in court during the Areewan trial. You can imagine what that means."

"Prostitution?"

"No," Barbara said. "It means child abuse."

Anatol arrived shortly after she'd hung up. "Hi!" he said.

"Hi!"

"The things you get up to!"

They had a brief, but oddly intimate kiss, then Anatol put the bottle of prosecco on the bedside table. They gazed at each other. He looked younger than she remembered. Over the past few days she'd furnished her image of him with crows' feet, a few white hairs and a couple of extra kilos. Maybe it was just that he didn't exude the same weary serenity as before.

He seemed really pleased to see her, relieved too. Shocked and relieved. Only in his eyes did she detect a strange exhaustion.

"Unbelievable," he said.

She stroked his hair. "What?"

"No idea. Just unbelievable."

They both laughed awkwardly.

His eyes drifted to the bandage around her shoulder. "I mean, what the hell?" he said.

"Come on, let's drink to it."

That night one nightmare followed hot on the heels of another. Anatol and Enni featured in most of them. They were naked and ten years old at most, lying on sofas, beds, floors and letting her do whatever she pleased with them. At one point Landen came and said, "You shouldn't do that." She replied, "It's good for them. They want it. Believe me. They're safe with me. They don't get ill here. They don't have to live on the streets. They get enough to eat. They're loved. Do you want a go too?" "No," Landen said and left.

15

Lederle woke her early the next morning. His hand rested on her un-injured shoulder. He seemed to have taken pleasure in touching her. "Get dressed," he said.

They had found Steiner. He lived in a secluded valley in the Vosges, to the southwest of Strasbourg. His wife and at least one man were with him. A man who drove a red Audi and had arrived a few days ago, according to eyewitnesses.

The raid was scheduled for 8.00 a.m. The Germans had permission to observe. But they weren't allowed to take their weapons across the border or interrogate anyone. In fact, they weren't allowed to do anything. As ever. Lederle shrugged.

Chervel, Justin Muller and Bermann had moved into a village near the valley the evening before. Which meant that Lederle must have known yesterday afternoon. She resisted the urge to comment. At least he was making sure she'd be involved.

He stood at the window while she got dressed. It was still dark outside. His head was in the middle of a snowstorm. "What about the children?" she said, slipping on Anatol's jumper.

He shrugged.

"Do the French know I'm coming?"

"Yes."

"What's it looking like on, um, the diplomatic front?"

Lederle giggled. "Bad. Almenbroich's going to have to go crawling to Paris to stop them throwing you in the Bastille."

She asked him to fasten the belt in her jeans, which he did. "Will you help me put my shoes on?"

Lederle held on to the table while he kneeled. His hands were cold and trembling. He eased her feet into her winter boots, then said, "Could you help me up?"

She placed her right hand under his armpit and he struggled to his feet. In the past he had been quicker to get going in the mornings. She linked arms with him. When they were in the corridor she asked, "What sort of a doctor is Steiner?"

"An eye doctor," Lederle said.

The snow on the ground had frozen. February had begun with a Siberian chill, and for a week now the temperature had not risen above 5 degrees in the daytime. She longed for her hospital bed. For Anatol. For Provence.

And for Landen. For the thousandth time she wondered why he hadn't come to visit her. She'd call him today and ask. Explain why she hadn't been able to stay for lunch.

As they drove along Matsuyamaallee she thought of Enni. Of the centre of the universe, of the roshi. As soon as she could, she wanted to go to the Kanzan-an and ask the roshi how you found *own-nature*. It might help her in the abyss.

Later they spoke about Taro. Lederle didn't hold out much hope either. The three Frenchmen hadn't shied away from killing a policeman so why would they have spared Taro's life? He had seen, heard, known something that might be dangerous for Asile d'enfants. He needed to be silenced. "He can't still be alive," Lederle said, sounding dispassionate again.

She nodded. Niksch and Taro. Two people she hadn't known for more than thirty-six hours. And yet they'd left traces in her life. The world felt different without them. She pledged to ensure it would remain that way. Her encounters with the roshi had made her realise how important it was for people to leave traces in another person's life. Even if you had known them only fleetingly.

At Bad Kronzingen they took the B31. There was scarcely any traffic, but Lederle kept to 60 k.p.h. Louise thought of the sheer thrill Niksch had got from driving. His glee when he let the back of the car swing out and then brought it under control again.

Niksch had been buried while she was in hospital. Almenbroich and Bermann were present, but not Lederle. In his situation nobody could expect him to attend a funeral, but he was the only one she'd have wanted to ask about Niksch's final journey.

They crossed the border at Breisach, then took the fast road between Colmar and Strasbourg, exiting at Sélestat. With almost no warning the mountains now loomed before them. They turned off to the north before St Dié. To the left of them it was pitch black, to the right it was beginning to get light.

Louise's father's family came from the Vosges. Friendly teachers, priests and grocers from Gérardmer, humble Catholics who slaved away in small, cramped rooms. For the first time she tried to imagine the seismic shock when her father brought a Protestant German woman through the narrow doorframe of the house in which he had been born. Had he known what he was doing? Had he only married outside the family tradition to afford himself some distance – peacefully, but definitively?

At any rate he was only successful to a certain extent. The Catholics from Gérardmer had opened their arms wide and welcomed to their bosom the girl twice punished by destiny.

A short time later Lederle took a deep breath and said, "Fifty-eight children since 1997. Where are they, Louise? What's happened to them? Do they live somewhere near here? For how many of them is life one big martyrdom? How many of those fifty-eight children were sold to parents who didn't want children, but a sex object? All the slightly older ones? That's twenty-one of them. Twenty-one of the fifty-eight children are older than six. Have these twenty-one children all been victims of sexual abuse, Louise? Were they sold? Or were they hired out on demand for a few days or weeks to child molesters or people who produce porn? These are the questions I've been asking myself for days. But do you know why I can't sleep anymore?"

She did not reply.

"I can't sleep because I can't answer the question as to whether you can pass moral judgment on someone who's so desperate for a child that they'll pay to adopt one illicitly, because it can't be done through legal channels. That's my question, Louise. Can you pass moral judgment on these people? Yes, I know, it means children are degraded, they become goods; the welfare of the adoptive parents is given precedence over that of the children, the demand determines the supply etc. All that is *right*. But I wonder: how can we humans be expected to have the maturity to cope with our desire for a child when we can just get our wallets out? If we know that we can give a new-born baby from Asia or eastern Europe or South America a better life than in their orphanage back home? We buy *everything*, Louise, we buy animals, health, land, leisure, beauty, love – how the hell are we as consumers supposed to understand that there's a line we must not cross? Where do we find the inner strength to place abstract values above what is possibly our *greatest* desire of all?"

Lederle broke off, exhausted, breathing rapidly. Louise could not tell if he was expecting an answer. And she certainly didn't know what sort of an answer she could have given him. She knew of only two people she could rely on to answer these questions: Barbara Franke and the roshi. Barbara might have said that the purchase of a child given up for adoption and child abuse were two sides of the same coin. The status of the child was the same: a commodity. The roshi might have said that you had to be at peace with yourself to muster the inner strength Lederle was talking about.

For the rest of the journey she wondered how she might find answers to those and other questions so long as she still relied on alcohol to make life bearable. And that the same thing lay behind the need for alcohol and the fatal longing to have an adoptive child: human desire, the root of all suffering according to Landen.

In a tiny village that still lay in total darkness they came across a convoy of French cars. Chervel, Muller and Bermann were with them. Bermann gave a grunt of surprise when he saw Bonì. Chervel and Muller shook her hand.

She got into a Citroën with Lederle. Two black, uniformed officers sat in the front.

"Didn't you tell him?"

"He doesn't have to know everything."

She looked at Lederle. He'd changed over the past few weeks, he seemed more defiant and more stoical. She wondered how Antonia's chemotherapy was going, but she didn't dare ask. And if his expression – the half-closed eyes and downturned corners of his mouth – was anything to go by, he didn't need to.

The convoy set off. One of the French policemen offered them a cigarette. They declined. He lit up and opened the passenger window slightly. The sun flashed between bare rock faces. Louise slumped in her seat. Her shoulder was aching, the smoke irritated her throat and ice-cold air lashed the right side of her head. She closed her eyes and opened them straight away. She felt a stir of excitement. They had Steiner! The first concrete lead to Asile d'enfants. To Natchaya, to Pham. Maybe there was hope.

But the excitement vanished as quickly as it had appeared. For Niksch and probably Taro too, the hope came too late.

The two French policemen took them to a low hill on the left-hand slope of the valley. Hugo Chervel and Bermann were waiting in an un-marked Peugeot. They looked over. Chervel gave her a cursory wave.

When they got into the Peugeot the Citroën turned and disap-peared. The first rays of sun arrived in the valley. They were a little way from the top of the hill and could not see the house in the valley. "Fifteen minutes," Chervel said.

They listened over the radio as the French officers took up their positions. Bermann couldn't understand everything; Bonì translated individual words. Lederle said nothing, it was as if his thoughts were elsewhere. He was right: when all this was over they had to talk. But she was beginning to worry about what he would say.

At 8.00 a.m. on the dot the order to launch the raid came over the radio. Chervel nodded to them and they got out. They walked side by side to the summit. It was freezing, but at least there was no wind. Chervel peered through some binoculars.

The snowy valley lay about fifty metres below, while Steiner's house was a hundred metres away as the crow flies. A simple, faceless, grey house, not particularly large with a pointed roof. The Venetian blinds at the windows were closed. Plain-clothes police officers crouched close to the outside walls like huge black insects. About halfway up the hill, three or four snipers squatted in the snow behind rocks. Twenty metres off to the side of the house was another large building, probably a stable or a barn.

Now the patrol cars approached. Uniformed officers leaped out and used their vehicles as cover. Via megaphone the people inside the house were ordered to give themselves up. Nothing happened.

Chervel lowered his binoculars and lit a cigarette.

"You might have thought to bring some chairs," Bermann said in German.

All of a sudden there was movement by the stable. Two officers brought a girl out and walked her to the nearest patrol car. Bonì's eyes followed them. The girl was wearing a skirt, and she was small and slim. Black hair, dark complexion. From the Far East? It was hard to tell her age from this distance. Not a child anymore, but not a grown-up woman either.

"Teresa, the maid," Chervel said. "A Filipina. Catholic, twenty years old. She's been working for Steiner for three years. Two abortions, and now she's been sterilised. It's more practical."

Teresa, Bonì thought. Niksch and Theres. Theres and Niksch. "You're well informed," she said, taking the binoculars from him. She held them up to her eyes with her right hand.

"I always thought you *flics* had fewer powers than us," Bermann said. "*We* don't know if someone's been sterilised, or how many abortions they've had."

Chervel didn't respond.

By the time Bonì had focused the binoculars the girl was already in the police car. Her hands were in front of her face and her head bowed. The car reversed then drove off.

She gave the binoculars back to Chervel. The house was still quiet. The voice over the megaphone reiterated its order, and then a third time shortly afterwards.

Nothing.

"Shit!" Chervel said. He lifted his radio. "Are you going in?"

"*Yes,*" a man's voice said.

Louise looked over at the French officers. None of them had a radio to their ear. Seconds passed without anything happening. Nobody seemed to be moving in the valley.

"I can't believe you didn't think of chairs," Bermann said.

One of the insects peeled away from the wall, raised his pistol and shot at the lock. Other insects snuck into the building. Panicked female screams.

No other shots.

"*Everything under control,*" the unknown man's voice said shortly afterwards.

Chervel tossed away his cigarette and looked at Bermann. "Standing room only here," he said.

A few minutes later the police officers led a woman and two men out of the house. The woman and one of the men wore coats, the second man only jeans and a jumper. The woman was wailing loudly and seemed to be in shock. Two policewomen supported her.

Bonì took the binoculars from Chervel's hand and focused on the man in jeans. Even though she hadn't got a clear sight of the driver of the red Audi, she was sure it was him. "What about the injured one?"

Chervel repeated her question into the radio.

"*We don't know yet,*" the voice of the invisible officer said.

The three people under arrest were put in different cars. More officers entered the house. The sunlight had crept a little further into the valley. A narrow strip of brightness lay on the side of the hill where the snipers were still in position.

"Can we have a brief chat with Steiner?" Bermann said.

"Not without official authorisation," Chervel said.

"Oh, come on, seeing as we're here."

"You're not here, Bermann. At some point there has to be an end to all these exceptions and favours."

Chervel took the binoculars that Bonì was holding out. "What about the children, Hugo? If we don't find out soon where the Asile lot are we'll never see the children again."

Chervel looked at her. His husky eyes didn't move. She knew what he was thinking. That the Asile people had disappeared a week ago. That in all likelihood the children weren't even with them anymore. "You'll get transcripts of the interrogations," was all he said.

"*Hugo?*" the man's voice from the radio asked.

"Yes?"

"*Steiner says he's dead.*"

"Shit!"

Lederle, who'd been standing motionless beside Louise, placed a hand on her forearm. She didn't know if he was trying to comfort her or stop her from running away. "It's O.K.," she said.

The second person to die because of her. But there were differences. Serious differences.

*

They returned to the car. Bermann sat in the passenger seat, while Lederle and she got in the back. Chervel put the key in the ignition, then turned around and said, "I've got to take you to the office."

Before she could respond, Bermann said, "Who have you got to take to the office? There's nobody here apart from you."

Chervel snorted and started the engine.

"No problem," Bonì said.

Chervel shrugged.

When they reached the road leading to Steiner's farmhouse the Citroën was already waiting for them. Chervel got out too. He came round to Louise and said, "Have you got a lawyer?"

"Yes."

"Is he any good at this stuff?"

"He's good at divorces."

Chervel smiled and kissed her on both cheeks. "I know someone in Kehl. I'll tell him to call you."

A day when everyone was looking after her. "Thanks."

They got in. Bermann opened the window on his side and said, "It was lovely not being here."

Chervel opened his arms. "How amusing you Germans can be. You're almost bearable this early in the morning."

On the way to Freiburg the excitement returned. They had Steiner, his wife and the driver of the Audi. They had the Filipino girl. Someone would tell them where Annegret Schelling, Natchaya and the children were. Where Pham was.

It struck Bonì that for her this was the most important thing. She needed to see Pham again, to know that he was in good hands. As he was the only one she'd met, he had become the face of all fifty-eight children on the Asile d'enfants lists.

But it was more than that, she felt. He was important for another reason. A bizarre reason connected to family, to a terraced house and a garden. To Landen.

"Try not to worry," Lederle said.

"I'm not." Louise blinked at the sun. Her shoulder ached, she was tired, she needed something to drink and she was afraid for Pham. There was nothing else worrying her. Apart from the fact that she was suddenly thinking about family, a terraced house and a garden. A 1970s role she was already too old for.

Lederle said, "These guys killed Niksch and shot Hollerer – Chervel knows that."

They arrived at the Rhine Plain. The sun vanished briefly behind winter clouds, before breaking through again. Family, a terraced house and a garden. Soft, cuddly dreams she'd had as a teenager while her parents were screaming at each other. Rose-tinted desires. Worse than that: Mick-desires. Not a week had passed without him urging her to give up her career.

"Besides, it was self-defence."

"It's alright, Reiner," Louise said, giving Lederle a reassuring pat on the thigh and wondering how she'd been able to communicate with this man for so long without touching him. "I'm going to have a little doze."

"Are you in pain?"

"No, just tired."

She closed her eyes and thought of the dead man. She saw him hurrying over to the Mégane from the side, then the passenger window shattered and he vanished. She couldn't recall his voice, only what he'd said. The pain, the panic in his words. *Shit, you've really got to get me to Steiner! Fucking hell!* She hadn't intended to kill him, but she felt no sympathy or remorse.

Then the dead man was standing in a garden and he looked like Landen. Beside him stood Pham. They were holding hands and gazing at Louise. They seemed to be waiting for her.

16

Her father was waiting for her at the hospital, sitting in the same chair as the day before, wearing the same suit. She could tell that he hadn't slept well. It made her dizzy to think that he had lain in the Anatol bedclothes. In a more hostile tone than she had intended, she said, "Papa, there's something we've got to discuss."

He nodded.

She sat on the bed. "I want you to move to a hotel."

"A hotel?" In astonishment he said, "-otel."

Slowly she lay down. Her shoulder throbbed, and only now did she realise how exhausted she was. How feeble and dispirited. Ever since her little, wicked friend had bored its way inside her she felt she was losing the will to revolt against the course of things. It had cut a swathe inside her where despondency and apathy were now thriving. An unfamiliar awareness of her impotence.

She heard her father stand up. Then she felt his hands on her feet. He untied her laces and took off her shoes.

She looked at him. "Thanks." From his expression she tried to work out whether he'd detected Anatol in her apartment. Tidied away her underwear, discovered her supplies of alcohol, glimpsed the abyss.

"Can I ask you something, Louise?"

"If you have to."

"Where were you?"

She mulled over whether to tell him about the Vosges. About how she'd thought of his family and Gérardmer on the way there. But she was too tired and said simply, "Away on duty."

He sat on the bed beside her and stared at her left shoulder, which was as bulked up as a rugby player's. "I don't want to press you, Louise, but what does away on duty mean? I haven't a clue about what you do. I know you work for Kripo and I know your rank and your colleague, Herr Lederle. But I've no idea what your office looks like, what cases you're working on or what precisely your tasks are."

"I never got the impression that these things interested you, Papa."

"Because I never asked. I knew you were a policewoman and that was enough, because I thought I knew what that meant. I was impressed, reassured and proud – it's a hugely important profession. More important than anything *I've* ever done. The idea that you were fighting crime for the rest of us gave me such admiration for you. My daughter is a policewoman." He smiled. "Whenever I read in the paper that the Kehl police had solved a crime I always thought, Louise is a policewoman in Freiburg. She keeps the peace in Freiburg. I never thought that she might die doing it."

"But I'm not *dying*, Papa."

She slid gingerly off the bed and went to the window. Outside everything was white, but it wasn't snowing. The sun reflected harshly on the snow-covered roofs and icy squares of grass. Out of the blue she found herself wondering if Chervel and Justin were interrogating the people they'd arrested. If Steiner was talking. If the Liebau task force had found more clues.

"I don't want to stay in a hotel," her father said from the bed. "I want to stay in your apartment. I feel I can get to know you better that way. And that we have a close relationship."

"Papa—"

"Please let me stay, Louise." He sounded solemn.

She turned to face him. Louise didn't want to think about these things. All that mattered to her now were Pham and the other children. Maybe Richard Landen too. She had no energy for anything else.

She nodded.

*

After her father had left, Louise fell asleep. With lunch came a doctor she had never seen before. He said, "We're going to take a look at that wound this afternoon, and if everything's O.K. you can go home tomorrow. Enjoy your lunch."

She sat up and took hold of the cutlery. "I don't want to go home yet."

He laughed. "Our food's not *that* great." Raising a hand in farewell, he left.

That afternoon the young, round senior doctor arrived with a junior doctor and a nurse, and eagerly unwrapped her bandage. In the evening the lunchtime doctor returned to say that the inflammation had gone down, the wound was healing well. She would have to take it easy, two weeks' rest at home, physiotherapy, I hope we never meet again, laughter, all the best, two manicured hands taking hers and sending her back out into the snow.

At 9.00 a.m. the following morning Lederle came and drove her home. When she saw her father waiting on the pavement her mood plummeted. In the lift she almost asked him if he remembered Filbinger.

A few things had changed in the apartment. Her houseplants were shining, her books neatly ordered and her items of furniture stood at right angles to each other, or to the walls. There were no dirty clothes on the floor, no fluff or hair. The apartment of a quiet, meticulous person in control of their life. "Welcome home, my child," her father said.

She curled her lip.

First she looked in her bedroom. The bedclothes had been changed. By the half-open window was a clothes horse with whites hung up to dry. A sheet and some underwear. Her underwear.

The bathroom had been cleaned too. No used towels on the edge of the tub, no hair in the hairbrush or plughole. No spare sanitary pads by the sink.

She went back into the sitting room.

Her father was standing beside the sofa, an odd glint in his eye.

She vaguely remembered that this was what he looked like when he was happy. "Sit down," he said.

She drew the curtains and sat. Had he discovered her stash of spirits? Would he try to stop her drinking? Would she have to drink in secret in her own apartment?

"Fancy a coffee? I bought some milk."

She nodded.

Her father filled the coffee machine with water. Instead of opening the cupboard where she kept the coffee he went to the fridge. Of course! Coffee belonged in the fridge. Besides Filbinger, that too had been a bone of contention in the seventies.

"I was in Günterstal recently."

"On duty?"

She gave him a reluctant smile. "So to speak."

"I can hardly believe there's crime in Günterstal." Her father poured milk into a pan, set it on the cooker and switched the cooker on. His familiarity with her kitchen was suffocating. It turned the kitchen into his kitchen, the apartment into his apartment.

She said, "Filbinger lives in Günterstal."

"Filbinger?"

"Hans Filbinger."

He nodded vacantly. Did he really not remember? Or did he not *want* to remember? Did he not want *her* to remind him?

She turned away. On the coffee table was Henning Mankell's *The Fifth Woman*. Near the middle pages was a scrap of newspaper – her bookmark. At the beginning was a piece of notepaper – presumably her father's bookmark. She took a deep breath, in and out. She needed something to drink.

In the cupboard beneath the sink were the vodka, the bourbon and the ţuică. In the tiny pantry was some red wine. In the bathroom cabinet was a 2-cl bottle of Jägermeister. But in front of her father? She couldn't bring herself to do it. Not yet.

On the answerphone flashed five messages. Five calls in a week.

More than there used to be in a month. She shuffled over to her right, turned the volume control down and pressed play.

One from Anatol, one from Enni and three from Landen. Three people she hadn't met until a week ago. Anatol said, "Hey, where are you?" Enni said, "Are you breathing regularly, Inspector?" Landen said, "You left so suddenly." His last call was from the day before. He asked about Taro and whether she was now on leave. He wanted to say goodbye as "they" were flying to Japan on Friday.

Friday was tomorrow.

She deleted the messages.

Nobody picked up at Tommo / Landen. After the sixth ring it went onto answerphone. She hung up and turned to her father.

"Hans Filbinger, Papa. It was because of him that you and Mama kept yelling at each other."

"No, that's not how it was. We didn't keep 'yelling at each other.'"

"What?"

"You might say we had a difference of opinion. You ought to know that at the time it was no longer possible to have a normal conversation with your mother. Perhaps that's why you . . ."

She leaped up. Her father froze. "I need the loo," she said.

The Jägermeister was where it belonged.

To be on the safe side she cleaned her teeth afterwards. Then she went back to the sitting room, and said, "What do you mean it was no longer possible to have a normal conversation with her?"

"She was . . ." Her father stopped, apparently searching for the right words.

"*What* was she, Papa?" She sat beside the answerphone.

"Wait, the coffee." Her father filled two cups. For several seconds he stared into the pan with the milk. Then he switched off the cooker, poured milk into the cups and carried them to the sofa. Like her mother, he hadn't remarried either. She hadn't met any girlfriends. Names had never been mentioned. It seemed as if they had destroyed each other for good.

When he sat beside her she got up. He handed her one of the cups. "She was ill, Louise. Psychologically ill."

"Rubbish."

"Very, very ill."

"That's such *rubbish*, Papa."

Her father nodded ruefully. She thought of her mother. Of the strength she still had, even after all those defeats. Why in spite of this strength had she always lost? Didn't it help to suppress or forget your own past? Did you have to change the past, like her father had? She gazed at him. Now he looked quite calm and self-assured. Nobody could pose a threat to him anymore. Doubts no longer existed. All of a sudden she understood that was why her mother failed. The victors are those who wrap themselves up in delusion.

She put her hands around the cup and turned to the window. "Let's get one thing straight, Papa. You say you want to get to know me better. I'm fine with that, but I guarantee you won't like getting to know me better."

"Don't say things like that, Louise. I'm convinced we can talk everything through, however . . . complicated it all is."

The telephone rang. She didn't move. "That's not what this is about. I'm asking *questions*, Papa."

"What do you mean, *ma chère*?"

Ma chère? She turned to face him. He hadn't called her that since the late sixties. "If you want to be part of my life, you're going to have to answer my questions, do you understand that, Papa? I ask questions, that's how I am. I refuse to be satisfied with not knowing or understanding something. *I ask questions*, O.K.? And I can immediately think of at least a dozen questions I want to ask you, questions you almost certainly don't want to hear. Can I be any clearer?"

Her father didn't look at her. "Maybe you ought to answer the phone instead."

"And after that, Papa? Can we get going with the questions?"

"Please, *chérie*, the phone, the ringing is making me anxious."

She picked up. It was Bermann. "We've got something," he said. "And I want you to come with us."

Her father said nothing as she got ready to leave. He was standing by the sofa, one hand resting on the arm, the other clenched. She kissed him on both cheeks and went out. She imagined he wouldn't be there when she got back.

At some point, when she felt like it, she would drive to Kehl and try to make him understand that the past always began in the present.

That the past *was* the present.

17

Bermann was double-parked with his engine running. "Are you sober?" he said when she got in. Wonderful, she thought: the old Bermann. Not the one who wanted to talk, but the other one, the simplistic, harmless Bermann. The Yin and Yang Bermann. Without using her left arm she strapped herself in. "Where's Reiner?"

"At the station."

"Why's he not coming with us?"

Bermann shrugged. She sensed that there was a reason and he knew it. Lederle was managing the back-room operation on the task force and those officers rarely went out. But Lederle loved going out. "Right," Bonì said. "Where are we heading?"

Bermann took his time, not telling her until they turned off for Günterstal.

That morning Steiner had begun to talk in the presence of his lawyer. Chervel had called Bermann and briefed him on the key points: Asile d'enfants owned a former farm to the south of Freiburg, a few kilometres beyond Horben. Steiner did not know who was there now.

On Schauinslandstrasse they joined a convoy of a dozen police cars, some unmarked. Bermann overtook them and went out in front. Bonì's gaze was fixed on Günterstal, which was rapidly getting closer. Mahler, Natchaya, Annegret Schelling, Fröbick, Lebonne, perhaps Berger, she thought. That made six. Maybe there were employees working at the farmhouse. And the Frenchman she had to thank for her little, wicked friend might be there too. "I want a weapon, Rolf."

"Yeah, right," Bermann said.

"I'm not going anywhere without a weapon."

He glanced at her. "You're not going anywhere in any case. You're not doing anything, do you understand? You're just watching to see if you recognise anyone. The Thai girl, the Frenchman, whoever. None of us has seen them apart from you. When it's all over someone will bring you home, and we'll see each other again when you're dry."

"Fuck you, Rolf."

"Not in this life."

Louise smiled. It was good to have people like Bermann around. Without them you might not realise the value of people like the roshi or Barbara Franke.

They passed through the town gate of Günterstal. On either side of it were trams that had been stopped by the police. White winter faces stared out of the windows. In front of the Liebfrauenkirche on the right a group of Japanese tourists had gathered around their tour guide, who was carrying an umbrella. They didn't look in her direction. Ten days earlier she'd driven along this same street with Niksch and thought of Filbinger, as well as the fact that Niksch wanted to be called "Nikki". Now Filbinger was no longer important and Niksch was dead.

Soon afterwards Wallmer got in touch over the radio. Bermann must have sent her and Schneider ahead. They were standing, she said *sotto voce*, a hundred metres from the farm on a narrow forest track. She described the road and the position of the farm. Hilly terrain off the road from Horben to Münzenried. Two buildings close together, surrounded on three sides by trees. Both looked occupied – curtains were drawn and one window tilted open. No animals, no dogs as far as they could make out. No cars. No tyre marks on the forest track, but that didn't necessarily mean anything. It had snowed a lot over the past few days.

Bermann picked up the radio and said, "We'll be with you in ten."

"*Should we take a look around?*"

"No, and don't let anybody catch sight of you."

"*We could try to go round the . . .*"

"No, Anne, please stay where you are."

Bermann put the receiver back in its cradle.

"Whose name is the farm registered in?" Louise said.

"Hans-Joachim Gronen."

"Who's that?"

"We don't know yet. Someone who doesn't live in Germany."

"Was Steiner ever there?"

Bermann shrugged.

She turned to peer out of the window. Who was Hans-Joachim Gronen? Another fan of the Far East?

A short, stout man was walking along the pavement. She imagined him as a tall, slim man who had just taken the decision not to fly to Japan tomorrow after all.

On their way out of Günterstal they passed the buildings of the Kyburg. As ever when she was here, Louise thought of how for five years she'd been called "von Kyburg" and at some point she'd come to terms with it. Unlike Mick. I've got a ridiculous name, he'd said before introducing himself to her. And after they'd divorced he had said, You're lucky, you can get rid of that ridiculous name now.

On the other hand, Michael von Kyburg: Swiss ancestors, counts related to the Habsburgs, all that had of course impressed the secretaries, cashiers, cleaning ladies, sales girls and waitresses. Maybe the writer too.

Above all it had impressed her father.

Halfway to Münzenried they turned off to the left. Bermann reached for the radio again. "We're almost there. Anything happening?"

"*Nothing. If you ask me they're waiting for us.*"

"Rubbish," Louise said.

Wallmer didn't seem to have heard her, and Bermann wasn't paying Louise any attention. Still, it felt good to be sitting next to him. It meant that they, rather than the others, had the initiative. That the ball was rolling. That they might have a hope of finding Pham and the other children.

Shortly afterwards they stopped behind Wallmer and Schneider's car. The farm was out of sight; they were obscured by a hill.

As they got out Wallmer and Schneider gazed at Louise in surprise. Wallmer managed a smile, Schneider said, "Hi, Luis." Even though he was in his late forties he was still the most handsome of the four inspectors at Freiburg Kripo. Servility didn't appear to have any effect on complexion or attractiveness. It might even be the secret formula.

She nodded to them.

"And?" Bermann said.

"Nothing," Wallmer replied. "I bet they've entrenched themselves in there and are waiting for us."

"Rubbish," Bonì said again.

Wallmer gave her an anxious look while Schneider's beautiful Roman brow clouded over. Bermann turned away.

The other cars stopped and their colleagues got out. Some nodded, others ignored her. Nobody said a word, but the tension was palpable. A task force on the brink of a raid was a highly explosive combination of adrenalin, fatigue, determination and nerves.

They grouped around Bermann, who issued instructions in a muffled voice. He repeated Wallmer's warning. Bonì repeated her observation. Someone giggled wickedly. Then the group dispersed almost without a sound.

Bermann held Louise back and ordered her to stay behind the others. "You're just going to use your eyes," he said. "Nothing else, do you hear me?"

*

Ten minutes later the task force and the additional police officers were scattered across the snow-covered area. Alone and in small groups, they waited behind trees, hillocks, bushes. After a while they stopped worrying about remaining quiet. Louise heard voices, coughing and cursing. The buildings were surrounded; nobody was going to escape. So why lie silently in the snow?

Bonì herself was perched behind a snowdrift beside the narrow track that led to the farm. Although she was freezing, the cold offered one benefit: her shoulder barely ached.

As she watched the two buildings she thought that Wallmer might be right. If the Asile people were here, they appeared to be waiting. But were they here? No cars, no smoke from the chimneys, no smell of burning wood. The curtains behind the windows were not moving. There was no sign of life anywhere on the farmstead. And yet Louise couldn't help feeling that people were inside.

Bermann, amplified by the megaphone, tore into the silence. As on that morning in the Vosges, nothing happened. A few seconds passed, then Bermann's voice boomed out once more. He was about twenty metres to her left, Wallmer beside him. He cursed. Louise knew that he'd wait three minutes at most before issuing the order to advance.

Who was inside those buildings? Or were they in fact empty? But if so, where *were* the Asile people? Had a week been enough time for them to get away?

Hardly. On the day after the "accident" near Mulhouse their names were put on the wanted list, which would have given them only a tiny window of opportunity to fly out undetected via an E.U. airport.

How would Mahler have reacted to the organisation being smashed? If he'd been here a week ago, would he have waited until today? Possibly. But they had to assume that Steiner would have warned him by telephone this morning.

Bonì slipped her hand into the pocket of her anorak and ducked. She'd refilled her supplies in front of her father. He hadn't said anything and nor had she.

Louise screwed the cap back on and put the bottle in the snow in front of her. She thrust it in so far with her finger that it was no longer visible. Then she cupped some snow over the top and patted it down.

So much for Mahler. But what about the others?

Annegret Schelling was injured in the accident, as was the driver of the Sharan, although presumably not seriously. It was highly unlikely they would have come straight back here. They probably went to see Steiner – together with the pregnant woman. He'd have attended to their wounds. Then Schelling and the driver would have gone to ground, either here or somewhere else.

What about Fröbick and Lebonne? The pregnant woman? Pham? The other children? How many children were yet to be passed on? Last Wednesday Annegret Schelling had said that Pham had eight more sleeps before meeting his new parents. They didn't know how many other children were with her at the time. Two days prior to that Schelling hadn't been able to talk to Muller because she'd supposedly been at the pony club with "the children".

Since Thursday evening everything had changed. It had become risky to travel through south-west Germany, Alsace or the Vosges with children from the Far East.

Assuming that not all the children had been delivered by Thursday evening, what would Mahler and his people have done with them after realising that their cover had been blown? That the children would now be earning them hefty prison sentences rather than a fortune? If Steiner had no concrete information and Jean Berger wasn't arrested, and if there were no records of the adoptions, it would be difficult to prove that Mahler, Natchaya, Schelling and the others had illegally sold children from the Far East to European parents or paedophiles.

If the children were with them it would be easier.

Bonì stood up with difficulty, and momentarily felt dizzy. Then she trudged through the snow to the nearest of the two houses.

"Hey," Bermann groused, "stay where you are!"

The building was about thirty metres away. It would have been easy for Bermann or one of the others to hold her back. But nobody moved.

"Shit, Luis," Bermann called out, resignation in his voice. Louise could feel the eyes of her colleagues on her. All conversation had stopped. She wished Lederle were here. He might have explained to Bermann and the others what she was doing and that they could trust her. But it didn't really matter. She was on double sick leave. It would be a long time before she was better again and could return to work.

But that was not important now. Only the children mattered. Pham, Areewan. Even Natchaya, who perhaps was only slightly evil.

She wondered how she would cope if there *were* dead children in one of the buildings. How she might have been able to prevent it. What had gone wrong when. Whether it was arrogant of her to think she could save the world if she couldn't even save herself.

Thirty, thirty-five metres, and yet she felt as if she'd been walking for an eternity. She was passing through a vacuum, a cold, white room where time didn't exist. Calambert, Taro, Landen, the roshi, Natchaya – they were all there.

Only Pham was missing.

Then Bermann entered the room too.

"I'm here, Luis," he said, two metres behind her, gun in hand.

She walked on. Nothing was happening at the house. Black dots moved in from either side. She could hear voices whispering, "They're dead." How could she have prevented it? What had she done wrong? In a moment like this the list of errors was endless. It began with the day she ran in the wrong direction near Munzingen.

Calambert's error was to have put a sticker on the rear windscreen of the car in which Annette had drifted towards death: IT'S A MAN'S WORLD. If the sticker hadn't been there he wouldn't have died. Perhaps it was that simple.

The sticker had been *his* mistake. Everything else had been *her* mistake. Every bottle of booze she'd drunk had been her mistake. And every bottle of booze she hadn't drunk.

Then she reached the end of the white room.

The front door was unlocked. She pushed it open and stepped into a dark, square hallway. All of a sudden Bermann was in front of her. Then Wallmer, Schneider as well as a few others jostled past. At once the hallway was flooded with yellow overhead light. Around her, doors were pushed open. More officers poured in, spreading themselves between the rooms and charging up the stairs at the end of the hallway. Muffled voices calling out orders, warnings. No shots, no screams. Above her the sound of rapid footsteps. Out of the blue she thought of the garden where Pham and Landen were waiting for her. She wondered in what sort of life the two of them and she could have been a family.

The ground floor was quickly made secure, followed by the upper floor and finally the basement. Nothing. The house was empty.

She went back out through the front door.

Bonì was almost at the second building when a police sergeant approached her. He hesitated, then stopped. She walked past him without saying anything. Behind her she could hear footsteps in the snow. Someone was running from the big house. Then she heard Bermann say, "Where?"

"Top left," the sergeant said.

"It's the Thai girl," Bermann told her. A voice was talking on his radio. Louise couldn't understand what she was saying. "Stay where you are," Bermann said. "I'm on my way."

He kept running and she hurried after him. The sergeant overtook her. They entered another square hallway, smaller than the first. The stairs were to the right. Bermann and the sergeant beat Louise to the first floor, then Bermann intercepted her. "O.K.," he said. "She's sitting in there with her sister and a pistol and a corpse." His right hand gripped her forearm.

"Who's the dead person?"

"No idea. A man."

"I'm going in."

The pressure of Bermann's hand intensified. "You're *not* going in. You can talk to her, but you're staying outside."

"Fine." She turned away. Bermann let go and she walked past him. From his expression she could tell that he knew she'd do what she thought was right. Perhaps he didn't even think that was bad. Perhaps he thought it would clear up some messy issues.

Nobody was standing outside the room where Natchaya, Areewan and the dead man were. The door was half open, the wall made of wood. The officers had taken up position on the stairs, in the bathroom next door and in the room opposite.

She stopped a couple of metres from the door. "Natchaya?"

When there was no answer, Louise took a step forwards. She saw a small right foot, a slim leg in blue jeans. The foot was slowly moving back and forth. Natchaya was sitting on the floor against the opposite wall.

"I'm coming in," Bonì announced.

"O.K.," Natchaya said.

A movement caused Louise to stop. Wallmer was standing to her right by the door to the bathroom. "No!" she begged with a whisper. Bonì pursed her lips without knowing what she intended to convey by that. Taking another step she opened the door wide.

Natchaya and Areewan were sitting side by side beneath the window, their eyes fixed on her. Natchaya was holding Bonì's service weapon in her lap, her other hand was on Areewan's thigh.

Louise pushed the door behind her, leaving it slightly ajar. Her gaze roamed the room. The red curtain was partially drawn. To her left stood a cupboard, to the right a bed. Otherwise the room was empty. Apart from the man lying on the floor near the external wall. His left eye was shot through. Probably a bullet from her Walther P5. A narrow trickle of blood had formed beside his head. It ran into

238

the middle of the room, creating a small puddle.

The man was wearing jeans, a jumper, sturdy shoes and an overcoat. His shoes and the turn-ups of his trousers were dry. He'd been planning to go outside, then had been shot by Natchaya – or Areewan.

"Sit beside door," Natchaya said.

Bonì obeyed. When she leaned against it, the door clicked shut.

The sisters stared at her in silence. They looked similar, as if they were twins. Areewan too was strikingly beautiful, in a more childlike way. You could hardly detect the age difference of seven or eight years. Only in their facial expressions did they differ substantially. Natchaya looked calm, whereas Areewan seemed to be on the verge of panic. She was trembling and making high-pitched, barely audible sounds. Louise thought again of dogs. A puppy, abandoned by its mother, beaten by invisible hands. She wondered why comparisons with animals made human suffering so much more striking. Then she said to Areewan, "Hello, I'm Louise."

Areewan lowered her eyes. Natchaya said she only spoke Thai. The sisters' beauty was beginning to beguile Bonì. She felt the urge to touch their faces, their bodies. For an instant she was convinced that this might be a way of conquering her own loneliness.

"You saved my life," she said at last. "Why?"

Natchaya shrugged. "Killing . . . not . . . good."

"You killed him." Bonì jerked her head towards the man.

Natchaya's expression remained unchanged. "He . . . wanting . . ." She switched to English. "He wanted to leave."

"The country?"

"The country, me, Areewan."

Louise nodded. So the dead man was probably Harald Mahler.

Natchaya's right foot had stopped moving. "He said, 'Go home. Go back to your family. Things have changed now.' I said, 'You are our family. It's too late for things to change.' He said, 'Goodbye, my love.'"

"And so you shot him."

"When it's too late, things cannot change anymore."

"Is that a reason to shoot your husband?"

"He took us into his world. We cannot live in his world without him. Without him we cannot stay, we cannot leave." Natchaya was speaking with extraordinary patience. A teacher explaining simple things to her pupil. Such as the course of life. Fate. Explaining why life sometimes has to end in a room like this.

Louise said nothing. Natchaya knew what was awaiting her and Areewan. She would go to prison and be separated from her sister. Areewan would be put in a home, with foster parents, or perhaps be sent back to relatives in Thailand, if there *were* any relatives. Years would pass before they could be together again. And even then others would determine their fate. Those wanting to help, those who'd sexually abused them. The living as well as the dead.

Things cannot change anymore. In one way she was right. In another she wasn't. "The only things you can't change are those that have already happened. You can change everything else, if you want to."

Natchaya simply smiled.

Bonì stood up, suddenly filled with a bleak anger. Anger at herself, because she was helpless and offering up platitudes. Anger at Natchaya, who looked so determined and seemed to know more fundamental things about life than she did. At least about one part of life.

She asked if she might open the curtain and the window. Natchaya nodded. As she crossed the room she realised that something was happening between Natchaya, Areewan and herself, but she didn't know what.

She opened the curtain and pushed up the window. Cool, white light blinded her, but the sudden cold was agreeable. Outside she could only see Schneider between the two buildings. He was looking towards the forest, but there everything seemed quiet. He appeared a little lost, as if Bermann had forgotten him in the snow.

Seeing Schneider made Louise remember why she was here. But something was stopping her from asking about Pham, Taro and Annegret Schelling. She felt that at this moment she had to devote herself to Natchaya and Areewan. She imagined that everyone else would have understood by now what was happening between them. Not her. Louise was finding it more and more difficult to understand anything at all. Her mistakes were coming with greater frequency. She'd thought they would find dead children in one of the houses. But they'd found the two sisters and a dead Mahler.

What was happening in this room?

Then she thought of the last thing Natchaya had said. *We cannot stay, we cannot leave.* Where did you go if you couldn't stay, but couldn't leave either? What did you do?

Then she knew.

She turned around. Her gaze wandered from the pistol in Natchaya's lap to Areewan, who was now looking at her. "What about your sister, Natchaya? Doesn't she have the right to decide for herself what she wants? Are you going to decide for her? Like your husband, like all the other men? Are *you* going to decide if she . . ."

Natchaya interrupted her. "There were no men. I took Areewan from Thailand to protect her. Now I cannot protect her anymore. Now the men will come."

The teacher, the pupil. Everything was so simple, so logical. She wondered if this kind of logic was part of Natchaya's religion. But which religion did she belong to? Was Thailand Buddhist? Muslim, like Pakistan? Were there Sikhs, Hindus and Christians in Thailand? Did they believe there that it was right to kill people if you couldn't stay but couldn't leave either? Did they believe that in certain situations it might be too late to go on living? Was that karma, assuming that Natchaya believed in karma? Or did everything just seem very simple to her, whereas in fact it was much more complicated?

Natchaya turned away and muttered something to Areewan in Thai. Her voice sounded soothing. Areewan nodded and tried to smile.

"She's scared, Natchaya. She doesn't want to die."

Natchaya looked at her again. "Can you protect her?"

"I'll make sure she finds a nice family."

Natchaya nodded. "But can you protect her?"

Bonì shook her head. "No, of course not." Her anger returned. She closed the window. Schneider, still standing alone between the buildings, turned and looked up at her.

"Then the men will come," Natchaya said. "In this life Areewan and I belong to the men. Maybe in the next life we will belong to ourselves."

"Then explain one thing to me," Louise said. "Why did you marry an arsehole like Mahler? Why did you help him?"

Natchaya hesitated, and said, "Because I am part of the men."

"What the hell does that mean?"

"I cannot explain. Maybe you can?"

Louise tried to keep her composure. "Because you didn't resist?"

"I don't understand."

"Because you didn't fight?"

"Yes, maybe."

But why? Louise thought. Why didn't you fight.

She moved away from the window and sat on the floor beside the four small feet. Areewan froze. Natchaya half closed her eyes. "Shit," Bonì said. "I don't understand a *single word*." She cursed herself for having started this conversation. Why Natchaya had done whatever it was she *had* done, all that would come out in the interrogations. There would be time enough for philosophical or psychological discussions then.

But now there was no time. Now she had to stop Natchaya killing herself and Areewan. And swiftly find out where Pham and the other Asile children were. But the thought remained: you should have fought. You shouldn't have done to other children what was done to you as a child.

She looked down at Natchaya's feet. Above the short socks were gold chains against her brown skin. The colour was dull and flaking off in places. Chains from a Thai beach, perhaps a present from her mother, or from a boy. From a time when she wasn't part of the men. Louise placed her hands on Natchaya's feet. As so often in the past few days she thought of what Landen had said about how impossible it was to really understand another person. But was it necessary? Perhaps it didn't always have to be painful. Perhaps there was a way in which you could respect or even love another personwithout the pain of not understanding them.

"You should go now," Natchaya said.

She looked up. "Not without my pistol."

Natchaya held out the weapon.

Bonì hesitated, then took it. Once more everything seemed so simple. The grip of the pistol was warm and damp. She ejected the magazine. Two bullets. Coincidence, or the logic of destiny?

Natchaya had placed her arm around Areewan's shoulders. Her sister's head was resting on her neck. Otherwise nothing appeared to have changed. No suggestion that in relinquishing the Walther, Natchaya had also relinquished control over her future.

Both sisters were wearing jeans and tight sweatshirts. No room for any more pistols. For a small knife at most. But a *knife*? Or would they use poison?

She put the pistol in the left pocket of her anorak. What was Natchaya planning? She felt the anger returning. So simple, and yet so complicated.

There was a commotion on the other side of the door. She heard footsteps and someone talking in hushed tones. Then Wallmer said, "Everything O.K., Luis?"

"Yes," she said gruffly, before looking Natchaya in the eye and saying, "Where are your people?"

Natchaya willingly told her that Paul Lebonne had absconded a week earlier, as had Jean Berger. Annegret Schelling had disappeared too. Klaus Fröbick had been here, but he drove off after a call from Steiner that morning. Her husband had spoken to him, but she hadn't. Fröbick was in a panic, desperate to flee, but unsure of where to go.

Bonì nodded thoughtfully and asked about Taro. Natchaya didn't recognise the name. "The monk," Bonì said.

"The monk," Natchaya repeated. She had no idea what had happened to him. The three Frenchmen had taken him away. "He knew."

"What?"

"He saw the men with me. He watched what we did."

When they discovered him, Mahler and Lebonne beat him to the ground. They thought he was unconscious. While they deliberated what to do with him he vanished. Mahler called the Frenchmen, who followed Taro and encountered Hollerer and Niksch. They told Mahler at the Kanzan-an and asked what they should do. Mahler said they needed to find the monk. He set off with Lebonne. The Frenchmen shot Hollerer and Niksch. Mahler and Lebonne found Taro, and the Frenchmen took him away.

"To kill him?"

Natchaya returned her gaze without betraying any emotion. Bonì sensed that she wanted to spare her the answer. For the time being she let it lie. Later, when everything was over and she was back in the department, she would hear the truth. "In the forest where they found Taro," she said, "there were children's footprints."

Natchaya shook her head. There hadn't been any children there. Louise pursed her lips. She'd been right about the Sharan tyre marks, but not about the children's footprints.

She put her hands back on Natchaya's feet. "Have you taken all the children to their new families?"

Natchaya shook her head.

"Where are the rest of them?"

"There's a barn."

"A what?" Bonì said, not having understood Natchaya's English.

"A barn," Natchaya said more slowly, raising a hand.

The barn was in the forest beyond the houses, fifty metres up a narrow path from the main building. Bonì ran ahead, followed by Bermann and some other officers, including Schneider. The snow was twenty to thirty centimetres deep. They could tell from footprints now partially snowed over that someone had been back and forth here hours before. An adult. No children's prints were visible.

Louise stopped to catch her breath. The cold air stung her lungs. She felt giddy, her shoulder was hurting and she knew she wouldn't be able to go on much longer. The time had come for her to recuperate. Two months, three months – as long as it took. She just needed to find Pham, talk to Katrin Rein and then her period of rest could begin. A time for contemplation. Of unrest.

Bermann, Schneider and the others overtook her, Bermann speaking into his mobile. He'd called Lederle back at the station and was telling him what car Fröbick was driving – a white B.M.W., according to Natchaya. They didn't know the model, only that it was an estate. And that Fröbick had several hours' head start, even if he didn't know where to go. Bermann put his mobile away and took out his pistol.

By the time she reached the barn the men had spaced themselves out around the building. Bermann and Schneider were standing by a door set in a larger double door. It was ajar. "Police! Open up!" Bermann shouted, kicking it open at almost exactly the same time.

Boni stood ten metres away. No children's voices. No crying, no screaming. Pham and a two-year-old girl from Poipet in Cambodia must be in there.

Bermann shot out of the barn and ran back towards the houses, followed by Schneider. Neither afforded her a glance.

She entered the barn, which consisted of a single room lit by a bright bulb that hung from the tall ceiling. Ranged along one wall were half a dozen mattresses with woollen blankets. Along the wall opposite were piles of clothes. Toys were scattered across the floor. It reeked of urine and excrement.

Pham and the girl were nowhere to be seen.

Louise leaned against the wall and sank to the floor. A young, female police sergeant kneeled beside her and asked if everything was

O.K. She nodded. She rested her head against the wooden wall and tried not to pass out. "You could do with some fresh air," the sergeant said.

Three of them managed to pull Bonì to her feet, and when they got her outside she felt a little better.

It took a moment for her to grasp two things. First, Fröbick must have taken the children with him. Second, Bermann was on his way to see Natchaya.

There was a ghostly silence back in the house. Half the task force had gathered by the door and in the room where Mahler's body lay, but no-one was speaking. It smelled of sweat, old clothes, stale cigarette smoke. Feebly she pushed her way past her colleagues.

Natchaya and Areewan were still sitting by the window. Areewan was keening again, Natchaya was phlegmatic, and both were staring at the figure of Bermann in front of them. "So?" he said menacingly.

"Rolf," Bonì said.

Bermann spun around. "Out," he hissed. "I don't want you in here!"

"They don't know where the children are."

"Go, Luis."

Wallmer came to her, but said nothing.

"Take her home," Bermann barked.

"Don't you touch me," Louise said.

Natchaya looked at her. "You should go now."

You should have fought, she thought, returning her gaze. She hated herself for having thoughts such as these. A moment later she asked in English, "Because things cannot change anymore?"

Natchaya nodded.

As she went down the stairs with Wallmer a tune could be heard, but only faintly. She stopped and turned around. It was coming from the room they'd just left.

"Come on," Wallmer said.

246

"Do you hear that?"

"What?"

They went on.

"What am I supposed to have heard?" Wallmer said.

"Beethoven," Bonì said.

Outside there was light snow. The cold seemed to have abated slightly. They walked in silence past the larger of the two buildings. Bonì asked to borrow Wallmer's mobile, then rang Lederle at headquarters. He had Chervel on the other line. "Call me back when you've found Fröbick and the children," she said. "I need to be there when you get him. It doesn't matter when. Do you hear me? I – need – to – be – there."

Lederle made her a promise.

Wallmer grinned as Bonì returned her mobile. "You always get what you want in the end."

"It only looks that way, Anne."

At that moment voices were raised in the smaller building behind her. With a loud bang a casement window crashed against the wall. Frantic male voices burst outside, with Bermann's bitter curses louder than all the other sounds.

Wallmer had turned to look. Bonì kept going.

The voices and the swearing stopped.

We cannot stay, we cannot leave.

18

Her father had gone. Louise searched her apartment twice, but he hadn't left a note. She turned all the radiators up high, undressed and switched on the radio. But even under the shower Natchaya hummed "*Für Elise*" in her head.

She was certain she'd used poison rather than a knife. If you were killing someone to save them from a worse fate, you didn't stick a knife into them.

As she dried herself she wondered why she felt so little sadness at the sisters' deaths. It made her feel a little melancholy, but no more than that. Perhaps because she hadn't witnessed it herself. Perhaps because she felt so sorry for their lives. Or because Natchaya had been so embroiled in Asile d'enfants' business.

For a while she tried to disentangle the questions relating to Natchaya's guilt and responsibility, but didn't get far. An underage Thai girl is hired out or sold to pimps. The girl meets a German sex tourist who's a regular visitor to Thailand, probably in a Bangkok brothel. By then she's a professional and still underage. When she reaches the age of consent she marries the German. Via a criminal organisation that procures children, she tries to bring her sister over. The mother gets the adoption annulled, but a few years later the sister is released and comes to Germany. While the girl protects her sister from a life as a child prostitute she helps with the procurement and sale of Far Eastern children to European customers. Is she forced to? Probably not. So why does the girl do it? She knows that what awaits the elder children at least is horrific, otherwise she wouldn't be protecting her own sister from it. She knows good from evil. So why does she do both good *and* evil?

Perhaps Katrin would find an answer in her textbooks. But perhaps you just had to accept Natchaya's answer: *Because I am part of the men.*

Whatever that meant.

Later she put the tin of coffee from the fridge back into the cupboard, crawled for a moment beneath the sink and sat on the sofa beside the answerphone. Two new messages.

Katrin Rein was requesting a meeting. Barbara Franke wanted her to call back. She dialled Landen's number. It was still only Thursday; there was plenty of time to talk.

Tommo answered. Louise apologised for her hasty departure the week before. Tommo seemed not to hold it against her and called her husband. Louise wondered where the telephone was in the Tommo / Landen household. She couldn't remember having seen it in the hall. On the little cupboard beneath "Happiness" and "Friendship"? No. In the kitchen? In the kitchen were the china cat and Niksch, but no telephone. In the living room?

"Ah, Inspector," Landen said.

"Hi," Boni said.

"How are you? Did you go on holiday after all?"

She grimaced. She had the third Richard Landen on the line, the secretive, depressive one. "Where are you now?"

Landen did not immediately understand the question, so she explained. The telephone was in the living room, to the right of the door. Not a cordless phone, because of the radiation. "Is that enough information for you?" He laughed softly, but was soon serious again. "Any news of Taro and Pham?"

She replied that Pham was alive but hadn't yet been found, and that she still knew nothing for certain about Taro's fate.

"Nothing for certain," Landen repeated.

Again she saw him and Pham in the garden. They were looking in her direction, waiting in silence. "And you're off to Japan," she said after a while.

"Yes, tomorrow morning."

She nodded and heard herself ask whether he'd put the telephone on speaker. No, he told her. "Good," she said. "That's good." She stood up and went to the window. Snow, frost and cold wherever you looked. The garden where Landen and Pham were waiting for her was green. She drew the curtain and sat down. "Why are you flying to Japan? When are you back? Do you love your wife? Why are you sometimes so likeable, and sometimes so dull? What do you mean by 'special gift'? I mean, is it a good or a bad thing? Are you still there?"

"Yes."

She got up and went to the kitchen window. Below was a boutique for plus size clothing. To the right was a small, unnamed square, where café tables, chairs and palm trees in plastic tubs stood in the summer. In winter passers-by crossed the square with their shoulders hunched, because it was open on three sides and windy. She drew this curtain too and said, "When will I see you again?"

Landen paused for a moment. "I didn't know that was important."

"It might be."

Another pause. "I'm back in a fortnight."

"Did you say 'I' or 'we'?"

No answer.

Apart from a small standing lamp all her lights were off. It was cosy. All that was missing was Barclay James Harvest. She brought the bottle of vodka over to the sofa and stood it on the coffee table.

"Is your wife staying in Japan?"

"Yes."

"For a while?"

"Yes."

"Is she beside you now?"

"No."

A fourth Richard Landen. A taciturn, surly Landen, taken unawares. One who'd realise only later what he had actually wanted to say. "How long is your wife staying in Japan?"

"Until the birth of our child, I imagine."

"Oh." She walked around the coffee table. From behind, the vodka looked even more inviting than from the front. Mysterious and full of promise. She sat down and said, "That gives us plenty of time, then. You called me three times in one week, so I assume you want to spend some time with me. Am I right?"

"I'm hanging up now, Louise."

"Fine."

"I'll call you when I'm back. Then . . ." Landen broke off.

"Then what?"

"Goodbye."

She spent the next few minutes not drinking. The desire and need were overwhelming, but Lederle might ring at any moment and tell her where Fröbick had taken the children. It would be reckless to have a drink before then.

She stared at the bottle for a quarter of an hour without touching it, and felt highly responsible. A few times she asked herself whether *fairly* responsible would be good enough too. But she didn't give in to the voices inside her head. To be on the safe side she put the vodka back under the sink. In the end, she thought, life is one big battle against human desire. What the soul craved destroyed the body.

When she sat down she noticed that only her bookmark was poking out of *The Fifth Woman*.

Later she pondered what "I'll call you when I'm back. Then . . ." might mean.

As far as Landen was concerned, it meant that everything they had to discuss could wait until he got back. But it also meant that there was a "then". A "then we'll see each other again" or a "then we'll chat about everything" or a "then we'll do it in my teahouse". The "then" meant that their relationship could not be adequately conveyed by the words "I'll call you when I'm back". That it went further than this.

Satisfied, she put her bare feet up on the coffee table and fell asleep.

When she woke it was still afternoon. The light in the room hadn't changed. Time had not passed. She looked at her feet and thought of the chains around Natchaya's ankles, the cool skin against her palms. She wished that "fairly responsible" had been good enough.

Lederle hadn't called. Fröbick was still on the run with Pham and a two-year-old girl from Poipet. What would he do with the children when he reached his destination or hideaway? Or if he had to continue his escape alone? Would he gag them, tie them up, and stuff them in his boot as Calambert had done to Annetta? Would he abandon them in the snow?

And what would he do with the children if he was surrounded?

Hollerer seemed to be making good progress. But he'd asked for the telephone to be removed from his room. He wanted some peace and quiet to think, Roman said. She understood that. "He doesn't want me to read to him either," the volunteer said. Louise was about to tell him he should try something less depressing than *The Outsider*, but kept her mouth shut.

"He doesn't want any visitors either," Roman said.

"I'm coming anyway."

"Please don't."

At around four o'clock she called Anatol. At five he was at her door with flowers, chocolate and prosecco. He looked even younger than he had in the hospital. "Hi," he said. "I don't have much time, I'm afraid." He went to the sofa and sat down. Bonì noticed that he moved like a stranger, unlike at the weekend. With a peculiar shyness, as if worried about being thrown out.

She put the flowers on the coffee table, the prosecco in the fridge and said, "Come to bed, but be careful of my shoulder."

Later, as they lay naked beside each other, Anatol spoke at length by his standards. He said that she was beautiful in an unusual way, in a "subterranean way", if you like. Not immediately beautiful, at first glance, because she wasn't "that slim" and "you don't really look after your hair, do you?" On the other hand, he said, the longer he gazed at her, the more beautiful she seemed, captivatingly beautiful in fact, because her expressions, her laugh, her smile, her look and her body all had their own particular beauty – something warm, wild, sad, unique, genuine. He couldn't keep his eyes – or hands – off her.

She wondered what he was trying to say. She had no idea.

Then Anatol said, "I've got to go."

At 6.10 p.m. she called Lederle. Still no trace of Fröbick and the children. If he had a mobile on him, it must be switched off. Bermann and Schneider were sitting beside the telephone in Fröbick's living room. Evidently his wife had known nothing. They hadn't told her everything either, but enough. "She's cooperating," Lederle said.

Fröbick's wife was convinced her husband would ring soon, because of his sons. He loved his sons and was a wonderful father. He would call. Especially as he knew he couldn't come home.

"A wonderful father," Boni repeated.

"Wait," Lederle said, switching to the other line. She thought he sounded harried, out of breath, as if he had been running. She went into the bathroom and fetched her dressing gown.

Lederle was back on the line. "That was Villingen-Schwennigen. They've got Annegret Schelling. Three guesses as to where she was."

"With her mother."

"With her *What*-is-Annegret-supposed-to-have-done-? mother," Lederle said grimly. "Fucking . . . *scum*. Did you hear about the Thai girl?"

"Yes."

"Terrible, Louise. Terrible. I . . ."

The doorbell rang. "Hang on, Reiner." Still holding the phone, she went to the door. Someone was knocking at it now. She ran through the possibilities: her father, Anatol, Enni, Barbara Franke, Klaus Fröbick. Richard Landen, whose wife wouldn't be coming back until she'd had the baby.

But it was Katrin Rein.

With a sigh Louise waved her into the apartment. Katrin was wearing a light-green blouse beneath her coat and carrying a black leather briefcase. She'd tied back her blonde hair and looked unusually determined. When she saw that Bonì was in her dressing gown she blushed.

"Take your shoes off," Bonì said. "Like a drink? There's prosecco in the fridge." She smiled in spite of herself.

Lederle asked who had arrived. Louise told him and ended their conversation.

She put the cordless phone in the pocket of her dressing gown. "Or you could have a coffee."

Katrin gave a horrified smile. "Oh, I can't take coffee; I've got a sensitive stomach. Do you happen to have any camomile tea?"

"Good God, no!"

"A glass of tap water will do then, thanks."

"You can cope with that?"

Katrin nodded. The tap water in those parts of town to the east of the railway line or Merzhauser Strasse, she said, came from the old water tower in the Sternwald – it was good quality and tasted excellent. The water on the other side of town came from the Rhine Valley – it was hard and didn't taste particularly nice. But here the water was so good that . . . that . . . "You could . . . um, keep fish from the Amazon in it."

"Fish from the Amazon?"

"Yes."

"Hmm. Could you imagine me with Amazonian fish?"

"Well . . . no. A few piranhas at best."

Therapist and patient laughed.

As Louise filled a glass she thought about which of her friends lived to the west of the train line. Off the top of her head she could only think of Bermann and Mick. Satisfied, she turned off the tap.

They sat next to each other on the sofa. Katrin had regained her determination and composure. She took a notebook and silver biro from her leather briefcase, drank some water, cleared her throat and said she really had to form a picture now.

"A picture?"

"Of your condition."

"I see." Louise got up and sat in one of the two armchairs on the other side of the coffee table. She pulled her legs up and rearranged her dressing gown. This wasn't the right moment for her definitive step into the abyss. She had to focus on Fröbick and Pham. On not drinking. But when *was* the right moment?

She waited in silence for the first question.

Three hours later she was back under the shower. Looking into the mirror she thought again that everything was perhaps quite different. What she saw didn't seem to correspond with the image that Katrin had assembled. Is this what Gamma alcoholics looked like in the pro-dromal phase?

The mirror fogged up and her face blurred.

As she sat on the loo it occurred to her that these strange terms marked the beginning of a new life for her.

She went back into the sitting room in her dressing gown. Katrin was lying fast asleep on the sofa. In her doll-like way she looked very pretty and utterly exhausted. Her cheeks were red and individual strands had come loose from her hairband. She'd made a huge effort over the past three hours as if having resolved to save Louise, whatever the cost. On a piece of paper she'd drawn a horizontal line and divided it into three sections: prodromal phase, critical phase and chronic phase. This is where you are, roughly, she'd said, writing "Louise" on the line between the prodromal phase and the critical phase. You're an alcoholic, but you're still in the initial stage of the disease.

The disease.

Beside the piece of paper was a list of telephone numbers of "volunteers helping people with addiction", the majority of them themselves former alcoholics. Alongside these were the names of self-help groups, specialist clinics and therapy institutions. Katrin had tentatively suggested that after a two-week or so detox in a clinic, she could complete the physical withdrawal as an outpatient. The path into the abyss was steeper than she'd imagined, but it might be less unpleasant on the way out.

Taking the woollen blanket from the back of the sofa, she laid it over Katrin, who briefly opened her eyes but didn't seem to wake up.

In the kichen she drank Sternwald water and ate a slice of wholemeal bread. Confused, she tried to recall when and why she'd bought it, then it came to her that it must have been bought by her father. She wondered how he was. Was he already hard at work changing the immediate past? Or was he trying to summon the courage to ask himself her questions?

She reflected on whether the questions about her family's past were really so important that they could be allowed to encroach so heavily on the present. Yes, she thought. The questions were part of who she was.

All the same, perhaps it was still possible to keep up contact with her father.

Just then the telephone in her dressing-gown pocket rang. She answered before it could ring a second time. It was Lederle. Fröbick had been in touch.

A patrol car was coming to fetch her.

"Call when you're on your way," Lederle said.

"Wait! What about the children?"

"No word yet."

She hurried to the sofa and put the telephone in its dock. Katrin was still asleep. On the table was the sketch with the horizontal line. She stared at her name.

Prodromal phase, Gamma alcoholic, disease.

As she got dressed she could feel the tears running down her cheeks.

19

Ten minutes later Bonì went down to meet the police sergeant who'd helped her to her feet in the barn near Münzenried. She introduced herself as "Zancan". "Italian mother," she explained. Louise smiled briefly and said, "French father". Zancan smiled back and asked if Louise wanted to drive. She shook her head. Zancan seemed to know where they were going because she didn't ask. She turned on the siren and crossed Werderring into Kronenstrasse.

Bonì stared out into the white night. Then she called Lederle. "Does Rolf know I'm coming?"

"He doesn't have to know everything, does he?" Lederle made noises that sounded like laughter or coughing.

"Tell him, Reiner."

"Later. Now listen."

Fröbick had first rung home at eight o'clock that evening. They'd begun by letting him talk to his wife for a while. He was in tears and sounded panicked. But he wasn't going to give himself up. When Bermann took the receiver he hung up immediately. As he hadn't switched off his mobile, they located him via the radio signal. He was driving all over Freiburg. But they weren't able to pinpoint him exactly – Bermann hadn't allowed them to deploy a helicopter and patrol cars.

At 8.20 Fröbick called home again. This time he agreed to speak to Bermann and asked whether he might strike a deal. Bermann told him they could discuss it, of course. Fröbick promised to hand over the children, unharmed, in exchange for 100,000 euros and his freedom. Bermann agreed. Fröbick said he'd have a think about how and where the handover should take place and he'd call again.

"Can he really be so naïve?"

"He's desperate," Lederle said. "He doesn't know where to go, or what to do. His wife thinks he won't be able to see it through."

Half an hour later he called again, saying the plans had changed. Now he was demanding 500,000 euros and said he'd keep hold of the children until he was sure nobody was following him. Bermann told him he'd only be able to get the 100,000 for now. If he wanted more it would take a while. Fröbick replied, O.K. then, 100,000 will do, I'll be in touch again. He made a note of Bermann's mobile number. Bermann said, You and the children need to eat, I'll bring you something. Fröbick said, Thanks, but for God's sake come *alone*. And then he hung up.

For the next twenty minutes he kept phoning Bermann in the car and navigated him through Freiburg, presumably to check whether he was on his own. On several occasions he had Bermann drive right past him, or he'd tail him for a few seconds. Officers in unmarked police cars could easily have intervened, but Bermann didn't want to risk putting the children's lives in danger. Until they knew where these children were, Fröbick was not to be arrested.

Then, just before Lederle rang Bonì, Fröbick instructed Bermann to drive to the car park at the southern end of the Opfinger See. He said there was another change of plan. Bermann was to bring a young, unarmed policewoman with him and head out onto the frozen lake with the money. Then he'd receive further instructions.

"He wants to exchange the children," Bonì said. "Good. That young, unarmed policewoman wouldn't happen to be me, would it?"

"You're not young."

"I'm sure Rolf wouldn't mind. There'd be a sporting chance he'd be rid of me for ever."

Subdued laughter. Zancan joined in too, quietly.

"I've got to hang up," Lederle said.

"Do I know her?"

"She's sitting beside you."

They were now beyond the residential area and driving along the Opfinger See through the southern part of Mooswald. The road had been cleared of snow. Dark skeletons of trees with a sprinkling of white flew past. What they could see of the forest in the beam of the headlights looked frozen solid. "You don't have to do this," Bonì said.

Zancan smiled. She was twenty-five at most. Not a Bermann woman – not attractive enough, too serious, too assertive. More like an Anatol woman, if such a thing existed. A woman whose beauty was subterranean.

"Are you frightened?"

"Of course I am."

"You don't have to do it."

"I heard you," Zancan said in a perfectly friendly voice.

Louise grinned. Zancan wouldn't be a police sergeant for long. She'd move up soon, or change career.

They approached the motorway which cut through the city forest almost vertically. A few kilometres to the south was Munzingen. Why had Calambert driven to Munzingen? Why had Fröbick chosen the Opfinger See?

Calambert had been on the run. Munzingen was pure coincidence. Just as it was a coincidence that she'd turned in the wrong direction. Fröbick, on the other hand, would have his reasons for choosing the lake. What were they? He needed somewhere to hide, and from where he had an easy escape route. Where he had the situation under control.

"He'll have been there for a while," she said.

"Yes," Zancan said.

"And because he knows that *we* know that, he also knows that we won't bring any back-up. We don't know if he's watching the motorway or Opfinger Strasse. We can't risk arriving with back-up. We can only cordon off a much larger area. Is that what we're doing?"

"Yes," Zancan said again.

"Good. What would you do in his shoes?"

"Split up the children."

Louise nodded. She hadn't thought of that. Why not? It was so obvious. One child in the car, the other one somewhere on the route he'd chosen for his escape. They wouldn't dare arrest him at the handover unless they were sure the children were safe. They wouldn't dare do it later either.

Splitting up the children was obvious. She'd have done the same if she were in Fröbick's shoes. But she hadn't thought of it. "I think you're the right woman for the job," she said.

"Thanks," Zancan said.

At that moment they heard Bermann's voice over the radio. "*Marie, stop!*" he shouted. It sounded close, furious, on the verge of hysteria. Bonì sighed and undid her belt. Good old Bermann. His concentration unseated for a few seconds. But she thought he might be right. In view of the situation Lederle's little game was dangerous.

Zancan took the radio. "What is it?"

Bermann screamed at her to stop. Zancan obeyed. "*Are you stationary?*" Bermann yelled.

"Yes."

Louise opened the door. Zancan looked at her in astonishment.

Bermann screamed, "*Luis, get out!*"

Zancan was calm. "Rolf, she's our only advantage. He doesn't know that she . . ."

Bermann yelled that he wouldn't permit any discussion.

"We need her," Zancan said.

Bermann bellowed that they didn't need a pisshead, this was about his life and hers, and the lives of the children. Why would they rely on a *pisshead*?

"*Fuck off, Luis! Marie?*"

Marie, Bonì thought – first name terms. Was Zancan another Bermann woman after all? She didn't really believe it. Bermann women never got themselves into situations in which they might defy him.

"*Marie!*" Bermann yelled again.

"Yes?"

"*Is she out of the car yet?*"

Zancan didn't answer. She turned to Louise, and Louise looked back at her. She understood Bermann. A hostage taker, two small children, two police officers nearby – even she wouldn't rely on an alcoholic in that situation, be they Alpha, Gamma or Delta. It dawned on her that she'd understood Bermann that time two weeks ago too, when this whole thing began. He'd told her that he'd had enough of her, and she had understood. Sometimes you understood best the people you didn't like.

"Your choice," Zancan said.

"Good luck, then," Bonì said.

The patrol car drove away slowly, as if Zancan were hoping she'd change her mind at the last moment. Then the red taillights disappeared.

Louise turned away. What would be the responsible course of action? Should she telephone her colleagues and head back to the city? Or walk the last few hundred metres to the lake to see if she could help? Which was the right direction, and which the wrong one?

From a distance Louise could hear the rumble of the motorway, but immediately around her there was silence. She was alone. Alone with two concepts: prodromal phase and Gamma alcoholic. And facing a future defined by these.

Asking herself the question, What do I do now?

From one moment to the next she suddenly felt frozen. The temperature had continued to drop; it must be minus 5 degrees. But Bonì doubted that this was the reason.

Not everyone ended up in such a situation, so why had she? At what moment, at what point in her life had she stepped onto the path leading her to this? What had gone wrong when? When had it all begun? Was it with Calambert, who might be alive today if it hadn't been for that sticker?

She suspected it had begun before that, when she'd decided to marry Mick. But she must have already been on the wrong path for quite a while, or she wouldn't have fallen for him the first time they met, when he'd told her he had a ridiculous name.

More important, perhaps, than the exact moment at which she'd set off on the wrong path was the fact that she hadn't realised it for years. Unaware of it, she hadn't been able to alter her course.

Bonì mulled over what she was feeling at that moment. Nothing that could have been of any help. All-encompassing fury. The cold. The need for a drink. That she was alone. A mild satisfaction that Bermann and Mick wouldn't be able to keep Amazonian fish in their tap water if they wanted to.

What else? That Niksch was no longer in this world. The worry that Landen wouldn't call after he got back. And fear. Fear for Pham, Bermann, Zancan.

She started running, westwards, wondering if it was possible that the right way and the wrong way sometimes led in the same direction.

The noise of the motorway had grown louder. Horizontal beams of light darted back and forth above the trees. She stopped to catch her breath then ran on. After about three hundred metres a car came towards her. She didn't stop, nor did the car reduce its speed. For the first time it crossed her mind that Fröbick might not be alone. Lederle had said he was close to panic. Out of fear he might have called the French professional, or Paul Lebonne, who had done a runner a week ago. There were, after all, 100,000 euros to go around.

A dark-red Porsche. A small, old face peered at her as they passed each other.

Then she was on the bridge that ran across the motorway. To the north lay the lake. In the light of the moon hanging just above the horizon, the snow shone on the frozen surface. Bermann, Zancan and Fröbick were nowhere to be seen. Had they already done the exchange? No, not enough time had passed.

She had never before been here in winter. In summer the lake was a recreational area with a nature reserve, but now it appeared inhospitable and menacing. A large expanse of snow surrounded by bare, black forest. Cordoning off this huge area, where there were barely any roads, was not hard. Searching it for a man on foot most definitely was.

Her gaze wandered along the shore of the lake and the forest. Even though there must be a dozen of her colleagues somewhere in the darkness, the whole area looked deserted.

Where had Fröbick parked his car? On the hard shoulder of the motorway, perhaps, which ran along the lake only a few metres from the shore. In the headlights of approaching cars she tried to make out if a vehicle was there, but she couldn't say with complete certainty.

Louise ran on, leaving the road just after the bridge and stopping in the cover of the trees. In the car park stood Bermann's Mercedes and Zancan's patrol car. The kiosk and surfing school were closed. Further in the distance, towards the gravel pit, a lorry was parked, covered in snow. Footprints led from the two cars and merged before heading for the shore. No other tracks were to be seen.

She didn't dare step onto the car park. If she were Fröbick she would be watching it. She would have separated the children, called the French professional or Lebonne for help, and kept the car park under surveillance.

She looked towards the lake. Bermann and Zancan were now out on the ice, a good fifty metres from the shore. They weren't walking side by side exactly; there was a gap of two or three metres between them. Bermann held a dark travel bag in his right hand. Zancan was carrying a smaller, lighter bag. Now Bermann lifted his left hand to his ear. They stopped, before changing direction and continuing northwards.

The fact that Fröbick was giving Bermann and Zancan instructions by telephone meant two things. First, he could see them and so must be somewhere along the shore. Second, if he was next to the car park she would have heard his voice. But all was silent.

She ran to the two cars as quietly as she could and kneeled down beside the Mercedes.

Where was Fröbick?

A path ran along the motorway on the eastern side of the lake. Groups of trees alternated with clearings. If he was there his only escape would be via the motorway.

The western side wasn't as easily accessible. He would have to find his way past the gravel-mining machinery, if indeed it was there in winter. Parallel to the shore and slightly set back, a path ran behind some trees through the forest. She couldn't recall if it was wide enough for a car.

Further to the north began the nature reserve. From there, especially at night, it was difficult to see the southern end of the lake, where Bermann and Zancan were. Besides, there were hardly any paths and it was much further to the nearest road, except for the motorway. Fröbick would need a road.

He must be somewhere near the southern shore. On the western side, she reckoned, perhaps beyond the gravel pit.

Should she look for him? Or wait?

Bonì was about to get moving again when she noticed that one of the figures on the lake had stopped. Zancan. Bermann had given her his bag and was now continuing northwards alone. This confirmed her suspicion. Fröbick would hardly allow Bermann to get close to him; he would send him in the opposite direction. He had to be somewhere here, close by.

Then she heard the sound of someone hurrying towards Bermann's car from the other side. A stifled panting mingled with the sound of footsteps.

Bonì pulled her pistol from the holster. Two bullets. She cursed. She ought to have waited. Ought to have stayed hidden behind a tree and watched where Zancan was going, then followed her. Zancan had led her to Fröbick. Now Fröbick was coming to her.

She narrowed her eyes to slits and concentrated on the footsteps. They ended abruptly. Fröbick – if it was him – had reached the car.

Seconds passed. Had he spotted her? Or was he just making sure that Bermann and Zancan were doing as he'd instructed.

Slowly she turned her head towards the lake. She couldn't see Bermann now. Zancan hadn't moved.

Louise could hear quiet thumping noises from the other side of the car. Fröbick grunted. What the hell was he *doing*?

Then she identified the sound. He was piercing the rear tyre, and at that moment she heard the hiss of air being expelled. More footsteps and a scraping sound: Fröbick crawling to the front tyre. She wanted to laugh out loud. A kidnapper crawling on all fours around a police car, on the other side of which was a Gamma alcoholic with only two bullets in her service weapon.

More thumping and grunting. More hissing.

She thought of Lederle's description of Fröbick. A desperate man on the verge of panic. A man feverishly devising plans only to discard them again, offering no resistance when Bermann beat him down from half a million euros to 100,000.

She felt herself beginning to relax.

More footsteps, and then she saw him. A short, fat man in a yellow outdoor coat. A penknife in his right hand. He hurried past Bonì, no more than two metres away, without noticing her. She smelled sweat, glimpsed a pale cheek. He fell to his knees beside Zancan's car and readied the knife.

But rather than thrust it in, he let his arm drop. It took her a moment to realise that he was sobbing.

She raised her pistol and said, "Hey!"

The man swung around. His mouth was open, his nose running, his cheeks wet with tears. She recognised him at once. The driver of the Sharan.

"Are you Fröbick?"

He nodded.

She stood up. "Lose the knife."

Fröbick folded the knife and tossed it towards her. He was shaking uncontrollably. "At last," he said.

"Yes," she said, sinking back into the snow.

Fröbick hadn't asked anybody for help. He was alone. He hadn't separated the children either – they were in his car at the entrance to the gravel pit.

Louise called Zancan on Bermann's mobile. Bermann and Zancan ran off to fetch the children. Fröbick was lying on his stomach in the snow beside the shore. She didn't think he should have a comfortable time of it. Besides, she wasn't carrying handcuffs.

She had searched him, but found no more weapons. Just the penknife. In his wallet were photos of his sons and four hundred and ten euros.

Bonì stood beside him and gazed out at the lake, waiting for Bermann and Zancan. All of a sudden the air was filled with the wailing of countless police sirens. The snow turned bright blue. There was frenetic activity. Uniformed officers took custody of Fröbick. Wallmer and Schneider were there, somebody asked her something but she could not bring herself to reply. The pistol was taken from her hand. Ambulances arrived.

The sound of a child crying blended with the noise of engines and voices. Zancan was carrying the girl from Poipet; Bermann carried Pham. The girl was crying. Neither child was dressed warmly enough and they weren't wearing hats. Both had red cheeks, but they seemed unharmed, at least as far as she could tell.

Zancan hugged her as she walked past.

Bermann stopped beside her and said, "O.K." To her ears it sounded as if a whole heap of other words were hidden in it. Words such as: You were right. I'm sorry. Thanks. Thank God you didn't listen to me.

267

You showed us again how much we need you. We'll be pleased when you're back. But now you've got to go. All the best for the abyss. Words like that.

"O.K.," she said.

Pham made a noise that sounded like "O.K." too. He stared at her, a finger in his mouth. Louise couldn't tell if he recognised her. She was waiting for Bermann to put him down. Then she would have taken his hand and brought him to one of the doctors. Put a blanket around him, warmed him up and made sure that he ended up with nice parents. But Bermann didn't put him down, nor did he give the impression that he was going to let go of the boy any time in the near future.

She raised a hand to stroke Pham's cheek. His skin was cold and smooth. Pham didn't react, he just looked at her with wide eyes. She let her hand drop and remembered what Natchaya had said about not being able to save the world. No, she thought, she couldn't save the world. But she had saved Pham and the girl from Poipet. To be able to save one or two people was definitely something. A big deal when you considered how quickly you could lose someone.

Pham turned to Bermann and touched his moustache with his finger, "You like that, don't you?" Bermann said.

Pham said something in Vietnamese.

"If only I knew what you were saying," Bermann said.

"He's asking if you're his new father," Bonì said.

By one o'clock the formalities were complete. Bermann had taken Pham to his house and then returned. Looking grey and drained, Lederle had driven home at around eleven. They'd postponed their conversation until this was *all over*. Without saying goodbye to Bermann, Almenbroich or any of the others she left headquarters. Zancan came running after her and said, "I'll take you home." The start of a wonderful friendship, Louise thought, exhausted. During the five-minute drive she fell asleep. "Good luck," Zancan said, hugging her again.

A light was on in Ronescu's kitchen. Television voices echoed in his apartment as she walked past his door. Katrin had left, and she'd taken the sketch with the line and the terms. Louise fell onto the sofa and lay on her back, stretching her arms and legs. Pham's dark eyes followed her. The telephone rang.

"Were you asleep?" Lederle said.

"No."

"Good. I want you to know. You're important to me and that's why I'm telling you this now."

It wasn't Antonia who had cancer, but him. He'd been fooling them for eighteen months. Only Almenbroich and, more recently, Bermann knew. Nobody else.

It wasn't Antonia who was ill, but him.

She sat down, but said nothing. Pham filled her head, not Lederle. No matter how hard she tried she wasn't able to summon any emotion in response to what he'd said. The only emotions buzzing around her mind were linked to Pham, Taro, Natchaya, Fröbick, the roshi and Richard Landen. Besides, she barely had any energy left to try.

It wasn't Antonia who had cancer, she thought, but Reiner. For eighteen months they'd seen each other almost every day and she'd had no idea of what he was going through. The person at her side had been completely different from the man she thought he was.

She wished he hadn't called. There was no space in her head for other people's problems.

"It's not very big," Lederle said.

"What?"

"The tumour."

"Where is it?"

"In my bowel. But we'll beat it, don't you worry. It hasn't spread yet . . . but I don't want to burden you with silly little details. You see, the two of us have to be strong now."

"I'm sorry."

"Me too. But we'll beat it. It's too weak for me. It doesn't have a chance. You have to look at it that way, Louise. We're going to win."

They ended the call. Yes, she thought, we're going to win. She got up, fetched the bottle of țuică from under the sink and went down to the ground floor.

20

February continued to be cold; it didn't get warmer until the beginning of March. When Louise returned to Freiburg the ice and snow had thawed. One of the coldest winters of the last few decades was coming to an end.

Hugo Chervel had the Mégane brought back. In her letterbox were the car keys, the bill and a card telling her the number of the house the car was parked outside. She set down her travel bag and stepped into the street. The red Mégane now had a blue bonnet and a blue driver's door. The entry hole from a bullet was still visible on the dashboard. Chervel's brother-in-law had even installed an undamaged stereo.

All the same she decided she'd buy a new car in the spring. Changes in one's life needed to be marked symbolically and a car was a good symbol. The changes could be seen, heard, smelled and felt with your hands. It wasn't a status symbol, but rather the symbol of a departure. A car for which it was always summer. A convertible.

There were nine messages on her answerphone, which was now full. Barbara Franke and Enni had both rung twice to ask where she was and why hadn't she got in touch. Her father said, "It's Sunday morning, Louise; where the hell *are* you?" Landen said he was back and "would love to know how everything worked out". Anatol and Katrin Rein had both left "Welcome home" messages. Katrin added, "You've managed the detox – now you're going to get through the withdrawal too."

Lederle said he was feeling a little better and hoped she was too. Once again he apologised for having lied to her for so long. His voice sounded drained, and less like "We'll beat it". He paused briefly, then said, "What sort of a society have we become, Louise? On Sunday I stood up on the Schlossberg, looked down at Freiburg and asked myself, What sort of a society have we become? When are we finally going to focus on our core beliefs? When will we go back to discussing values instead of tax reductions and the cost of prescription medicine and the stock market? Where are the children, Louise? I look down at *my city* and *my region* and ask myself: where are the fifty-six Asian children? And all those other children we know nothing about? How many ended up in Freiburg? How many are living down there in the claws of sexual abusers? What sort of society are we, that we can produce these illnesses and perversions, but then lack the courage to admit that we *have* produced them? Child abuse isn't even notifiable."

The tape was full.

She emptied her bag, repacked it and left the apartment. Like the other callers, Lederle would have to be patient for a few weeks more.

The Mégane started up as if nothing had happened to it. Another reason to ditch this car.

In Zillisheim she bought bread and fruit, and drank *café au lait* while standing in a dark bar. Old men sat playing cards at a couple of tables, cigarettes in their mouths and in front of them glasses of pastis and coffee cups. There was much laughter and chatter, and occasionally a card was played. She'd always imagined that one day her father would sit in a bar every morning, drinking pastis and playing cards. She liked the idea without knowing why.

As she left the bar it began to rain.

Over the past few weeks she'd had two telephone conversations with Lederle, one with Almenbroich and one with Muller. Jean Berger and the Frenchman who'd have killed her if Natchaya hadn't stopped him were still on the run. The driver of the Audi, who'd been arrested along with Steiner and his wife in the Vosges, was refusing to talk. The French police didn't care. From his fingerprints they could charge him for two serious robberies, in 1999 and 2002.

Paul Lebonne had been arrested in Casablanca at the end of February and extradited to France. He admitted to working as a carer for Asile d'enfants and being at the Kanzan-an and the farm near Münzenried. But he denied any involvement in illegal adoption and the selling or hiring-out of Asian children for sexual purposes. He believed the children had been adopted legally and had never heard of a monk called Taro.

Annegret Schelling also claimed she knew nothing about what had happened to the children she'd looked after at the Kanzan-an and in the farmhouse near Münzenried. She believed the adoption process had been perfectly legal. She said she hadn't had access to lists of names or addresses; these had been kept by Jean Berger in Basel. It was only after the confrontation with Bonì that she realised something wasn't quite right about Asile. After Steiner had treated her head wound she'd left Asile d'enfants and moved back in with her mother. And she'd never heard the name Taro.

Steiner, the German doctor, admitted having been responsible for the medical care of the children and failing to disclose his income to the tax authorities. Yes, he had specialised in ophthalmology, but at heart he was a paediatrician. The children had been brought to him with colds, flu-like infections, allergies, and once even with measles. He'd also paid the occasional visit to the Kanzan-an and Münzenried. He'd administered routine vaccinations, given advice on nutrition and psychological issues – etcetera.

Since her arrest his wife hadn't uttered a word. Teresa, the Steiners' Filipino housemaid, wasn't saying anything either, presumably out of loyalty towards the two of them. As she had no residence permit it would be only a matter of time before the French police found out what she knew.

The German police weren't particularly interested in all this. They had Fröbick and he wouldn't stop talking. What he said confirmed everything they'd suspected. Dozens of children from the Far East – he didn't know the precise figure – had been sold to western European adoptive parents or paedophile rings. At least four of the elder girls had for some years been hired out for sexual services to France, Germany, Belgium and Switzerland. Jean Berger had set up the organisation and run it from Basel; Harald Mahler was in charge locally. Lebonne, Schelling, Steiner, Fröbick himself – all of them knew what was happening to the children. Fröbick, Lebonne and Schelling, perhaps the others too, had also repeatedly abused older children who'd been brought to Europe exclusively for sexual exploitation. Although Steiner had been responsible for looking after the children's health in general, he'd also given the older ones regular H.I.V. tests, treated injuries in the genital and anal regions, and supplied contraception for the older girls.

As for Taro, Fröbick confirmed what Natchaya had said. Taro had witnessed Lebonne and Mahler molesting her. They'd discovered him, knocked him to the ground and he had fled. Fröbick didn't know any more details because he'd stayed at the Kanzan-an while the French professionals hunted for Taro, joined later by Mahler and Lebonne. Afterwards Mahler simply told him that "everything was O.K."

So Fröbick couldn't tell them what had happened to Taro either. Why had the monk not confided in the roshi? Why had he walked for days through the snow, going ever further from the Kanzan-an? Natchaya had said, "He saw the men with me. He watched what we did."

He watched.

The roshi had said, "In Taro doubt. Many questions."

What had been going through Taro's mind as he watched Natchaya and the two men? They'd never find out.

There was something else Fröbick could not – or perhaps would not – tell them: the names of Asile d'enfants' clients. These had been known only to Berger and Mahler. He was, however, able to shine some light on Hans-Joachim Gronen, the owner of the farm near Münzenried: he was an old friend of Mahler's, he ran a bar in Bangkok and was involved in the prostitution racket there.

The most difficult task now was to coordinate the investigations of the German and French authorities. Requests for assistance were exchanged, high-ranking officers travelled back and forth, while in the background the foreign ministries applied pressure. In spite of this, or perhaps because of it, the process was taking a bewilderingly long time. Now that their cooperation was official, everything became more complicated.

The strip of asphalt leading into the forest between Zillisheim and Illfurth glistened dully. It had stopped raining, but the sky remained overcast. The veil of light was grey. She'd decided to visit Niksch's grave when she came back. Then she'd talk to his mother and sisters, and try to make them understand that security had nothing to do with whether or not there was a policeman in the family.

The potholes in the gravelly road were filled with rain and melted snow. The car park was empty. She got out and looked around her. The cat was nowhere to be seen. For a moment her mind turned to Landen, but she thought it best to forget him.

She'd tried several times to visit Hollerer again, or at least speak to him on the telephone. But Hollerer hadn't wanted any visits or calls. Nobody, not even Ponzelt or friends from Liebau, had managed to get through to him. Roman, the hospital volunteer, said he was suffering from severe depression. As soon as he'd been fit to travel he'd had himself admitted to a hospital in Kaiserslauten. At the end of February he'd been transferred to a rehabilitation centre.

But she wasn't going to allow Hollerer to vanish from her life too.

The sight of the Kanzan-an brought tears to her eyes. From a distance the monastery looked the same as ever. Even the grey cat appeared on cue in the hilly meadow.

She stood by the entrance and looked up at the window at which she'd first seen Pham. She didn't have to worry about him or the girl from Poipet. The girl had been accommodated with friends of Barbara Franke. Pham would stay with Bermann and his family. But he wasn't called Pham anymore; his new name was Viktor. He had become a symbol.

For Bermann the order had been restored. The case was solved and they had won. The dead, the disappeared, the open questions were forgotten. Bermann was a master at focusing on what was in front of his nose and ignoring anything that wasn't. He'd assembled all the pieces of the puzzle they'd investigated, and written off all those that were still missing. You could barely tell that the picture which emerged at the end was incomplete, or even that it wasn't 100 per cent accurate. It reflected the visible reality. That was all that counted.

Bermann called it "data rationalisation". Anything redundant was eliminated. This maintained the effectiveness and operational readiness of the department. The next crimes had already been committed. The next dead bodies and missing people were waiting to be forgotten. That's how the system works, Bermann said, by which he meant society, the media, the West, life. The fact that fifty-six children from the Far East between the ages of one and nine were unaccounted for, that some of these children were suffering regular sexual abuse, was of no long-term importance for him or the system. It was an abstraction. The children didn't have faces. Those without faces didn't exist.

Bonì looked at the teahouse. This time she couldn't hear the sound of the gong. She wondered where the roshi was. On the phone Chiyono had said that half the monks and nuns had left over the past few weeks due to the events surrounding Asile d'enfants. Only she, Georges anda few others had stayed – as well as the roshi, of course.

We drink tea, we talk. She resolved to tell the roshi about the children and ask him Lederle's questions.

She found Chiyono in the small office. The nun bowed, then they shook hands and sat down. "I wasn't sure you'd actually come,"

Chiyono said. Her hair was a centimetre longer than the last time. A new plaster held the frame of her glasses together.

"Me neither. But I'm here now. And I've got time."

"I'm happy to hear that."

"I've got lots of questions, I warn you."

"Excellent! It'll do me good to be asked questions again. It keeps you young and makes you reflective. By the way, there was a man asking after you a few days ago."

"A man?"

Chiyono smiled faintly. A tall, slim man in a black coat. He spoke to the roshi in Japanese for a while, before the roshi sent him to her. The man asked whether Chiyono had heard anything about her, Louise. Whether Louise had called or been back to the Kanzan-an. She wasn't able to help him and he had left.

"He might come back," Chiyono said.

Louise nodded. She thought of Landen's "Then" and how this "Then" still seemed to be of importance to him. "Tomorrow", "later", "then" . . . What a man! "If he does, he does," she said.

"And then what will we do?"

"Talk to him."

Chiyono laughed. She got up and went to the door. "Follow me. We've prepared a cell for you in the nuns' wing."

Bonì grinned. So she had ended up with the nuns. If only for the beginning.

Dear Reader,

The following short story, "Dark Death", recounts the Calambert case repeatedly referred to in *Zen and the Art of Murder*. For Louise Bonì it's a traumatic case that's largely responsible for placing her where she is: right on the edge of the abyss. For this reason I long toyed with developing the ideas that crop up in the first two Bonì novels into a story in its own right, as a sort of prequel. When the *Welt am Sonntag* asked whether I would like to write a short story featuring Louise Bonì as part of a small crime series, the opportunity had arrived.

The story solves one or two of the puzzles surrounding the character of Louise Bonì and I suspect it makes her more understandable for the reader.

I hope you enjoy it,

Oliver Bottini

OLIVER BOTTINI

DARK DEATH

LOUISE BONÌ AND
THE CALAMBERT CASE

A nnetta was fourteen when she disappeared. A wild girl, teeming with energy, still too much of a girl and already too much of a woman for one body and one soul. She was bursting with contradictions and she contradicted at every opportunity. As if it were the flag of her own little country, she held out before her everything she thought and wanted, and who she liked and who she didn't. Truth was her only friend. Nobody followed her too closely; they kept their distance.

"She's tricky," her mother said.

"She can never keep her mouth shut," her father said. Louise Bonì looked from one to the other; she knew the thoughts that were going through their minds and made them speechless with shame: the truth spoken once too often, the wrong person provoked, the child's causing trouble again. They were sitting in her office at police H.Q. in Freiburg – serious crime squad – for the third time since the wild girl had disappeared. On a good day you could see the Vosges from the window up here; when it was snowing, like today, you could barely make out the old post office building opposite.

"Are you going to find the bastard?" the father asked. He was short, round and important for a number of reasons. His grey three-piece suit rustled in a rather frosty way and had the whiff of an internationally renowned couturier. Her gaze wandered across perfect seams and sublime creases. His cheeks were glistening with sweat. When a child was abducted it turned a lot upside down, perhaps even the rest of your life. But his right hand was holding on to his left index finger with such desperation that she detected even in this man some goodness and vulnerability.

"Yes." What she neglected to say was that generally they found the perpetrators, but the victims did not always return.

Annetta's mother, even shorter than her husband but slim and wiry, muttered, "We've been having problems with her."

Bonì nodded. She knew about these kinds of difficulties from neighbours, Annetta's teachers and friends. Many thought it possible that Annetta had had enough and from now on had decided to lead her life without her parents.

"But she wouldn't have just run away with a man," the mother said.

"Running away is cowardly," the father said. "Our daughter may be many things, but she's no coward."

"She would have told us straight up."

"She'd have said, 'Papa, Mama, I'm leaving.'" The father gave a weary smile. There was a hint of admiration in his voice.

Louise suspected the parents were right. Girls like Annetta didn't run away in secret; they looked for a fight. She glanced at her conversation notes and at once understood why she was so affected by this case. The parents had described their own daughter, but also her: Louise Bonì, forty-one, chief inspector at Freiburg Kripo, on a journey to nowhere.

Everyone was still unsettled by the changes in security since the September 11 attacks. The snow and the exhaustion did the rest. Although Rolf Bermann, head of the department, had been reinforcing the "Annetta" task force, none of the investigators was getting enough sleep. Whenever they were outside, the snow assaulted their eyes, and when the light had vanished from the short winter days they moved through the seemingly perpetual darkness to follow up the dozens, hundreds of leads from the public.

"Are you bearing up?" said Bermann, handlebar moustache and chauvinist – the last of his kind in Freiburg, for the time being at least.

"Of course," Bonì said.

"Maybe a case like this helps. It's a distraction. Less time to spend at home."

She frowned. "Who was that blonde who came to meet you the other day? One of your wife's cousins?"

"Alcohol is never the answer," Bermann said.

"Nor is extra-marital sex."

He laughed.

No, alcohol wasn't the answer, just a sort of cleaning fluid. Was there still a Mick stain on the bedroom carpet? Use a bit of alcohol and the stain was gone. After almost six months there were far too many Mick stains and residues in the apartment. On the floor, on the walls – the ones on the mirrors were particularly stubborn and those that lingered in the odours were especially painful. She couldn't cope without her cleaning fluid at the moment, four weeks before the *date*. "You should move," Bermann had said in the summer.

Where do you expect me to get the energy for that, arsehole?

Then the snow came. The sad winter light mercilessly revealed stain after stain and all the residues that a cheating husband could leave behind in the pores of a half-shattered life. Suddenly there was always something to drink to hand.

I went to lunch with a friend, Louise said.

It was a neighbour's birthday party last night, Louise said.

New perfume, not great is it? Louise said.

When Annetta vanished, everything else went out of focus. The parents rang after twelve hours, after twenty-four the case landed on Boni's desk, after forty-eight Bermann assembled the task force.

Soon afterwards they found out where it had happened.

In the picturesque Fischcrau district a tall, handsome man had been leaning against the railings of the canal. He called out to a girl who was skating over the ice. The girl had laughed, so had the man. "Oui, oui!" he'd said.

Two witnesses had heard the man speak French. A further witness had noticed a white Peugeot 306 with notchback in a nearby car park. Its number plate ended in "75" – Paris. Another witness had seen a tall, handsome man and a girl get into the Peugeot.

Louise called her colleagues in Paris. They promised to keep their eyes open. A tall, handsome man driving a white Peugeot, who hadn't gone to work or come home for three days. Greying, unshaven, wearing a dark parka, jeans, blue trainers. Louise pictured the man and Annetta skating to the car together.

"Don't get your hopes up," Paris said.

Hopes? Far too risky in this life. Louise survived only on anger, energy, determination and overindulgence.

The snow fell and the memories of Mick's confession the previous winter crept coldly beneath her skin.

And every day Annetta's parents came.

"You promised," the father said.

"We'll get him."

"I don't care," the mother said. "The main thing is that nothing's happened to our child." Three days, four days, five days. Everything had happened to the child, except perhaps the worst thing. Louise said nothing. The mother asked no questions, wanted no answers. All she wanted was hope.

"Does Annetta speak French?"

"Yes, very well," the father said. "We've been to France a few times, which was enough. She's got a great talent for languages."

"I imagine she's making a long trip," the mother said. "We can't see her, but we know she's there somewhere." She raised her hands towards the window. "And at some point she'll come back and maybe she'll tell us about her trip, but maybe not."

"He's killed her," the father muttered. His eyes had landed on the photograph of Annetta in the file open in front of Louise.

"A sea voyage." The mother smiled behind tears.

"If someone like that is after money then they . . . torture and kill." The father bowed his head and stayed in that position for several seconds. Louise heard him moan softly and his virtually bald head twitched.

The mother stood up and went to the window. "My girl's strong," she said in a kind voice. "My girl's alive."

Louise looked at the photo. Annetta on a sofa in a yellow flowered dress buttoned to the neck, a pretty, intelligent fourteen-year-old, large eyes, serious mouth, and yet you sensed she was about to laugh out loud, she was just posing for the family album and then she'd jump onto a skateboard in cut-off jeans.

The mother sat down again. The parents looked at Louise in a detached way. "Don't give up hope," she said.

"She's dead," Bermann said late that evening and his words reverberated in the deserted corridor. His eyes were staring at her from deep sockets, his face was grey. It was the first time Louise had seen him like this, no longer a speck of healthiness or freshness in this bear of a badly brought-up man. "How can you think she's still alive?"

"Some people just aren't so easy to kill."

He shook his head in disbelief, unamused. "I've rarely heard such crap. Go home, Luis, and get some sleep."

Back home she crouched by the cupboard below the sink and counted, using different rhythms and melodies, the endless empty bottles until the counting had become a sweet game and the terror had dissipated. For a while she fell asleep where she was, on the kitchen floor. When she woke up a ghostly Mick was waltzing through the apartment, talking of children and a little house out of town, and the *date* had come one day closer.

Hey, who's that? Mick asked in a low voice.

She struggled to her feet. On the countertop was the photograph of Annetta. Pretty girl, Mick said, and now, in her dark delirium, a fourteen-year-old girl was added to all those secretaries, cashiers, cleaning ladies, saleswomen, waitresses and the writer, who he'd itemised in his confession on the chairlift in Scuol.

Early in the morning the telephone rang.

"Someone saw him yesterday," said Reiner Lederle, her favourite colleague. "The Frenchman with the blue trainers."

*

A tiny grocer's in a village on the way to the Rhine, hidden beneath the snow. Behind the counter a wrinkled old lady, Hermine Schwarzer. In front of her a copy of the *Badische Zeitung*, open at the page with the request for information from the public.

"I remember because I can't speak a word of French, and he couldn't speak a word of German." She tapped the paper with tiny, withered fingers. "A tall, slim man, not dressed warmly enough for minus twenty, but he was good-looking and very, very tired. He had a car, a light car, yellow or white."

"A Peugeot?" Bermann asked.

Frau Schwarzer shrugged.

"Did you manage to catch sight of his shoes?"

"Dark and soaked through."

"What did he buy?" Louise said. She was standing in the narrow passage by the counter, wedged between Bermann and the smaller Lederle, who always smelled a little of illness and decay.

"Fruit, bread, cheese, biscuits. Lots of biscuits." Lederle wrote it all down. "Loo paper. Tissues. Cough sweets. Tampons." Louise felt Bermann and Lederle tense. Annetta was alive.

A helicopter came from Stuttgart, a hundred uniformed officers from Lahr, and there were dogs too. Starting at Hermine Schwarzer's grocery, they checked and searched houses, farms, sheds, meticulously combed white woods, icy valleys, increasing the radius metre by metre, terrifyingly slowly, far too slowly for Bermann, who like everyone else knew that it was now all about hours and minutes, and he was barely able to contain his anger. Boni was pleased this was the situation, that everyone was captivated by his energy, because it meant no-one was paying any attention to her minor afflictions. The shaking, the lapses of concentration, disorientation, cold, hot.

"Coffee?" Lederle said, filling his cup from a thermos.

"No, thanks."

A break to warm up in the car with the engine running at the end of a thoroughfare where the village came to an abrupt end. The white plain merged with the white sky. Perhaps there were a few invisible white trees over there, maybe a few white houses, and maybe not. Maybe this was where the world came to an end, it could go no further. Lederle hummed a tune to himself – this nice, sincere man was always cheerful, Louise thought, even here, even now. Where did this cheerfulness and confidence come from? But his humming was slow and measured, and she could tell how tense he was. "I need the loo." She got out and ran back through the burning cold to the warm, narrow shop. Lock de-icer? No, she didn't keep anything like that, said Frau Schwarzer, at a loss. Oh, don't worry, Louise said, alcohol sometimes did the job, high-percentage alcohol. A miniature would be perfect, it's more portable.

Becalmed and yet heavyhearted, she ran back to Lederle thinking, Jägermeister – master of the hunt – weren't they hunters right now, masters amongst hunters? You see? Everything was relevant somehow.

Lederle had got out and hurried a few metres in her direction, the car door left open. Into the muffled afternoon he yelled, "Munzingen!"

He was driving through villages and across the countryside, leaving more and more traces, a tall, handsome Frenchman dressed nowhere near warmly enough for this arctic spell, buying food for two, but only ever seen alone, shopping, in a supermarket car park, in his white Peugeot. Three witnesses over the past few hours, he seemed to be getting panicky, there was no method to his route: around the Tuniberg, as if he couldn't get away from Freiburg from where he had abducted Annetta. Yesterday evening Frau Schwarzer's village, this morning the L134 near Gündlingen, then Bötzlingen and most recently close to Munzingen.

"She's dying on him and he's going crazy," Lederle said as they drove with their blue lights flashing on barely distinguishable roads towards Munzingen. He was a safe driver; no icy, snow-crusted road surface in this world would cause him trouble. "Why doesn't he hand himself in? Then it would be all over."

"He's scared about what comes after that," Louise said.

"And so he's making everything much worse."

The girl in the photograph flashed in her mind, Annetta on her parents' sofa, then racing on a skateboard across a snowy field, all of a sudden on a sun lounger on the deck of a ship, her father running through the picture, the mother, both of them calling a name, but not their daughter's – they're calling, "Louise!"

She rubbed her eyes, forced herself to concentrate.

Only ever seen alone . . . Either Annetta was lying on the back seat – or in the boot.

It went on snowing. Lederle turned on the windscreen wipers, clumps of snow were massing beside the mudguards, you couldn't see much further than that. Bermann called, Louise put it on speaker. One of the new witnesses had noted the beginning of the registration number, so now they knew who the white Peugeot belonged to, and because the descriptions given by the other witnesses matched that of the owner, according to the French police, they also knew who they were searching for: René Calambert, a teacher in Paris, married with a daughter.

"I don't get it," Lederle said.

"Has he got a mobile?" Bonì said.

"Yes," Bermann's voice said. They were trying to locate it at this very moment, but it was probably switched off.

"He might call his wife," Louise said. "He's in a panic, he doesn't know what to do."

Soon afterwards Bermann rang again. They couldn't pinpoint Calambert's mobile. "Where are you?"

"Just outside Munzingen," Louise said, her finger on the map. Coming from thingummy . . . Tiengen."

"Wait just outside the village."

They glimpsed Bermann's car when they were only fifteen metres away. A heavy, black saloon huddled in a snowdrift. Bermann was standing, mobile to his ear, in the midst of clouds of breath and snow-flakes, between the circles of light that shone too brightly and hurt Louise's eyes. Three or four heads inside the car, members of the task force. Raising his hand, Bermann pointed westwards at the sky.

Turning her head Louise saw nothing, but then, tiny and scarcely visible, a blink of red, followed by a blink of green. "The helicopter's got him," she said, excited. She leaped out before the car came to a stop. A faint clinking in the right-hand pocket of her anorak as she ran to Bermann. Clinking as she ran, she thought, that was something she'd have to get used to. In the distance she could hear the helicopter. "Have they got him?"

"They *had* him," Bermann said, putting his mobile away. "And lost him again."

"*Shit!*" All of a sudden the cold crept into her warmed body, into her innermost layers. Her teeth chattered for several seconds before she brought her muscles under control.

A third car with police colleagues had joined them. In convoy they followed a little road that ran to the south-west, towards the helicopter that hung almost motionless in the grey sky. Out in front Bermann's car braked abruptly. They all stopped. To the left a slightly wider track led through deep snow to nowhere. To the right was the edge of a leafless wood.

After they'd gathered around Bermann he pointed to the left, mobile in hand. "A hundred and fifty metres from here is an abandoned farm. House, shed, barn, all pretty dilapidated, but O.K. for someone looking for a hideaway and a bit of warmth."

"What about the car?" someone said.

"It would fit in the barn."

"Is this the drive?"

"No," Bermann said testily. "This is a fucking footpath in summer. But it'll get us there quicker than the drive."

"It doesn't make any sense," Louise said.

Bermann raised his eyebrows in irritation. "What?"

"He's not thinking straight anymore, he's in a panic – he's not looking for a hideaway or shelter. The girl's badly injured, but he's not taking her to hospital. Instead he's been driving around the area for hours, maybe even days. He can't just park up somewhere, look after her and wait to see what happens. He's got to keep moving or he'll go mad."

"The helicopter saw him; he *must* be here somewhere."

"I know," Louise said. "I'm going to wait in the car."

From the waning warmth of Lederle's car she watched her colleagues, ten dark shapes labouring their way through the snow, making slow progress. One man out in front: Bermann. For Annetta's sake she hoped his assumptions were right. With his willpower and strength Rolf Bermann cleared up matters where most others would fail.

She reached for the map she'd tossed onto the back seat earlier. The track to the farm was marked, as well as a long driveway from the other side. To her right was the strip of wood with only footpaths going through it, but a forest road ran along its northern fringe. It was worth a try, she thought. In any case, she needed a pee.

She got out and trudged over to the trees through thirty-centimetre-deep snow. Breathing heavily, she pulled down her trousers and squatted. Bermann and the other officers had shrunk to scarcely visible dots, now moving forwards at greater distances from each other. One hand in her anorak pocket to stop the clinking, Louise walked on. She came to some sort of path marked by animal tracks, animals with hooves, deer perhaps – she didn't know. Mick would have known. One of his lovers had been a vet, the woman who'd concluded the confession in the ski lift when they arrived at the mid-station near Scuol. Picturing a busty, stupid beauty in a white coat, Louise had whacked her ski stick against the side of his head and brought their marriage to an end. But it wasn't easy to get rid of someone like Mick, who could preserve the illusion of stability and an everlasting "We", and now he haunted Louise through her nights, her dreams, her drunkenness and the snowy undergrowth of a wood near Munzingen.

When she heard a sound she froze. A metallic click she'd heard thousands of times before, but she couldn't place it. Disjointed images and feelings blustered about in her mind, her legs were aching, her lungs crackling. Why did the physical and mental exhaustion and despair have to overwhelm her right now, as well as the cold, the fear? At least her discipline was still intact; her right hand had automatically reached for her Walther.

And then she worked it out: a car door had been shut.

Summoning every last reserve of energy, she followed the path as quietly and quickly as possible. A shape appeared between the trees – a tall man, standing ten metres in front of her with his head bowed. She heard a gentle rippling and then the man looked up and noticed her.

She held her weapon so he could see it and said in French, "Don't go making any mistakes now, Calambert."

"She's alive," he said hoarsely, "but she's in a bad way."

"Where is she?"

He gestured behind him with his head.

Louise could see nothing but trees. Trees that wouldn't quite keep still. She blinked. "In the car?"

Calambert nodded. "She's not made for this sort of thing. Those girls are looking for wild adventures, but in the end they bite off more than they can chew and then it's all whingeing and whining."

"*What* did you say?"

He yawned. He shrugged.

"Let's go, arsehole," Louise said, aiming the gun at him.

Calambert laughed and raised his hand, which now sported a pistol, the barrel pointing to the side. He looked at it uncertainly then shook his head. "Not me, I'm going somewhere else." Pointing the weapon at Louise he retreated, step by step, moving ever further away, disappearing momentarily behind trees, then emerging again, becoming a tree amongst trees. Against the white the dark swayed, staggered and wobbled.

Louise pointed the Walther into the air and fired; her colleagues would hear the shot. She ran off down the path which must lead to the road where the Peugeot would be parked. As she ran she notified the ambulance service, then Bermann, who barked orders at her, all of which began or finished with the words, "Wait for back-up!" Although Calambert didn't re-emerge, she found the white car soon afterwards, half in the ditch. She peered inside: a chaotic jumble of clothing, food packaging, bottles, blankets. No Annetta.

She caught sight of a sticker on the rear windscreen: IT's A MAN's WORLD. Fury flew through her arteries. She turned her head, scanned the edge of the wood, the road, but there was no Calambert. She wasn't going to leave him to her colleagues. She – a woman – wanted to put the handcuffs on him herself.

She opened the boot.

A brown blanket, a gentle whimper. All she could see was the top of a forehead encrusted with blood, hair stuck down. "It's going to be fine, everything's going to be fine, sweetheart," Louise whispered as she carefully stroked Annetta's shoulder. It took her a while to realise that the girl's wrists were tied to her ankles; Calambert had literally folded Annetta in two to fit her into his boot.

She untied the scabbed hands and feet, then cut through broad strips of packing tape with Swiss Army penknife. Without really knowing what she was saying, she spoke to Annetta, stroked her and finally ventured to take the blanket from the girl's face – here too were traces of horrific abuse: swellings, blood, and a deeply disturbed look in her eyes.

When Bonì heard a police siren she straightened up. She fetched two more blankets from the back of the car, laid them gently over Annetta and ran.

The snow flurry was growing thicker; on this narrow road she could see barely more than ten metres ahead of her. She heard

Calambert before she saw him. He was battling his way noisily through the wood and broke through onto the road no more than eight metres ahead of her. She was about to shout a warning when a shot rang out. Calambert had fired more or less in her direction, but she couldn't tell precisely with the snow, the anger and all the other emotions inside her throbbing head. Another shot rang out, an acrid smell tickled her nostrils and the Walther had jerked backwards. Now Calambert was bent over his thigh, screaming. Around his feet, red was flowing into the white. It's a man's world, Louise thought. His arms were flapping about, his head flew up again, as perhaps did the hand holding the gun, perhaps not; it was hard to tell. Once more the Walther jerked back with a bang, Calambert stopped screaming, lurched backwards and toppled into the snow. She went to him and seconds later watched him die in a rapidly expanding pool of crimson crystals.

Annetta lived for four more days. In intensive care she drifted towards death in an induced coma. Each day Louise stood by the large, square observation window, the mother and father beside her, both as motionless as the girl on the other side of the pane of glass. At some point the mother put her hand on the window and said, "She's on a long sea voyage and that's the porthole, and she can look out whenever she wants, and we can look in."

"Why don't you go to her?" Louise said.

"She wouldn't want that."

"No," the father reiterated, "not our daughter."

Louise entered the dark ship and sat by Annetta's bed so she didn't have to bid farewell alone.

"Thank you," the mother said when it was over.

The father took her right hand in both of his and said, "Thanks for shooting the bastard."

Did I? Louise thought. Even the next morning she couldn't remember her encounter with Calambert. An unreal nightmare of cold, despair, fear and exhaustion, where there were no thoughts, only emotions, reactions and the occasional clinking of a little bottle against the bunch of keys in her pocket.

"What did I say afterwards?" she said to Bermann.

"That he was going to shoot at you again."

Bermann asked no questions, nor did he allow any. Not even a bullet in the thigh had stopped the kidnapper and killer René Calambert from pointing his gun a second time at Chief Inspector Bonì, he decided. Once again his colleague had aimed at his legs, but because of the visibility and the wounded man's erratic movements, her second bullet unfortunately hit his stomach before he was able to shoot again. Regrettable, but clearly self-defence.

Thus Bermann brought order to the chaos, and this order helped Louise get over the next few days and weeks, Annetta's funeral and the *date* in the spring and on into the summer. It was not until the following winter that Calambert reappeared with the snow. It's a man's world, he said, and died time and again in a pool of crimson crystals.

AUTHOR'S ACKNOWLEDGEMENTS

I would like to thank everyone who has helped me with this crime novel, in particular Dr Petra Eisele from O.W. Barth Verlag, without whose initiative it would never have seen the light of day; Freiburg Kriminalpolizei, and especially Karl-Heinz Schmidt for his phenomenal assistance; my agent Uli Pöppel for his detailed feedback and friendly support; and my wife Chiara Bottini for the very many intense conversations about the manuscript. Any remaining errors are entirely my responsibility.

OLIVER BOTTINI was born in 1965. Four of his novels, including *Zen and the Art of Murder* and *A Summer of Murder* of the Black Forest Investigations, have been awarded the Deutscher Krimipreis, Germany's most prestigious award for crime writing. In addition his novels have been awarded the Stuttgarter Krimipreis and the Berliner Krimipreis. He lives in Berlin. www.bottini.de.

JAMIE BULLOCH is the translator of Timur Vermes' *Look Who's Back*, Birgit Vanderbeke's *The Mussel Feast*, which won him the Schlegel-Tieck Prize, *Kingdom of Twilight* by Steven Uhly, and novels by F. C. Delius, Jörg Fauser, Martin Suter, Katharina Hagena and Daniel Glattauer.